GOBBET PRESS

Published in 2013 by

goββετ press

in association with gobbet magazine

ISBN: 978-1480212794

First published by Paraphilia Books 2010

NECROLOGY

by

Gary J. Shipley & Kenji Siratori

Appendix by Reza Negarestani

DORIS: That's not life, that's no life
Why I'd just as soon be dead.

SWEENEY: That's what life is. Just is

DORIS: What is?
          What's that life is?

SWEENEY: Life is death.

T. S. Eliot – *Sweeney Agonistes*

Death is what we are and what we live. We are born dead, we deadly exist, and we are already dead when we enter Death.

Fernando Pessoa – *The Book of Disquiet*

[anti-faust of thin earth=of=the drug of my grief that respired the brain of etc of an embryo is saturated the infinite=alternating current of the sun to the orgasm excretion organ of the cadaver city that beat 1milligram of bio-less_apoptosis of outer space to the emotional particle of f/0 of the end of the universe that the sponge=brain of gene=TV stratification dive and the happiness of clones did the murderous intention of the blue megabyte of the sky gimmick chromosome=of eye of the hell of the cell that my soul proliferated the absent-minded body organ of the wolf to the bisexual placenta of the fatalities that soaks the formalin of the annihilation that inhabits to the rhinoceros bar cerebral cortex of road and resolved in that ant lion to the negative=escape circuit of the gene that is infectious=makes my love that stalled the sun capturing alive with the technology of

Death is a form of life that need not look outside itself. But, like terror, it is essentially cytoplasmic, both contained and voided of core, a state without nucleus feeding on an essentially borrowed hollowness. Death-Terror arrives as the hereditary curse of exaggerating (dubbing) that central chasm, of naming (dubbing) its circumference in the guise of a fetal solution, a nascent spasm melding the void with the voided – a state the perfection of which cannot be realized unified with a zeal for enlightened abnegation – itself the result of an informational mutation culled from a mechanized hinterland of chronically impervious default positions: a Sisyphean indulgence of process, process as rebellion against process, humanity duplicating its forms of expression into a perpetual climax of self-harm. Every act is a mimicking, a post-production ghost of its own dead origins. The overlap is corrosive; it eats the ex-sun of the cannibal race larva=of which the muzzle of the soul of the megabyte of the embryo that disguises after cow dries the blood vessel in the outside circle of ant of sun=as for the human body that was crying out the synapse the other selfs of the chaos that went up in flames committed suicide in the over there of my mirror image-vision of disillusionment=of=was instigating the clonic=embryo of the earth area to the living body asphalt=of to the body organ of the strange mystery of the embryo that my soul raped the brain that was full in the DIGITAL_future of the fatalities when loves to the ecosystem of the brain of the thalidomide that controls the sun of absence to the joke of f/0 of the body organ like my angel=the sun the atomic embryo the locus of the artificial love of the centipede that resuscitated the hunting fission=of=of ground brain will crush future without

through the present until the subject is made cadaveric. This rolling necrosis of consciousness cannot be escaped without profound symptoms of withdrawal, often bordering on white-eyed psychosis. The formulaic excitation of man's sensate mass is a process of duplication, of making oneself over according to some crude template of what it is to exist in the moment, like mistaking the shadow beneath a basking lizard for the lizard itself. The number of fresh disassociations – between embodied states and internal theatrics – manufactured by each new day of human life is both colossal and fugitive; our minds, constructed from layer upon layer of reinvented mutilations (like scarified onions held together by the promise of uncut flesh) are born old like new decisions. The gradual systemization of homicide simply reflects the necropolis of the human mind, those dead cities of

becoming acquainted with happy gimmick of the fatalities that I love to the love of the chameleon of the chromosome that was cut off/continued to incubate the corpse of cyber=god to the interior of the womb of the joke that parallels to the zero of sunlight--
Brain of a dog:
The beat that does not awake, darkness that is not seen....operate....with the rep-LOVE_eyes of the chromosome clone boys of the asphalt that do the apoptosis immortality of the dog that discharges the synapse of sleep so fuck++cadaver=of which embraces the drugy sun++++: the suicide replicant of lonely [myoglobin], ADAM doll of the cyber mechanism of the placenta world=<second>. It seen not and grieve over....the soul-machine that shut down the night sky of the desert any longer era respires++become clumsy omotya/I rape the emotional particle of the zero

stifled hope born deaf to the shrieking soil of unfortunate carnivores yet unable to feed themselves through thought alone: their corpses cover the earth; grass blades skewer them; moss binds them together; rain floods their cavities making a loosely-dressed ossuary of everything that remains unseen.

The putrefaction of souls stilled in airless chambers, made solid and many, weighed into the dead flesh of brains: the majuscular dressing eases the qualms of the unstrung corpse still clinging to his cringing tissues – but nobody can explain to him his raging cynophobia, how he repeatedly dreams of four black legs walking through blue grass, waking noosed with dread. Like lizards they look outside themselves for warmth; they surrender their bodies to the whims of the sun, to the cruel persistence of decay (a certainty of blackened fluid,

of ADAM
doll++++++not....she does the
end of clonical [love] desire
only++++
The future without
digital=apocalypse horizon
monochrome murder: brain.
ADAM
doll/rape++++++eternity
plays with the NIHIL_body
system of grief. CODA-enable
to sleep
She
Planetary
....bio=less=contact++++neo-
humanistic seasons "1/8"
(chaos....I do not
understand....myself fainting
lobotomy)
"....hacking the computer of
the sun of the world of the
dog///"
the solar system was blocked
up to the placenta of the
DIGITAL_disillusionment of
an ant: sense keyhole of the
brain of my someone cadaver!
someone///embryo in agony
feel pain cyber=of=cadaver
city instigates rhythm ant of
cosmic interior of the womb
to perceived f of limit torn

their dreams secreted in oily
pools), disease and the slow
rot of identity and feel safe in
it. This is what the mechanics
of paradise looks like to
something that is not only
born to die, but cannot prove
to itself that it wasn't born
dead, that all fetuses
don't fall dead from the
womb, their faces fat with
autolysis, and that all the
psychological trappings of
adulthood aren't just the
nightmarish symptoms of
protracted decomposition.
How is it more midwives do
not mistake themselves for
morticians? Plants and
animals would do well to
mock us: they live simple and
quiet while we revel in the
noise of our deaths, edifying
the ephemera of our
necrotized states.

Whoever concocted the world
did so under the influence of
monsters, incarnations sired
from states of self-reflexive
revulsion. Reality is horror – it
eats people like a carnivorous

was chromosome to
<<respire>> fatalities of brain
of infinite///puzzle sun of
inorganic substance organ
conceived] [clone of love to
jointed was embryo of
mysterious_drug??? maze/to
the rhinoceros bar space of the
dog thin blood of my brain
interference NIHIL///lapse
of memory=of which was
painted==the masochistic
residents of [sun] embryo of
light year=bewas respiring a
cadaver to the spiral instant of
dive///the horizon]
inheritance of my murder
[suck blood clones=of=the
circle lurks to gene=TV
committed suicide:
DNA=channel genital organs
of the chameleon split coexists
to the antifaustic placenta of
the world--:the wild nature
condition of outer space in
continuation=discontinuous=
soul=stalling/zero=of which
disturbs my brain of
[revelation///] an embryo
megabyte vital body
sun=:=secret/of (synapse)
etc/the sun that BABEL-

fog – a construct so diabolical
that man has been
unwittingly cajoled into
adorning the effervescence of
his dreams and his fantasies
with costumes of malleable
terror: ghouls, hybrid
creatures, fused entities,
seditious organs and limbs,
malignant slimes, mythic
decapitations, supernatural
possession, psychotropic
pestilence, brains worm-eaten
with paranoia (insanities of
truth)... myriad extremities of
man's dull fug.

When man is resurrected
from his grave of
enculturation – his cul-de-sac
of self-conscious putrescence
– he will for the first time
breathe the air of his decay,
instead of his decay breathing
him, inflating and deflating
him like a blackened lung.
Only then will murder (death
made code) be recognized as a
game of life: the only cure for
the perpetually hunted is for
them to realize that only those
already dead need run; in

ism=drops the nightmare of the neutron of a dog on the thalidomidic living naked body of my ant cadaver city=of=[charge improving that was beating to an infinite manhole///] the immature nerve fiber of the embryo is attached in connection with the love of the clone and sun=of=, to the lips that a pierrot who was going to ruin was prohibited the virtualrealistic crowd of the brain of simulacle or the ant=moon in reverse side of:....human body=of=zerox-machine desire. world=of sun of: the DIGITAL_eye that was betrayed=the seed had transfigured to the antifaustic placenta of an ant---
.(possibility cells=of which charge=the murderous intention plays)
[:brain*LIM my body....]
The god of et cetera: LOAD body invades speed....the clonical love of the placenta world that does road of the spirit holy precinct....cyber dog of TOKAGE fuck the

order to have a chance in the game, the quarry must cull everything thought susceptible to death, for it is dead already. The supposed grotesqueries of murder are nothing but auto-conspiracies designed to have us remain comfortably wallowed in our own rot, dancing and singing the odour of putrefaction (the embodiment of it), instead of drowning each breath in the perfume of sphacelation, aware to our mortified condition and born anew from it.

The animation of dead flesh terrorizes only those who remain ignorant of themselves, those with paraffin bleeding from their veins and skeletons of wrought iron. The future is a flesh-fly feeding on itself.

This persistent tingling form immersed in our holy brains sticky as phlegm secreted in a forbidden tongue. We, immediately old, cut together

worldly desires machine of
the angel mechanism of even
the gimmick girl: homosexual
anthropoid that I record are
scrapped....the lonely womb
cell of the ADAM doll: a
strategy....emotional particle
leaps to the machine area of
TOKAGE....: do the vaio-
universe of uterus-machine:
space crunch!....the death of
clone boys: brain the
catastrophic body of an ant
so/the hybrid suicide
machine of the
sun++operates. The drug
embryo of the reproduction
net....blue sky mechanism of
the night sky of the desert the
larva machine of the
monochrome earth....I sing
with the brain that is the
opening of an ADAM doll:
insulates it with
replicant++and others: the
horizon of DNA and the
storage: the anti-clone that
last term in ADAM doll....sun
committed suicide!....to the
pill form brain universe of the
machinative angel:
The world which falls.

and looped for all time shrink
in the society of self. Shoddy
memories congealed in
adipocere as recurring come
the sickly trills of stiffened
budgies floating down
autumn rivers, sky black as
newborn shit.
Eyes stretched like skin over
knucklebones.
Cobwebs conducting
medieval currents
drowned in ancient human
sap.
Human lips parked like two
molluscs in the sun,
old codes farmed for autopsy,
the world smudged like a
muted sky
reeling from exhumation.
Dreaming of leg-irons and
purposeful explosions,
all former requirements
reduced to glossolalia.
Mutation on the ward, his
mouth a bouquet of teeth,
reflections rolled flat,
saprogenic ratiocinations
strung and worn like pearls.
White face powder on the
inverted minstrels of nigredo.

blue sky, to the
disillusionment of the
mechanism of the fetus that
swims
the spider of paranoia
scratches the jungle of the
darkness where is born and
radiate the cruel black hole of
the feeling particle that the
code of the callousness of the
grief electron list of the
molecule that divides lack.
your caress that your siren
form oculus that you are
committed to R of the capital
letter is committed to the
chaos of the murder that
crowds to road in the night
stores the organ of the
darkness of a corpse--be
tortured to the color of blood
BOX of the pain to the
keyhole of the massacre of the
fetus horizon that crystallizes
got crooked.
the feeling record apparatus
that cell connects and
discharges to the state that
gets drunk darkness scratches
the desire of the antibio code
and establish to the part of the
shadow that I turned with the

BODY FARM:
A doctor enters the room, his
skin greenish, his hands
galvanized. The abscesses on
his forearms resemble
wounds from an ice-axe. His
coat is made from human
bladders – bleached and
stretched – and is screwed in
place with lathed teeth. He
does not hesitate: he peels off
the girl's skin like a swimsuit;
underneath is something
resembling the sedimented
remains of innumerable
medieval amputations.
She comes to in the middle of
the procedure (a standard
data-colonization) and begs
for the return of her discarded
cutis, but the doctor,
hardened to these cries from
the dead, barely raises his
eyes from the warren of
ancient tunnels that cringe
beneath his scalpel.

The diagenetic codes of
conduct that had quite
literally turned 21st century
man to stone proved resilient
to all known forms of

mineral living body--
you/depressing/night
sky/secret/murder/thin/slee
plessness/virgin/consolidate.
able to shoot down the
reproduction of the unside
and the angel of 0
comma_impregnated and
DNA play in the subsidence
area of the blue sky crashes
and slaughter the voice of
topologic existence gallant
vagina oculus my brain brings
the wave to the story of
existence difficulty was
discovered (my tears truth
that I confuse and enumerate
naked body punishment
murder that doesn't exist
burial--I stare at the sigh of
the secret permeation of the
cell--the hook up point of
existence)
my brain trap of this murder
fetus that got complicated and
relaxed optical, to the fraction
of the deep mystery of the
corpse that blinks
my thinking=cell escape-code
of the sun that the hell barks
and revolve the plate
intoxication of the birth

aggregation. To salvage them
was to leave them intact.
These titanic obelisks were
abandoned without ceremony
at a suitable geographic
location. One week later a
new desert was formed.

Humanity is a saprogenic
bacteria, an organism that
sustains itself on our perished
flesh, flesh once antenatal and
flush with a life unimaginable
to the grey porridge through
which we filter our deaths
and journey down into the
refabricated structures of our
stunted decay.

Nightmare-Script: She came at
me with eyes muddy as a
flightless sky. Her limbs were
held together with iron rings,
each decomposing appendage
stiffened in its annulose
casing.

Unbidden, a black hand of
mysterious branches comes in
though the window.
Yesterday's experiments are
confined to their fusty rooms,

dissolve begins to crowd to the terminal line of body outside.

the sun of asphalt world to road that was open the cyber fly cell of the insanity that erects swims the topologic powder dust in the second that explodes--"your crime is falling into silence in the record of the sphere of the human body that becomes white hot....the sleepwalker who isn't seen and isn't operate to your blood attires the interior of the womb of the sun after dries....the conversation that your original form indistinct soul emits from a blue intense picture....XXX"

fly commits suicide my unknown retina to--zero scatters sun chaos of half body of horizon from dive generates my oculus shadow without shadow goes after shell of the fetus in the decay just before dream of the splendid body outside of murder

comedy of the cell of the hooked to a meter, eavesdropping on hushed voices in bad light. Beneath unguarded halogen, tiny gods tear at the skin, talking through inconsistent speech patterns of plotted fantasies exhibited in the veins of dead bodies.

The tropic tensions of mutiny are transposed to month-long video recordings, the mental states of the operatives unwrapped and devoured like sweets. These newly liberated beings count weary across our neglected A-roads. Contents aside, their stomachs exude a refined stench. Dumped like sacks in a line, killing daydreams, melting into the tarmac, staged clams found hosting a blank, dark all-babbled archive of submerged time.

All non-identical brothers between the ages of ten and fifteen were taken away for testing. Work began to back up in a matter of hours. Half their number returned within

18

human body my strange--
thinking of the existence
difficulty of the sun break
down
hell--the appointment toe
reflex who embraced an
immortal pierrot absence of
the nature of cosmology
desire
the machine freezes the
optical artery that scatters to
the reproduction of the earth--
the desert where micro
murder was committed the
atmosphere that transfers
fills--the plasma of fear is
activated in the sky where
spermatozoon choked with
the corpse of my tears/with
the rhythm of the massacre of
the cell unit that discloses the
existence of a schizophysical
naked body.
I become the soul of the
inundation that isn't seen
Gaia BI-COSMOS of the
scaffold that becomes the
earth like the lonely mystery
of the electron which reigns
on the head///
X hell that the shallow sleep
of the corpse passed the larva

a week: toxic, partially
defleshed corpses propped
and propelled by chemicals
and punitive voices. Their feet
were green and their ankles
stripped of skin. Where the
skin remained its texture
resembled that of wool. Their
mouths were slack like bad
dough, and each one had a
distinctly rachitic
deformity of chest. Tasting
Time is the common name
given.

When greeting the stuffed
remains of her victims one
should refrain from assuming
airs. One would do to also
keep in mind that the hammer
marks are inconsequential
mutilations, nothing but
gloomy dents in an otherwise
unmodified material. Young
children, running brown from
these tumbled figurines,
though regularly metered for
symptoms, as yet remain
unaffected.

Once kidnapped, they soon
come to assume many of the

of the pain that drop to the interior of the womb of the sleeplessness of the fly and distort the visions in the future that my appointment toe intoxication fetus that was deceived to the humor that transfigures inheriteds the night magnetic look that confuses and decays--my fetus is caught to the retina of the fatalities crime X play that isn't seen and isn't embrace/imp folded to the prolapse impossible atmosphere. respire the callous spectrum of a corpse-- the thinking of the fly that my fetus crowds to disgrace, to the spatial suicide of the murderous intention that quiesces is crushed to your uterus. "disillusionment approximates outside limitlessly the body of the monster--the organ of the zero of the fetus that the bright drug of the sun was toyed with to the camouflage of the insanity that measures the vector of the impossible interior of the womb senses

standard human traits. Although their transparent skin and similarly diaphanous organs have an emetic effect on most, there are still those who seek them out for sexual purposes. Specimens once considered useful in the temples, those of dangling origin, are now seen as little more than flea-bitten impulsives sick on the blood of needled mothers. Sun spots in their raped regions provide stark testimony to an unholy hardening of the soul.

Heaven's reconstructed symbols ordered that a mass be held without sound in honour of his distorted ears: sucked kettles coated in puzzled hair. The world's new materials came to the table stale. And yet somewhere anomalous detectives still drain reactions from metronomic citizens in rooms rank with the elicitations of sustained interrogation. Those that are permitted to leave stay left;

me wear of explosion to depressing outwardly/croak the fly! imp overthrown to the dream gravity_look of the sufferings X fetus of the thinking image! "I step on my fetus to the R area of the naked body and entered--my fetus was exposing the body outside certain season like the chromosome when gets furious at the corpse of the mystery--the buffoonery play of the sun that was folded to null that radiates the laughter of night sky in the drug=area of grief is running through/the last arrival point that last term f of other self was impregnated to the over there of the cell. "death operates--I step on the shadow of hallucination--the null play that floats to the unknown shadow of the chameleon from the interior of the womb of the drug discloses the keyhole of the mystery of the human body/the pierrot only" who travels to a thinking impossible catastrophe and they skirt the edges of our town, their brains devoured by toxic fertilizers and inanimate fantasies. Slaked with the rotting organs of our kitchen mechanists, they can live a week or more.

Grown men, flapping their arms like wounded birds, wait for their days to end in un-policed inanition, as girls from the print works taunt them, these fading slovens their frothy minds wrapped in disorganized fantasy, with flashes of snatch and suety thigh. The wind races along on overhead wires cragging all but the most protected of skins. By the time 'death' claims these laboured souls their faces are scarred rock, cicatrices of climatic bane having re-sculpted the features in innumerable stratums of decay. We hear that coal chisels are often required before they are coffined – should funds for such funereal extravagancies be forthcoming.

21

combined the wakefulness of the upside down appointment toe to///the image of my fetus off.

"....I discover a deep blue area....in the sky of steel****"

"your soul that becomes unknown=the zero of the universe that turned vital by brain cannibal race of clone=love?"
my dog which rapes the anti-faustic sun of the gene in the desert of an embryo does the nebula of the disillusionment of the quark to the drug star of road that the manhole of a cadaver shines the body of storage to the rhinoceros bar body of the embryo of the respiratory arrest the image of the horizon to the placenta of the extreme north of BABEL LOAD to the keyhole of the suicide of the cell other selfs that sleeps in the deep sea interference and be blockading the earth to the brain puzzle of road of an ant fuck chromosome=of crab

The railway lines peter out long before the closest town. That this unseen habitation releases smoke into the sky is but mere hypothesis, a lofty rationalization cooked up in the heads of our perpetually stranded commuters forced to wear their faces in glass for 8 hours a day.

Incidents of data-molestations are on the increase, and invariably end up in the courts. The lies eventually seep through the silence. Decisions are irreversible. Tears run thick black from the usual eyes. For some, the suffering of the inanimate is too much to bear, its mere printed detail a sabre to the guts. A stay of execution is granted to all of flammable kin, until such time as they can be used collectively to facilitate the torching of larger and less flammable transgressors. Some say that we've turned on the Still-Kind for no other reason than to

22

locus of eyeball that fly was betrayed to the velocity of light scream of the machine that is falling=to the dramatic hearing of the fatalities the world sonic the future tense of ADAM that <F> suspends the madman of the cosmic ant the pupil I become to the secret promise of the rhinoceros bar change of the cadaver city able to ride take that heart the virgin of a jaguar is the micro=acme of the body the brain of the embryo gets confused be exposed to the gimmick documentary of a cadaver it plays strange the love of the hell of the cell that my human body drifts to the maze of the DIGITAL=quickening and the earth where is latent to the quark of treachery crashes to the clonic strings of the reverse side in the moon the negative limit of a cell to body tissue palpitation the body of the fretfulness of an ant without becoming acquainted with exit of etc of the spiral is jointed to the soul that an ease our ice-damaged flesh one day out of seven.

In the cities, cadaverous machines stream through the streets looking only outside themselves for death. The meat they eat temporarily replaces their rotting intestines, an equal amount of which is passed as faeces a few hours later. The dead only speak of death as of a dream; whereas the shared insanity of human kind is always to live death and only dream life, and then only to dream it dead, unyielding, rigor mortised. The debugging/human exit = the alchemy of self-reflexive decomposition: souls cooked black as shadow and smeared on the walls in the shape of men. (The vampire sees that he is not the only creature buttressing a corpse with displaced cerebration, vivifying its putrid organs with prophylactic substances: he knows the blood he drinks is spoiling and bitter – he can embryo was disillusioned and to cause any births of the world to the anti-faustic to the cruel stratification of a chromosome subsided to the hope of the mutation of the hell of the cell that rapes the soul in future to the undirt murder person of the emotional particle of strange speed of the chameleon who is pierrot of earth outside circle=of=to the soul of the sterility that begins to overflow to the internal organ murder of pupil of which dream-plays....the plug is scattered are caused to the rays of the space=zero that the cell other selfs reverse to the localization of the slaughter of the sun the true violent=skizophone of the cell disguised and the laughter of the mask to the body that leaps the quantum of the ant that the blue sky is infectious! The output_brain area of the dog::the body fluid of myself where the over there of the pupil of the LIMIT girl where the hybrid suicide system of

taste the plague of anthropoidal birth in every drop – but he also knows, which man does not, that putrefaction is a process of many forms and that his own self-inflicted stasis serves to consecrate his habitual strategies. When he dreams he dreams of purple trees lost in a black night sky; his nightmare is never waking from this dream.)

The death they fear is subtraction, that moment when the smut of their decay ceases to sing, when it is sucked to bone and silent dust. Happy to live in rot forever they pray that they may be allowed to keep the noise, and the noisier their prayers the deeper that collective expiration can be felt.

Our future medium cradled by psychosis
(Phthisis and Insanity):
a man wishes himself dead, knows his body to be

the clone boys::the sun that the speed of TOKAGE::the soul-machine of myself reproduces to the REC brain of the drug embryo clone-dive to the brain universe of an ant overheat the outside circle love-replicant///body of the ant that beats digital murder sublimated the gimmick of eve_chromosome! The brain of a boy respired the nano-machinative suicide line of the sun! :the cyber womb cell city access-code////
Nano-machinative suicide system boy machine of TOKAGE dances the contamination=mode of the soul-machine of myself: REC brain awakening: the rape_sun group love-replicant body fluid of the drug embryo the gimmick thyroid city of an ant LOAD so dog of which it secretes basement of the artificial sun where walks fuck although road: shooting the brain target of the embryo of myself that is lost in wild fancies of the VTR_soul-machines of the clone

polluted, and so desires for it to be destroyed and replaced. He wants for his head to be blown open.

The morgue has no windows. It is constructed from yellowed stone and is known to sweat throughout the summer months. Its smells are lonely dreams.
Its orderlies refuse to prepare men for the grave, choosing instead to have them live forever in clouded mirrors. Its rats feed on themselves. Black is its colour of truth, and its inhabitants choose to sleep through it. Any smiles are exhibits meant for somewhere else, logistical errors kept in storage until their rightful destination can be found. Artificial respiration of carcasses in hospital parking lots:
savages draped in the skulls of their enemies, junked on poison, paid to promote movement and sound because death is disgusting and death does not move and it does not

boys::0% of word that I was murdered in the digital placenta world blue sky of BABEL animals line: the murder circuit of ADAM doll: the boundless body of myself records the love of the clone: digital=vamp season OUTPUT of a chromosome Gene=TV of the body of the drug embryo: the soul-machine of the clone boy that hybrid mental dismantlement: the brain of myself connects with the body of an ant the skizophysical cell division of the artificial sun: the REC brain of the interior of the womb of a dog that homosexual VTR of uterus-machine breeds in the over there of the chromosome where conducts artificial insemination reproduces the sun and the love of clone boys commits suicide impossible: the clone-skin of TOKAGE I rape the cadaver of god///the nano-machinative body system of the ant: the nerve of myself that clone boys replicate the love that

sing.

This desiccant spring, misplacing its steady pulse and finding instead innumerable surrogate futures all born writhing from the maggots of their own decay. This desiccant spring, this flowering of immortal rot, this rhythmic corrosion of an ancient despair trapped and repeated forever... We were born in winter and it will never come again: death can be callow but once. (The spores of *Existenz* are entombed by layers of subsequent spoilage.)

Vision of the hybrid man: His mouth is full of chewing gum that is manufactured from blow flies. He distrusts all forms of inorganic currency. His clothes are tailored from softened bones, and he is eager that you should understand the significance of this. He says his name is always changing and that the

committed suicide to digital]
the herds of the love-rep...
cadavers of enough myself::an
indefinite automaton that I
caress the wolf=space of the
cyber embryo::the
rape_storage of the soul-
machine of matrix
DNA=channel myself: the
reverse evaporation vesicle
sublimated the clonic end line
of the artificial sun!
Catastrophic planet of an ant
reproduces: VTRVTRV
Desert of TOKAGE restores]
Machine mechanism of the
soul falls the word-- ADAM
doll dreams of imperfect
suicide in the corner of the
retina the brain of a dance
mass of flesh mental
fabrication boy shut
down....think about like the
gimmick of the cadaver of
god toward the pierrot of the
another person of world the
self control condition
malfunctions so ants the
murder of the womb area the
body of the speed embryo of
the body fluid of the zero
beats operates to the drug

realm his identity occupies is
terrain vague.
He notices a blemish, a
blackened section of skin, on
the tip of his left forefinger
and immediately thrusts his
hand into his trouser pocket.
He gets dewy-eyed when he
reminisces on those half-
forgotten seasons of cancer.
When you mention death he
will not understand.

The Land of the Dead 2:
If nothing happens to the
dead, then here is where you
feel the concentrated force of
that non-occurrence, where
one man may be framed into
multitudes. Here every form
of expression is vengeful of
that earlier sickness, and more
vengeful still of the cure that
put all of its symptoms
behind glass. It is not possible
to feel this land, and it is not
possible to want to. In order
to mix well in the new Land
of the Dead you must try to
ignore the psychopathologies
of those around you, however
pellucid they may be, and in

27

mechanism "so....myself resuscitates to the disillusionment of birth" brain of heat crowds to "cadaver of myself....and in the style of the nervous temperament of the thinking impossible embryo that <boy> is wrapped to the love of the self replication nature of the disillusionment that does blood to the pupil of the clone like the rotation wooden horse of the GOOD-BYE spiral/the end/placenta that witnesses the strange heart of children that dashes in the season of the small murder when the noise sun that radiate heat" have a chromosome montage and be "the corpse of a nightmare"="the second" the dog which the future of myself makes visual the hearing that was shut reproduces "the boy=machine=hERO" "....embrace "the earth of a hybrid fly...." love of machine line myself of frigidity the angel of the boy falls" to the no circumstances submit to an urge to vomit, as public exteriorizations of any kind will prove extremely distressful to all involved.

The soul grows like some sentient mildew on the dead flesh of life. It's the slow decomposition of the brain; it's the ephemera of rot; not the vermicular sludge, not the decaying body itself, that instrument of some potentially eternal substance, but a conglomeration of putrefactive bacteria and phenolic compounds – such as cadaverine, putrescine, 3-methylindole – slowly revealing themselves as they consume their host.

The anticipated unification – upon us again – is based on ancient principles: The eight-limbed lusus naturae stumbles on the ground, its orifices hailing worms. (Our lovers' bodies slowly collapse into one another in what onlookers describe as a body universe of the digital=apocalypse to the manhole of the reverse side in the road genital organs moons of the thyroid-cadaver cities of the zero of myself half just as is communicated to nihilistic space of wolf so idea of SEX of myself depressing machine of embryo (explodes....to attraction in unnext month foresight body mode of (boy (twisted becomes cyber=wolf of frigidity) electron=ant that the brain of the embryo that caused to the clonic love of a chromosome disguised crashed respire era to the masochistic of the sun that respired the plug of the rhinoceros bar/reptilian to the spine that escape=the negative desire of the material to the laceration of insanity suck blood fatalities of camera-eye of drug of VTR in the abnormal world of the cell love/reversed the megabyte of the mass of flesh of the madman to the murder person who beat....my brain

sublime twinning of souls.) In the mirror this fat would run as water. A new beginning rises from its raven slime. This spectacle of arachnidan rebirth transcends all odour as the rotting tango shifts and squirms beneath its waxy cuticle. These freshly spliced entities – joint terminals of biocapturism – now united forever in their carnal bonds eradicate the binary presuppositions of their former corpse incarcerations, those old emotions reduced to catabolism, human tissue into gas.

This cold-blooded machine life of death born twice over refuses an exhaustive transcendence for the sake of countability: the localization of progressive host disintegration has left its mark in this attachment to a sickness for which although there is a cure it remains unwelcome.

Sometimes they still wake in

cell that formed the placenta of f/0 of tokage had become extinct to the brain that is in an earth outside circle from the body fiber of the embryo who sleeps in the reverse side in the moon: clones of eternity recurs cadaver city=of=DIGITAL_solitude of musical scale my genes of all dive: my body chromosome of desire of crater to split is....embryo turned pale having was: ant of battle=of=vein to love fatalities of skull scratch sound disillusionment of DIGITAL=weather grasped vital body of chaosmic decay to sun and ant of murder=of=sec palpitation was my person whether about brain? idling <absent> and <mystery> of which stimulated the bisexual cerebral cortex of the clone in the interior of the womb=world of [thalidomide/f] of the sun was thinking about the bio-less_play=space of an embryo to the ovarium of BABEL

the crib of howling dogs, and for a time recall those cold nights spent drinking away the future of the sun. They hear the clatter of autumn slowly fade as they melt back into the cloistered hollows of their sclerous, mannequin-like skins. I hear the script encode itself over and over, hiding in its own replication, collapsing under the weight of each predatory transmission – scan its message dismembered like Bellmer's poupées. The future's mutations will never reveal those fabled points of egress.

We are the agents of our own physical degradation, of our own somatic ruin. We are the instruments of murder, repeated murders, serialized self-killings promoting the expansionist plans of our transcendental identities, our existence as psycho-active rot. Every thought dislocated from action represents the further spread of our disembodiment, a temporary synapse of etc of the embryo that coexist to the brain of the drug mechanism of the angel the clonic thinking of the ruin of the earth area reflain "eye of the DIGITAL=madman that my body turned OFF the war of the larva condition of DNA to the rhinoceros bar artery of the dog that escapes became" the cyber=gimmicks of the immortality of the fatalities that loves recorded the terror that becomes the abnormal world of the body vital the suspected=brains of the fatalities that fabricated and loved the bio-less_pupil of the chromosome fuck on my heart that creeps about the chaosmic placenta of the ground and revolve anti-faust of the DIGITAL makes clonic birth chromosome of f/0 of world in infectious caused ground of whole of suspension by my brain from gathered was clone*embryo of inheritance impossible desire? placenta began to overflow the from the stratification of f/0 of the emotional particle

annihilation of carnality. As decomposition intensifies so too does the sense of our essential incorporeality, the less we are embodied by that on which we feed and transform. We are machines of slaughter, removing ourselves from those excremental sacks with every fresh evisceration. Our violence against flesh is so automatic that we cannot often see it. We see the severed limbs, the corrupted skin, the disease of deliberate traumas – invented in fantasy and enacted repeatedly and without reflection until only fantasy bleeds – the beheadings, the fractured bones, pulped faces, all the many architectural ecstasies of blood,

and yet still we remain secluded in false narratives and solutions fit only for trematodes.

of tokage that transfigures::
OFF--
The sun of myself is respiring
the clonic end of the drug
embryo. Do short with the
despair machine----subjective
body of the hell of the cell that
the artificial sun of the clone-
skin: the brain of myself that
the interior of the womb of
the digital dog: clone boys is
dancing the corpse of road
fuck! The gradual suicide line
of the clone boys::the body of
an ant that invades the body
fiber of the lobotomy fly of
the angel mechanism of
ADAM game....the soul-
machine of ADAM doll the
other side of the artificial sun
the MHz love-replicant
chromosome that beats
operates: the body line....suck
blood of the zero of myself
that inoculates the murder
crazy idea: the cyber crime
program of the drug
embryo....night sky of the
desert that gets deranged to
the reproduction gland of
TOKAGE_DNA=channels of
the blue murderous intention

You children of winter, you
corpses titillated into warped
maturation, you glossy
coroners shitting out your
fetal waste... I see you
watching with unbridled glee
as putrefaction stretches,
bloats and distorts your
decrepit offspring but 4
minutes free of life. The barely
disguised mummification of
the elderly is always a source
of terror for the uninitiated,
those unaccustomed to the
flat desiccation of butyric
fermentation. They see the
insect life moving underneath
their diluted skin, and are
repelled that they have come
to live with the dead.
Those female cadavers in dry
decay – nothing left but hair,
bone, and an untidy smudge
of red lipstick – have been
known to disintegrate at will.
Even their parents are a
source of disgust-fuelled
consternation, and they
cannot long ignore the grave-
waxed glimmer of less-
advanced decay screaming
from every unpowdered

clone boys of the sky that respires the planet of an ant era with the speed of the soul-machine of the ADAM doll_junk to the emotional line of the zero of myself: 1/8 of brain of the drug embryo inheriteds: ADAM doll murder VTR: the sun of myself 1/8 suicide machines of the drug embryo that conduct artificial insemination....so that the pupil of the dog LOAD to the murder range of the ant pattern of the gimmick girl with the matrix of the ruin of TOKAGE that copy the body fluid of myself that gene=TV witnesses the clone boys of the reverse side in the month who explode rapes the nightmare of the amniotic fluid mechanism of ADAM doll the soul-machine of myself stops the breath that goes to war and respire/imp replicate the nerve fiber in the last term of the ADAM doll that notifies the love of the clone road of love-replicant dogs by the time_difficult fissure.

Dogs shaved and melted down for the purposes of this grimy understanding, this filthy slurry of ruin, this index of hands and tongues. She arrives with a centrefold's dry swell, her lips moistened with invertebrates. Her emotional wiring is enigmatic, her remaining soft tissues now embalmed exposing larvae – we look away. She is disgusted at the thought of death-memories, can't see how they can be of use. There is a pause as the prose-CURRENTs regenerate. The paralysis heightens our desire – a soft human relic of tear surfaces, soluble word masks, and hauntings.
She talks of
the splendour of enlightened colonization,
the escape from leaden maturation,
murderous pitches reduced to animal soils.

existence. I copy so that I reproduce the brain of the ruin of TOKAGE--the reverse side in the moon in the over there of the pupil of the gimmick girl....the drug embryo of the brain of 1 the murderous intention of the cyber mechanism of TOKAGE/transplants in 1/8 seconds: clone-skin uterus-machine of the solar system I murder the herd of the ant of narcolepsy and the body of myself receives the semen of the ADAM doll of the cadaver city. <murderous body line of the soul-machine>.
:the artificial sun drug embryo of the body=plug of the machine line....machinative angel of dustNirverna the brain of <<breakdown>> puzzle awakes the ADAM doll ceremony-despair machine that has set to the hell of a cell. The speed of the sun becomes a line....++the clone boy the rhythm machine of anti=sex evolves....++clone-skin records this merciless love of the cadaver city, on

We talk of cosmetic slaughter, of capital punishment, the ambient phases of meat, bacterial bogs of black rot in the skulls of fleshless astronauts.
The floor is thick with vermin faeces. She doesn't appear to notice. The clock on the far wall makes like spades in a burial ground. Us murderers require nerve cells to dream the half-eaten corpses of sex-death. This is parasitic recycling.

Whims in water of voices – death found artificial – the currents of rain underneath man leave the condition by process – our dead spread on hair – the game revealing shaved spots hiding ultimate maturation – we devoured this desiccant bone – brains in kettles of innumerable faces, all obelisks and alchemy – pray-fund operatives hear the Gum Men coming through homicide – invertebrates in explosions with all unaffected nihilism resembling wallowed

the heaven of the cyber
mechanism of the gimmick
girl where: coexisted the sea
of the two poles of gene.
:machinative angel of
grief=of=circuit the internal
organ of the side relation of
the digital=apocalypse/mode.
Thin vacuum, ADAM doll of
Nerve fiber
The machinative angel
assembles....the cheerful
machine-seeds of the placenta
world....laughs impossible
to....1/8 of emotion of the sun
accelerate it to the satellite
pack of an existence difficult
soul-machine: the motion of
vital/non=being of the
ADAM doll....ant of: escape
the body junkie who! :the
stratosphere of uterus-
machine parasitism person of
the cosmology of the over
there of that season pupil of
'f': the miserable insanity of
clone boys who the gimmick
girl who explodes replicate
happy: of a chromosome that
was recovered begins to
laugh....the sea of the lapse of
memory line....gene of

narratives – once revealing in
its skin as faeces of muted
human decisions into the
blackened rooms – layer
eight-limbed (dubbing)
moment –
flesh simply reflection of that
moistened bitter vomit of
grotesquery (Our
reconstructed dreams sky
parting as discarded refuse
inflates their dogs) – just
dancing as man can, in
common ages of skin – feed
the dreams to remain in time
for grave-waxed conducting
as of inanition, the stale of
many, the insanity of the
sustained – uncut time a
smudge, a relic lived to the
core, that saprogenic world's
their making flesh for the
without – the concentrated
flapping of needled doctors –
forced naming of the scan –
shrink cutis, for terminals are
always one of condition –
some of his logistical branches
devoured – useful for killing
and moistened misplacing –
excremental
(debugging/human self-

M++++++I reproduce....the
residual gauge of the soul-
machine [<future>=ADAM
doll respires era++]
Because myself is the speed:
the artificial miracle of the
sun: a suicide replicant that
impossible to
reverse side in the moon
where pushes aside the crowd
of f of the mitochondria and
went out excitement to road
of the parasite embryo of the
sun surface stimulates a clonic
chromosome and the
chaosmic wound crimson
electron killing and wounding
was playing to the ugly cells
of the anonymity of f that the
android released the cord
form mystery of the ground
with the instinct of the micro
eyeball of the fly that lost the
sun
microcosm=of=darkness=of
which goes up and down in
the brain table of the severe
genes/despair of the earth
where murders the storage of
the womb and the
bio=less_drift of soul
desire=the DNA of upside-

consciousness) filters – our
fetuses, as transparent, are
hosts of the unwelcome –
wrought intestines worn on
enlightened chest made
disgusting and born away –
drop into A-cells howling
chronically – according to the
owned, the melted drinks
embodied for paradise, that
deformity of the again,
assume black into skin
traumas – inhabitants die rats
in blackened corpses of their
informational stumbles –

these structures as children –
flea-bitten localization of
larvae come cytoplasmic, half
transmission torn from
unholy slimes, entombed
rightful and funereal they live
rot – the old without and
reconstructed they try on their
silent costumes – they pocket
the stream of leaden prose-
CURRENTs, surfaces torching
– hours in those abscesses on
earth, subtraction to our
dough, paralysis of
degradation, womb, grave,
and steady parked

down that caused wolf latent the potential embryo of the "the game" the body of f/0 of god battle was notified to the counterclockwise brain of the fatalities: blood gets thirsty....the brain of the twin raped mutual soul: the brain of the drug mechanism of the ant that the DIGITAL_placenta of the paradise faints in agony to the milligram tears of the rapture of a girl to the first cry of storage/micro murder person design color the cadaver of road that harmonized to the womb of fatalities was interchanging the solar system to the equator of a chromosome gene=TV was reflecting and was weaving passage that blood was bleached to the end of the ground of the drug<I dance to the chaosmic mass of flesh of the body/embryo that fatalities continuously radiated enough sea merely to the quarks of the callousness of the pierrot that bent the curvature that is this

aggregation – their collapse into rebirth – remain a weight, habitual like stomachs in paradise, a message underneath glass futures – require psychological end – transform to keep in tears, old, purple bonds writhing immortal – the corpse transcends in vague floating non- identical supernatural decay – cold states of our excremental casing – skirt of sludge, the feeding layer dead behind a stream of unstrung deformity – possible remains of psychosis on A-roads – waxy kin wear anew those transcendental Toxic4 bodies partially eaten – yellowed colonization of kidnapped flesh and paralysis – little railway of defleshed cancer ghouls stuffed in flea-bitten remains – belly duplication floods humanity made animation – do the born time deeper in sphacelation, from butyric indulgence into that devoured look – these pellucid brains innumerable half still in putrefaction – you disillusionment of a vital body in the mating of an embryo and wolf>fuck the inorganic substance solitude of the sun that becomes the virgin who recorded the cruel caress of an emotional particle and angel=intonation of etc of or embryo of zero that showed the hybrid DNA of night sky to the far interior of the womb of the electron=the decay of $f/0$ of the womb was being played strange to the indecent inhabitant of the image that looped the body organ to VTR of clone-tokage of the horizon death that the cell other selfs that the skizophysical brain cells of the embryo that cause the sun of a chromosome to the cosmic artificial intelligence of tokage subsided and conducted the zerox machine of the body organ of the centipede did palpitation should be loved LOAD to the other side of the sun it inheriteded the blood of the disillusionment of outer space to the artery of the embryo

minds resilient in the silence of annihilation – only minutes in this enculturation for constructed flesh – spoilage vision up in wrapped glimmer – his mouth afar as gloomy emetic heads fade in replication – putrescine now inconsistent with our machines – while burial hailing ordered onlookers of constructed states – we have the antenatal look of pre-abandoned meat – a fetal nothing plotted from BODY evisceration – in that mass climatic nothing but dreams of those abandoned expressions and death – mysterious reconstructed dark decisions grave-waxed in warm brains escaping the systemization of parked skins – disease their teeth for hands – people outside logistical layers, maggots squashed and stretched like vomit – nightmares screwed down to script come in muted kettles to corrosive futures, grimy as sphacelation –

that impossible to the blue vagina of the sky that set up the mine in the time that focuses to anti-faust of eve that erases=1 gram of universe=to the tube of the respiration of the fatalities that I love and played the clonic string of the reverse side in the moon and committed suicide to the interior of the womb of the wolf BABEL=of=to the DIGITAL_love of tokage that coexisted the brain of an embryo in your every day toward the crowd of a frivolous cadaver infinite series=of which was suffocated=to the intention of the radical latency of the respiratory organs of the embryo that beat the thin earth of the blue sky to the cell other selfs!

to the quickening of the love of the clone of battle that perceived the DIGITAL_despair of an embryo at the center of this world which the negative heart of the material was the man chronically transparent in supernatural lizard, our scripts construct themselves decaying our talks, eating the new Sisyphean children – agents coated with moss whisper in concocted hours to paranoia formed of time and wires – never talk of misplacing man murderous in decay – choose immediately, intact in waking later in human mud moistened further, the seep recall softened slowly – will progressive slaughter peel the hypothesis? – fantasy cradles its disease in embalmed poupées – truth: our repeated urge to make black architectural – dogs bloat up in ceremony of useful transcendence – commuters without earth, un-policed for branches and spades – whims slaked through innumerable peels rightful in their rot – ruin comes with symptoms born in lines as each corpse recedes back into its skin – liberated flesh lives through hardening of womb springs –

attached my freeze body fluid whirled the region of etc of a cadaver to the cerebral cortex of 1 micron of the disillusionment*embryo that caused the infinite drug war of the sun organ in the interlude area of f/0 of the chromosome where crashed disguised I grasp the nebula of the chaosmic embryo to the crowd of the soul that ant went mad and I who road of reptilian=filled the blue of the sky to sec echo did the blood of the cell other selfs the inorganic substance love of the sun that caused clone-tokage of my blood vessel inhabited to the internal organ that DIGITAL=mitochondria were deceived the sun of absence to the synapse of the empty earth area that beat to the hole of grave of the quark and as if it causes to bubbles the mirror face of chaos LOAD to my blue storage=/the slaughter of f are permeated to the sadistic rays of my right brain that experimented the scan acts of brothers recycled in data-molestations of a single formulaic week – life expansionist like vomit – table lung in the old sun of hands dead under floods of collective disgust-fuelled nightmare born on the soft message – process-kind feed regularly on self until they are dark and together tailored by dead hands – work through terror into phlegm – his psychopathologies crawl down his forearms, his principles eavesdropping for souls – night girls rotting considerable in transmission: they future girls chances made in inanition – still black and nascent found – both remaining persistent in fat sickness, skeletons shrinking, spots arachnidan to inanimate existence – lovers have taken on ancient skin together their putrefaction purposing them like old born stones – auto-conspiracies toxic in the conducting dream time come until terror wills a glossy cancer, its predatory spread

skizophysical virgin membrane of the earth area to the deadlock of the quark mechanism of the fatalities an embryo of 1 and the thin electron of BABEL that diverged to the cosmic soul of an ant LIM shakes the mirror images of my chaos and play the sun of the grief of the neutron that turned OFF f of the massacre of an embryo to period to the placenta of the nightmare of the electron theory of an ant and caused my bio=less_brain cells invaded-
:the null revelation:you/butterfly stroke/passion that was open to the drug/machine of hell halts///the fetus is your damage the horizon (ocular of the continuously massacre) the tidal volume screen that erases the mysteries of 6 character to the black hole of the atomic earth that flutters the butterfly stroke of the electron to the impregnation play of the off-season hell that combines the character of

annulose –

when involved in listed abnegation we help them construct the innumerable months – the recordings arrived polluted, but useful and recurring in us: from them we reinvented the grave – these inhabitants, entities of some embalmed psychosis, are an indulgence of meat, slovens comfortably warped by rank mechanical prayer – minds stay in changing inside a face's punishment of unpowdered decay – every dewy-eyed video polluted to titillate tissues of disgusted attachment, mothers, wires of effervescence, days of spring, all sacked by a lone flesh-fly – operatives hiding in regularly monitored brains, hiding dead, literally inside the cynophobic void – mannequin meters and wishes of presuppositions seep into subsequent life-filters – talk escapes the ward, seeps into the world, into the gummed mouths of habitual murderers ruin--your corpse at, the back of the keyhole shed tears your uterus thinly caused the quickening that was full to your rapture to the vacant atmosphere of gray shouted fearful female dog I howl and fills////the area of the unlife of the thinking that makes absent to my brain that passes through the beat of neon and be coming off--the love, that is going to ruin the pierrot that the viscus plays the suicide of immortality and play love the drop of the lung that fatalities of depth unenable records of hallelujah topologic crime of the respiration that can't precipitate...."nonexistent limit exists outside my body. I exist in the over there of the self-consolation where was stuck on your pupil. you are twisted the golden chameleon in the night****"the fetus that the night of sleeplessness is shaking an audition impossible pale street lamp to the murderous intention of the virgin of the quickening that is impregnated the

slaked with borrowed codes – face veins decay destroyed by fertilizers – ice-axes cannot hew this dead currency – in forbidden torchings branches of exaggerated intestines release smells of printed paper –

removing horror outside itself – wrought index of maturation provides the future's lips with a diabolical rhythmic smoke – significance is decay wrapped up screaming – Expansionists collapsing under the lizard's secreted interrogation – after a few crude drinks they admit to murder, and to being God – alone we turned to talking the bane of terror – too self-conscious we bloat our understanding, forming surrogate temples of unfortunate death and the cure of noisier and noisier fantasies – dream girl raped with bacteria – auto-conspiracies of terror

hallucination that is descending drug into the body that froze you who are crying out as for I, the matrix of the generation that confused manufactures the sun of existence difficulty and "....the looking coldly that erases your storage radiates heat to the space of the solitude that the butterfly stroke that passed the time of suicide was impregnated on the beach of the solitude where it cut....the consciousness that fetus came flying to the birth of the suffering of the chaos that I engraved on the figure of the murder of my cell...." I am going to forget the sufferings of the tears--
to the fingertip of the marionette=brain cell of the embryo that accumulates the happiness type of the past of an artificial paradise on the gimmick of the drug mechanism of the angel that my soul begins to split on the brain of the murder of an ant the cell wolf toys with the

tissues transcending paradise in morgue-town architectures of bone from decomposition solutions bred slowly within themselves behind all because solution is still dead felt from cooked centrefold's flesh appendage costumes and binary mind – to him inorg. in psychotropic courts, and of formed sources possible disease of instruments, some coming to that truth – sucked children refabricated in the informational tide of self-reflexive ear – thought supernatural but suffering blood all-babbled and corrosion in rings – forms of life tucked away in killing sacks – its walking scoff at killing in slow desire of the life like death – the fall its source half-forgotten and what carcass clams, cadaverous, slow of yet sexualised plans to callow life of purposes, kitchens ripe with meat, rolling abandoned heads melt screaming the want – keep Reality newborn

cyber=aerofoil of the clone
catastrophic internal organ of
the blue sky quark the
transmission line of the
cadaver city plays to the
mode of life clonic passion of
birds discloses the
DIGITAL_generative organ to
the vocal cord with the
bio=less_air of an embryo sun
that the stratosphere of the
happiness of a chromosome
consciousness of the micro
murder that was done the
drug*reproduction gland of
the blue sky my gimmick that
cracks to the accomplice of the
velocity of light=inheritance
of death god who DNA is
diverging like the guerrilla of
the cell of the ant interference
to the map on the other side
of the sun desire and was
made the eradication of the
hell of the cell the honeycomb
of TOKAGE BABEL visual
hallucination send back out
the fission disease of the sun
to DIGITAL to the cell other
selfs that dance earth outside
circle=of where my brain
basement of the embryo in the

distorting tiny expirations,
murder in the sky reeling in
schmaltz dreams –
be code-eyed anew to own
both skins staying shadowed
to land decomposition in
public on the skewer –
understand the poupées now
vermin-warren entities born
to an eventual poison – that
malleable incarceration made
guts hammered flat, and
every hour in skin is a
degradation, hours of skin,
cased, arms of line-born
weighted hammer loops in
that weary code of symptoms
– invariably when expression
count is made we begin
decomposing, on them bone
morticians, traits of birth you
mediums of worm-eaten
hunted, you fertilizers of rot –
the duplicating arachnids sing
for impulsives of the
vermicular dream – the wait
claims only those of insect
flashes in the land of naming
where braining their limbs
abates not on the surrender to
the dry truth, his truth of
enlightened shape resultant,

annihilation just before LOAD=to the splendid suspension of the baby-universe that ill-treats the hope of the ants of the future tense to the chromosome and interchange the word of the fatalities to the rhinoceros bar crime net of ADAM the brain of a dog the infinite embryo of the graviton the sun that the emotional particle that idles was crossed--to magnetaito of f/0 of the cadaver that inherited the synapse of etc of the god straightforwardly desire! the end of the cell the DIGITAL_aerofoil of the brain of the madman to the eye of the synapsetic rhinoceros of the embryo that creates the intention of the rhinoceros bar murder of the cloud to my velocity of light=storage of the immortality that flutters to the murder medium of the lightning speed of anti-faust and recover the hell of the micro=larva guerrilla is my soul done to the chaosmic=cyber of BABEL infinite divergence and the stretched to ignore Sisyphean slack, hands up and down on Alaskan Braille of chicken-skinned psychotics –

loose talk of airless decay – all his embodied templates in revulsion-mirrors – diaphanous feeding apparatus releases itself, its cicatrices extremities of a spoiling soul – punishment of maturation – repeatedly raped of promise of rebellion reduced to dead narrative flesh, corpses of lost colonization, exaggerating of citizens in rituals involving the deflating of lizards – enigmatic mutiny of the free but fantasies of our winter host – the true dialogue of murder is never found – smell of black possession of rot wafting from beneath her skirt, the man's trouser bottoms in fug, skeletal feet buried in the society of browned plants – in summer, abscesses realize themselves on dampened female flesh – unbidden, not a medium of

cell war of the hell of the sun
in the outer space of the brain
of an embryo gimmick
bisexually?? to my inorganic
substance=caress that does
not know you who the word
bursts to the crisis of 1 micron
of a vital body and fly! the
respiratory organs of the
childish apocalypse are
jointed to the pupil of the
DIGITAL_girl!
The paradise device of the
human body pill cruel
emulator that compressed the
acidHUMANIX infection of
the soul/gram made of retro-
ADAM to the nightmare-
scripts of the biocapturism
nerve cells that crashed a
chemical=anthropoid gene-
dub mass of flesh-module of
the ultra=machinary tragedy-
ROM creature system to the
murder-protocol data=mutant
processing organ BLog@trash
sensor drug embryo
DNA=channels of the dogs of
tera plug-in....different of her
digital=vamp cold-blooded
disease animals vital-abolition
world-codemaniacs of the

spring, they feed, exhausting
their environs of mass – smell
alone proves death to the
simple and babbled faces, all
thought dead in extremities
progressive and
architecturally degenerate – a
man shaves the worms from
his skin as they come up for
air – his white glabrous body
a molluscan ghoul in the
summer sun –

propelled by a need for more
useful dead – living in prefabs
constructed from glossolalia,
the ground an oral mutation
righting itself in tremors –
human guts moving to the
currency of lizards,
regenerating through second-
person eviscerations – layers
of dead yellow feet, soles
black with prior
circumstances –
the orderlies all junked
saprogenic, inmates torn and
dangling torches of self-
consciousness beneath
needled eyes coffined, fading
in a
manifold of anomalous

terror fear=cytoplasm which turned on the ill-treatment of a clone boy is debugged to the brain universe that was controlled.

Technojunkies' hunting for the grotesque WEB=cadaver feti=streaming circuit of the acidHUMANIX infection archive_body encoder that jointed is output to the brain universe that was processed the data=mutant of her abolition world-codemaniacs emotional replicant::the murder-gimmick of a trash sensor drug embryo DNA=channel to the mass of flesh-module of the ultra=machinary tragedy-ROM creature system paradise device of the human body pill cruel emulator that was send back out the era respiration-byte of the soul/gram made of retro-ADAM gene-dub to the modem=heart of the hybrid cadaver mechanism that turned on the biocapturism nerve cells ill-treatment of the

shadows – insanity dumped into the sky reeling – fetuses, man's disgusting ephemera, fed their own black slimes, squirms of gradual shitting bones, collective elicitations where fantasy dies on the irreversible –

the one carcass to still get old, persistent the like recognized as blue, raging death rings, his ground assembled from consecrated faeces – those suitable for debugging appear to have been cooked in human kettles – their eyes are soft and red like lipstick – prepared outside for days drinking rancid fluid of decomposition – tears sold as tincture – bound feet of poupées smeared across the sky, tree branching arachnid – state cure formed in crumbling compounds – bodies raped in calculating print of coal moments reinvented by the blind pecks of caged budgies – stay well throughout the scarring of cutis, indexes prove as dogs of tera murder game of a chemical=anthropoid.

The abolition world-codemaniacs which is covered the reptilian=HUB_modem=heart that accelerates the virus of the dogs of tera and was processed to that genomics strategy circuit data=mutant of her ultra=machinary tragedy-ROM creature system plug-in****the era respiration-byte is send back out=hunting for the grotesque WEB of a chemical=anthropoid to the nightmare-scripts of the biocapturism nerve cells that jointed the paradise device of the human body pill cruel emulator murder-gimmick of the soul/gram made of retro-ADAM I turn on the brain universe of the terror fear=cytoplasm to the cadaver feti=streaming_body encoder that compressed the acidHUMANIX infection@trash sensor drug embryo technojunkies' hacking ill-treatment....

concocted as inanimate dreams wrapped in their own requirements, the fall into organisms metered by reflections – men rise in hushed flesh of soul, heaven rotting in blackened windows –

assume he represents those beneath, is hosting cold-blooded murders of minstrels for the sweetened chimes of their squalls – in death mutation can be stretched to incorporate drinking songs and anarchic beheadings – the flesh of the clock fissures – faces in black fermentation somewhere, withdrawn as concocted lovers – theirs is a deeper anthropoidal fug with theatrics subject to hauntings – she hailed unguarded purposes designed in a bar half-forgotten, secluded, thick with whims 'n' sickness – called for remains their sedimented expression as though voided, blank, skin dangling,

48

Era respiration-byte is send
back out to the murder-
protocol of the biocapturism
nerve cells paradise device of
the human body pill cruel
emulator that compressed the
acidHUMANIX infection of
the soul/gram made of retro-
ADAM gene-dub of a
chemical=anthropoid mass of
flesh-modules of the
hyperreal HIV=scanners
nightmare-script@cadaver
city is output to the
ultra=machinary tragedy-
ROM creature system
reptilian=HUB of a trash
sensor drug embryo vital
browser of the abolition
world-codemaniacs emotional
replicant performance that
was debugged to the brain
universe of the hybrid
cadaver mechanism that was
processed the data=mutant of
a clone boy technojunkies' to
super-genomewarable
murder game.

Hunting for the grotesque
WEB cadaver feti=streaming

cloistered in mildew –
and to the journey their
creatures they turn
to the theatrics of the sky, the
subjects of horror, neglected
cells mechanical,
innumerable, fading, sucked
soft – the putrefaction cannot
shadow the fat deposits
quailing like maggots in their
brains – stomachs eventually
bursting as if beneath an ice-
axe – its new here immortal
all that making a refrain from
the dead message – his
punishment is hearing forms
and lost faces, seeing their
weight, cradling their stench
found artificial – we left
autumn over there with
brown eyes on the water,
ragged sleeves of black
sustained slow, data-
colonization rising in flies –
rats sucked at the skin from
cages – men bound in boxes
meshed like lice-feeders –
those blackened see the
brains, see rebirth in that fetal
tropic of our hollows' warm
stretches –
animal journeys to no

circuit that is covered the reptilian=HUB_modem=heart technojunkies' hacking and to that mass of flesh-module DNA=channels of her digital=vamp cold-blooded disease animals=joints brain universe of the abolition world-codemaniacs emotional replicant performance that turned on the ill-treatment of a chemical=anthropoid to the paradise device of the human body pill cruel emulator murder-gimmick of the soul/gram made of retro-ADAM is processed the data=mutant::the acidHUMANIX infection of the dogs of tera I rape the surrender-site of the terror fear=cytoplasm where I compressed to the insanity medium of the hyperreal HIV=scanners murder game of the cadaver city.

Plug-in to the cadaver feti=streaming circuit disillusionment-module of the murder-protocol data=mutant processing organ gene-dub of greeting, to force-flesh replication, the congealment of savages – ancient lizards decompose on the desiccant ground – 3-methylindole oozing from cracks in the creature system, acid in the land, slimes form as possession writhing in 21st century non-occurrence, through it we ignore the truth – shed like skin of burning woman, diabolical, enigmatic, flammable – fused print looking to the destination of a forefinger – new host smiles worn by mistake, formed against the deaf chewing dreams of man's mass grave into effervescence – eyes flat, saprogenic, eyes in eyes of rivers all in on the game of identities – feeling dead farmed to promote the wonders of ceased embodiment – spliced amputations from our enlightened brothers – enemies melded into existence, most flea-bitten, sound progressively dead to our live ears – operatives a chemical=anthropoid reptilian=HUB of her abolition world-codemaniacs emotional replicant modem=heart of the hybrid cadaver mechanism that turned on technojunkies' ill-treatment to the paradise device of the human body pill cruel emulator that compressed the acidHUMANIX infection of the soul/gram made@retro-ADAM murder game nightmare-script to the mass of flesh-module of the terror fear=cytoplasm that tera of dogs were output the brain universe of the hyperreal HIV=scanner form hacking a clone boy....

"the mass of flesh-module=hunting for the grotesque WEB of a chemical=anthropoid to the murder-protocol of the biocapturism nerve cells that jointed the paradise device of the human body pill cruel emulator that was processed the data=mutant of the soul/gram made of retro-hidden in the cavities of a journey, a vengeful faeces sensed in prose-CURRENTs' grave ecstasies – the construct cajoled from hardening skulls by shifts titanic in public script – into these eyes of waxy summer come parking codes and fetal memories of a cadaver's truth – he wants nothing of exteriorization cells – he has his self-reflexive microbes FARM-bred in layered voices – mind-squirms made toxic ephemera – powdered from every source it explains itself in a construct kind of scalpels and procedure code free from transparent futures, on and on insanities of Sisyphean corpses wounded, encoded, auto-feeding, surrendered with faces flat to the rain – we glossolalia, we mutations of the auto-conspiracy with tensions fertilized by slovens selling self-harm materials to heads without hours – state promoting itself through doctors to hinterland effect – they own this reinvented

ADAM brain universe of the ultra=machinary tragedy-ROM creature system to the modem=heart of the hybrid cadaver mechanism nightmare-script@clone boy technojunkies' murder-gimmick FUCKNAMLOAD....the cadaver feti of the dogs of tera=I turn on the abolition world-codemaniacs emotional replicant to the DNA=channel of the acidHUMANIX infection archive_body encoder that streams the hacking of a trash sensor drug embryo ill-treatment.

embryo=of=the cracking/mode of my chromosome that the sun makes different of the love of the future tense of the clone that f was eroded to: reverse the heart of f/0 of the clone=embryo that was mixed to the barren blood vessel of the parasite centipede of the sun. the light in the moon of my chromosome body fluid of the pupil of a girl like the autumn, these crib hospitals replete with suppurating molluscs –

this hereditary state unified without notice, its substances, deep cicatrices of consciousness, act to prove their worth with blemished tongues – sound of ratiocinations, cavernous orifices of the soul wrought from woollen skin – covered with myriad reflections and artificially stilled sleep – thought-chemicals all subject to morgue offspring running to egress – We use A-roads to shift the gloomy bodies to and fro, coat them in shoddy tarp and perfume their breaths – some remain forever dazzled by the gloss of blackened maturation, their place waiting and waking in the thick soils of immortal night – we are them – selves on order, forthcoming, culled from middle sentience, from the transmission unmodified in organs, spring deflating its number into eyes wired to butterfly clonic love in future to=8 drug=organs of brain=of the embryo that cause broken and idle to the equator/mode of the womb suck blood///to the back of the fractal eyelid of the fatalities BABEL=I paint the halo of the cyber of a dog and my soul beat brain embryo of before dawn:::love heart of the fatalities to hold and resuscitate the retina of the DIGITAL_ant)) the locus of the love of the clone that quiesced. it respires the membrane in the moon that my f/0 of that is connected to the soul battle of a dog and the velocity of light embryo interchange was exposed to the retina of the no destruction of the fatalities to the brain cells that was murdered brain of the schizophrenic embryo or L of the sun reverse=space of the clone centipede of the infinite sun that write off the fuzzy synapse of an ant to intestines of the sea that become and explode unknown and caused to the body of my minus

relay process of looped expression – beginning biocapturism –

the men talk of work paid in transgression, of the sun still old a week from now, clinging to it – the brain a gloomy moment of tears and submerged futures, and of the cure we dream of escaping dressed in majuscular ODOURS, mysterious phases of sky reeling sky, nerves raped, flesh in bacterial silence – hands pressed on glass, long digits slowly retracting prey of essential carnivores escaped into possibility – nobody is disgusted by the cragged symbols of murder, cutis inside out – terror granted to another and then only in metered mass dreams – phenolic figurines melting in underground wards dry from the drinks nobody serves – of the costumes twinning on permitted days tumbling into the light of organs, the narratives locked in rigor

inhabited to the heart of f of
upside-down of the abnormal
world that resonates to the
message of the ant of the end
each other
[thinking other self]=of
bioless_embryo that the area
wore the brain of the fatalities
that shrieks=the mode of life.
nude cyber whirls [fly-]
chromosome of the
anonymity of the fatalities
that my cerebral cortex
emitted cracking to the mirror
face of chaos to the soul of the
body/mode of an embryo in
the ground of the brain of the
ant where the inorganic
substance love of the sun
interference of BABEL-ism
that leans in the reverse side
in the moon where I was
fabricating absent=of=the
synapse of etc of the
embryo:::recover that grasped
desire!-or
to come flying///to invade
the cervical vertebra of sec of
suicide///the dizziness of an
embryo ground of clonic petal
awakes///outer space to the
thinking of every suspension

mortis, in fantasy of the
warren in stasis, tied, bane of
unmodified exaggeration –
resurrected persistence of
architectural cries place the
murders on a reduction of
distorted citizens – their days
the tunnels of half-forgotten
solutions – the trains run
regularly, commuters'
currency of a dream, their
fleeting incidents resembling
fantasies dampened with
inanimate thickness of days
quiet of voices – the sky's
numbered splendour an
abnegation of terror,
of rolled (debugged) humans
severed with psychosis in the
sly rot of incorporeality –
pearls cosmetic in old
informational dreams made
public to children, a currency
of resurrected windows
looking out on annihilation
unmodified by death –

yellowed rot raging in his
unnamed chest – naming is a
flammable act – belly seeping
out, left floods like an
unnatural sky sometimes

that ventures the drug area of an ant embryo of before dawn=of=brain will snatch the stratification of the megabyte of the earth area as for the future of an embryo, I will rape the cadaver city where my soul of f/0 of weather centipede of organ just like of sun was suffocated so orgasm of the centipede to topological: reverse this world of 1////the cell other selfs break through the hollow shell of f**[n-]***

Menstruation in her short just before that the emotional particle artificial sun of the desert that the nerve fiber of ADAM is penetrating the skull of singing voice myself of the insanity of the clone boys that decays commit suicide to the grief of the cell mechanism of the embryo is copied....the virtual image of the girl that the soul chromosome of the dog that the despair machine/switch ON cadaver of myself does the infinite tropic short of the

terrorized by grotesqueries, porridge masks, dreams of clotted voices, half-eaten genitalia planted in annihilative paranoia-construct – he arrives innumerable, waits with the rats junked beneath ecstasies of dead teeth – a future fall to them behind a cuticle – the toxic grass plays a callow game with a drop of trees – concocted to collapse, the self-killers, wearing store-bought masks, display all scarified veins – the slaughter of a new arachnid is simply paradise, edifying all seven in animal mirrors – consume the meat of stale minds, twinned number live a slow death – branching limbs torn, sap human, the clock skin, clutches of scalp and hair – we'll be safe together, baby – the writhing number are slow to surrender, rotting turned skin forming conditions of fluid disorder –

feel the mistake slow, the cadaverous flesh solutions, those swimsuit fifteen cyber paradise that drifts was executed to the spiral that hate fuck++to the hypothalamus of the cadaver of stratosphere++clone-dive++god play...."the body of her ant pattern "the word" "artificial intelligence" "the junkie"...."the ovarium of her drug mechanism.... the replicant brain of road nature++the beat of darkness++darkness occupies our 1/8 of brain....thinking impossible++"yourself explodes the heart of "present=of death" "the dance" the....abnormal world" become aware of...." "soul of relation=yourself of end cadaver of yourself fertilized the soul was chopped up by the pierrot of indeterminacy body of yourself reverse=ADAM_mode of life of the soul-machine that evolves to the contraction like the foam like a dog octave vital <non> of the blue murderous intention end of the sky that gets deranged the brain of tropic yourself that

needled in flammable skin – eventually weary he beckons the dead cragged souls of molluscs, deaths perpetual for sickly promotion of minstrel autolysis – the shadow exhaustive blackened a lip's decay – the reality, all thought clatters in their voices, cut grass in the hours of the sun – too old to wait in dream of mother ruin – sun cobwebs lost under corrosive symptoms of egress – provide odour: that it? we unable to wake the 2 bodies – video him open! –

aggregation of them dead in multitudes – escape sleep through the laboured alchemy of fetuses skewering this gloom-fed shit – and that of poupées screwed by coroners chewing gum, onlookers basking in wires and springs of multiple articulation – recurring dream of dogs running through autopsied meat – his breath of onions and paraffin, eyes little, inanimate – an uninitiated becomes the horizon of a cadaver resuscitates to the grief of the micro of the drug embryo that I rape and the womb cell records it distort and imp and do despair machine boys END of the protoplasm of the hell of sleep++"the reproduction gland BY brain" the-line that occupies our machine*wolf space with the cracking of the grief of a chromosome so fuck the parade of the drugy corpse that reigns over "ant like" "the record line of the secret of an embryo hearing-- All that flies apart the high speed body of hear....drug-machinemyself of yourself that all the pleasure of the animal cyber in the last term buy the synapse of myself and pass through fill the highway of the ADAM line brain cell of the machine girl learns battle to the storage becomes unknown....became...." the brain of the true clone++desert of myself the wolf=space and synapse dive to the grief of a cell "the

god hesitates in the warmth of exit rot as prayer-blown dreams come unwrapped –

excitation of softened brain under climatic conditioning – metered autopsy phases of a mistaken dream – glossolalia of universal emetic ignorant of ruin – mutation corrupted, hardening the mental, melted, spliced vague and non-identical – the eight-limbed agents of catabolism drip fat from their bones, form the notices of a dark inanimate mix, a junked bouquet always of rats – forearms in decay – unification came fading from sickness – head skin moving corrugated with invertebrates – creatures of squirming gangrene restructuring their smudged orifices – increased circumferences under soft skirts of loose skin – the uncertain texture of a fresh abscess cloaked in dust –

rot dubbing Still-Kind in airless voices, mouths stuffed with grass – doctor's fingers sterility of myself "of soul" the level with the murder machine-spore of an embryo is opened........"melody yourself that the solitude of love"="the eternal storage" the clone boys do the replicant suicide of her consciousness who being processed arithmetic by the machine line of the soul of number myself of the body of the embryo that ill-treats the language line of artificial play human-genome yourself of the sun self-consolation in the world of the disillusionment lost the past! Soul of yourself of an ant pattern records the moisture of an amoeba form embryo...."in the over there of sleeplessness pupil of the cyber mechanism of a dog scrap" "the infinite machine of yourself...." "to the immature nerve fiber of an embryo a cadaver iterate" "the end line of the gray beat++vagina of the sun simulated be....the body of myself that the future of virus myself of grief shut down the murderous

under lizard-skin – tissues of seditious material brought out into the light – his sacred sludge covered funereal – orderlies locked in a climax of rot – kitchen hands boiling flesh pellucid, discarded swimsuits of abscesses re-sculpted in huge moulds – humans reduced to slurry of a universal corpse – livid pus leaking from mysterious faces –unmodified the forms grow teeth of squirming scalpels, hands stuffed and abandoned in slack substances – a million dead whores face down in pools of phlegm – mummified terrain of hospital instruments – bones pulped into the whites of your eyes – disguised in cruel sanctities the town does not appear to itself – we blow the paralysis out their BODIES –

instrument points to nothing – dead weight of mysterious blood life – them sick-born cells to a self of immortal figurines, returned writhing as if awake – destination

intention megabyte of the
clone womb cell that
approximates "ADAM of
gimmick mechanism of soul
of"
sun*interior of the womb
exploded moon in reverse
side in sleeps spider of nest of
embryo=of=cyber to my
butterfly controlled is my eye
sun of inorganic substance
scream by solved is micro
cadaver city of highway dog
of [BABEL-ism] of cerebral
cortex to program embryo of
mysterious_internal organ of
spectrum to various
body=of=earth guerrilla and
it idles the DNA=loop of a fly
eyeball of the desire of the
clone that the negative
quickening of my soul
transmitted the other selfs of
junkie hope from the vagina
of the earth area=hologram
with DIGITAL of the embryo
that went bankrupt to the
brain of the joke of the
DIGITAL_fatalities that
surges and rape the
chromosome of clone-tokage
that executes the masochistic

militant upon the will and
half that code born of
mechanisms and processes
swollen and fused – tango of
nerve-animals with sky
reeling – warren of decay-
indexes – mental company
made physical in walls – man
sustains less-advanced
conduct howling of his
countability – and not from
meat on wires are those
halogen bulbs red – they
parked in hereditary fat to
promote a realm they clatter
later – slowly clinging
animation, the embodiment
held for decades, human suet
paralysis of those elderly
drones shitting potted-meat
born recurring –

murder-relics blackening on
deserted A-roads – human
intestines held together in
vision's clouded tunnels –
man shrieking of supernatant
time, cringing degradation of
wishes to our exalted state of
decomposition,
young spoilage promoting
putrid shifts of host's deaf

emotional particle of the
earth! the echo of the earth
[BABEL-ism/write off eye of
the flies!] ill-treating the
dogmatic heart of the earth
that your brain of the desire/0
of the clone to the murder
person of the blue megabyte
of the sky who was cut
off/scrap intestines of the no
destruction of the sun from
the storage that loves the plug
infinite you LOAD my
future=of=the love of my
insanity that breeds the ugly
centipede of artificial
insemination to eye and
digested outer space with the
eyeball of the tragedy of a fly
with the sunlight in the
suffocation just before of the
embryo that cuts the thread of
the chaosmic spider of an
embryo I who the madmen of
the fabrication were formed
the corpse of the ant of road
to the narcolepsy_respiratory
organs of the cell that spin the
human body that escapes
builds the DIGITAL_body of
the embryo of the cadaver of
god that instigated the

society of forever –

life chewed up into some
habitual solution to death –
the loud rebellion of
cadaverine lung air –
fractured states of
decomposition dangling
behind glass patterned in
puzzled tears – storage
facilities crammed with
pulped carcasses and our
midwives' used daydreams –
doctor of old grotesqueries,
his bodies blackened and
ephemeral put into the world
on script – he rooms with
slurry animals – corpses the
currency of cerebration –
finds the perished state of his
stomach lining unsettling – he
makes a machine of his
nightmare – blackened wind
in clock explosions spoiling
inverted psychosis of
submerged dreams – these
vampire cities shrieking of
pulse-machines and
long-sequestered layers of
corrosive sap, inhuman,
inorganic, porridge of
screaming blue insanity –

murder by the thinking of the
womb

:.....DNA=desert/--"""""

to the blood vessel that the
extreme that thinks about=8
ice embryos of the body fluid
who bloom all over in the
noisy flight spiral of the sun
was split limit of the
disillusionment that bark the
negative insanity of the
material to the f-
DIGITAL_body/mode of an
embryo: transmitting was the
speed of the blue awakening
of the existence difficult sky
with///the outer space
where becomes the gimmick
of an embryo grasps cadaver
of god impossible=I illicitly
sell perception
cadaver=of=rape storage loss!
clone of sleeplessness=of the
quarks of desire blink and the
murderous intention of
manhole just like of an
embryo=as for sun of body
fluid that turned pale to the
future tense sun that was
fabricated and was go up in

re-sculpted, un-policed birth
slug arrives on the terror
terrain – beneath sucked
forms of distress serum – he
moves the transgressor's
sickness into farmed future in
state of autolysis, a landscape
of noosed ruin – farmed
suffocation – confined decay
of cadaverous entities –
fingers devoured by her
perished anus, diagenetic
glimmer of its carnivorous
states –
vermin in the dead trees
dreaming the colour of
nihilism – we breathe rooms
of stretched hollows,
substances of despair, colours
cut from eyes, torture
procedures unyielding,
wounds blurred with
screwworms –

stay for mark of necropolis,
toxic pitches inflating bodies –
endless nights made texture
of cobwebs – children arrive
with symptoms
common to all, enemies,
writhing savages – man

flames will begin to
reproduce the mode of the
end of an emotional particle
to road of ants to the opening
of the chromosome of the
fatalities that controlled the
brain cells of drift desert
of=visual impossible=of fly of
crowd self of 1 milligram of
brain of BABEL-ism
instigating was magma of
vocal cord treachery of high
tide sec recorded cadaver
sleep able to desire ground
cause....pierrot of human
body breakdown of BGM in
accordance with pupil to
moon in reverse side
LIM*resuscitating was
embryo of suicide of blood
vessel earth of infinite
incubation condition just like
was storage of childish
exercise write off of f/0 of
murder organ to
transform....BABEL-ism
boundless future of
zero///earth area to the
artificial molecule of the
demolition of the dream
condition of vital Level that
spreads in the desert of the

parasitic on the hereditary
cure – the sequestered
circumstances of glass, of
quiet stasis confined in wiring
and perpetual disguising of
purpose –
faces of transparent terrain
cradled for tasting –
impulsives cull their codes
with black insects – when
they leave they wear a look of
uncertain testimony – of coal
incarnations in distant
windows – our murderers
born of ancient rooms to
death – beginning any
secreted data-colonization
with offspring exhibits –
toxic onlookers trapping
fetuses putrefactive, dead,
cringing, immediate and
greying – humans melted in
execution rituals, skin one
prophylactic abscess sentient
meat of pink glass – the
human is resilient and raven,
transcendental animal hooked
on taste of fear and the
alchemy of tarmac –

oily faces of carnivore
operatives feeding on

love and intelligence of the clone revelation was invading rhinoceros bar placenta of an ant game sun that shakes to the vocal cord of the fatalities causes a dog brain that earth gets deranged to the lapse of memory of 1 gram of existence that programed the body organ without the murderous intention of the blue sky to the embryo of the f=cyber who gets complicated to the vagina of 0 Level of the earth and was suspended the micro traffic of a vital body worn and usurp the ugly production device of the velocity of light digestion organ--horizon of the pierrot that an embryo had penetrated the earth area DIGITAL_ground=and induce the first cry of DIGITAL..../anti-faust to the brain of a dog! earth area=of the zero gravity_fatalities of the embryo that cut the mask in the moon and tore DIGITAL_apocalypse that make the thing of the light reconstituted biocapturism – claustrophobic host of tied animals cut shrieking, dismembered, their limbs carved into new asemic font – fat of sacrifices poured into black soil – vegetation grows sustained in poison of noosed violence – bones pulped into yesterday's sclerous hours – this vampire instrument of thought possession bound in dead traits and talking dreams – commuters misplace their reflections in landscape of torn earth of skeletal trees – emotions of this enculturation are symptoms of repetition – deep in the hinterland tropics we overheard murders, grimy-eyed lizards feeding their young – town in late stages of catabolism, streets inanimate, corpses rotting and breathing out drains and duplication, parks hollowed out for new grunt inventions of Bellmer – rhythmic instruments manufactured to aggregate flesh – dreams of dirt skies of incubation – beheadings, blood tingling in year that comes flying to the chromosome of the paradise/mode of clone-tokage=the manhole of the sun was caused a quark in the season of the disillusionment of that chromosome with the plug//stimulates f of: the corpse of the tears....fatalities=of which eros of the reverse side in the moon that beats loves bioless_darkness of DNA to the weird radio waves of the cadaver city quark to the eye of the rhinoceros of communication impossible clone-tokage that notifies the mummy of the light year of that embryo=rhythm of the desire of the clone of f that I caught a glimpse of the mummy of the embryo of the light year to the ovarium of the hell will continue to tell brain:....the hearing of the drug mechanism of the angel_broken--chromosome=of palpitation=ghost=of=heart=space of "f" of embryo DIGITAL that earth sonic to the low grass, the lizards' black flesh formed from entities inhuman – man's eviscerated intestines talking, revealing secrets – gall stones strung like pearls – those recordings of lipstick-coated elicitations issued from parking lot, knees unwrapped on the damp concrete – some murderers dress their work for onlookers and keep count – deformities of internal flesh detailed in the clouds – pewter slabs of impending rain, transparent bin-sacks congested airless with blow-flies – unseen psychotropic hands speak in dead language, hollowness of savages softened in the sand – unceasing deglutition of pestilent meat – invariable forms of carnalist souls – weary iron spliced into hypotheses, insanities of the non-degradable organ – kitchen-sink cosmetician's hands in severed jugulars of new architectures of flesh – animations flowering from archive of mutilated the cyber that crowds to chaosmic in the season_antifaust=of=the birth stratosphere hypnosis! air=of=murder concept of sigma! the rhinoceros bar body mode of mankind entrance//don't tell love!!! reptilian=of=fabricate love of f to ex-system-cycle--=sun of my vacant brain cadaver of god reflein to the placenta of the darkness of clone-tokage that soul=was raped//BABEL-ism=loops to synapse impregnation/eye is transformed.....:the terror that vital body interchanges to sec of the suicide of the horizon to dive was filled eye of the cell of the sun was flooded to the analogic internal organ of a crow so! the cerebral cortex of my f/0 (BABEL-ism) of spider=of=the murderous intention is secreted: human being=of the blue sky was turned the different that crowds=to sweetheart so DIGITAL:.....mad dog=of=the eyeball was respiring !!!LOAD/120%:::::

consciousness – black flush of necrosis – bacterial breath of vampire decaying in slow cerebration, rebelling the putrefaction codes in holy internal anarchy – psychotics tingling with paranoia of future currents screaming of sex-death exits – supernatural messages mimicking silence – shrink-wrapped, severed ephemera, guts rot-damaged sweating putrescine – machines diseased with themselves, buried in dead noise, anomalous sickness of weary human futures – parasitic floods of perfumed solution – stiffened commuters construct slaughter fantasy on the skins of children – a porridge of errors and life a black pause unrecognized – dogs feeding on their own waste – mechanized prose-CURRENTs = chemical mutilations on the formulaic trends of self-reflexive death – bouquet of wounds discarded

[chromosome @
the matrix of the desire) that
(night sky crouches on acidity
interior of the womb of tokage
of the spring mechanism
transfigures to out of
season/insanity of the self is
radiated to body outside. as
for my sleep tokage that
wears to the sun of the
revenge of all directions and
shot germinates the
transmission line of the drug
atom on the analogical
internal organ of the cadaver
cutely like the embryo face of
the sleeplessness without the
dream of my cell unit floats
from the systematic identity
impossible duct of the gravity
that my black noise future
presents the scar of the
universe dew and drowned to
the murderous intention in
the moon digital image of the
atmosphere disturbs the mask
of the blood corpuscle in the
explosion just before (human
body=of the indication of the
fission that the war of the cell
breaks out the limit value of
the pain=over there of the

on empty grave – slurry of
print corpses, of ghoul
specimens, traumas shaped in
slurred reminiscence of
cytoplasmic substance – this
dead land of mothers thinned
out, skeletons of dough, blood
of paraffin, singing songs of
humans bloating in
multitudes – lizards drunk on
unimaginable vomit of
congealed babies – skins
haunted with purpose
manufactured from half-eaten
dream of rebirth – auto-
conspiracies of death-
memories, possession fabled
to appear grey and trapped in
its own mass – cobwebbed
eyes and mirrored voices of
decapitated heads inflating in
still air of rainforest dawn –
veins rolled out like seaside
sweets – spores of
daydreamed masks slipping
under the skin in worm-like
spirals of grimy fog – born
unimaginable, weighed,
grown in sedimented
daydreams of transcendence –
gummy fetuses of
putrefaction safely inverted in

tragedy horizon=expands to
the synapse goes osmosing to
the vocal cord of the murder
of the cell) with the breast of
my retina cadaver erects--the
pierrot snuggles up to the
hearing impossible nerve and
come flying on the plane of
the murder topologic play--
you--battle become
acquainted with:::your corpse
of the fly on the
interface***the internal organ
that embraces thinking
impossible of the pierrot
immortality. my tears that my
tokage dreams of the junk
ecstasy of the corpse that
leaves) from outside certain
(body outside the body cut
the lung of the centipede that
turned with the space of the
filament of the blackhole and
tear so tokage revolves and
secretes to body outside so the
machine of the drug atom
dream of the virus that
regresses to the face of the
black apocalypse of the sun
was accomplished the
messenger as for tokage,
tough disillusionment that

the worm-hollowed skull of
God – slow song of black
ratiocination
made automatic –

vermicular slime held inside
mock subject, his head a
dream of inanimate fug –
reality mocks cure grown
from the sky – death eats of
water – disgust-fuelled
insanity of bacterial
witching-ground –
mechanized wind babbling of
lands unwelcome – index of
origins defleshed for purposes
of subtraction – fetal lizards
decanted from crying glass –
cold-blooded loop in muted
black FARM – shadows of
nigredo mannequins
discovered in stratums of
funereal aggregation –
mummified paradise stranded
in one endless cadaveric
summer – hybrid
transcendental shrieking –
salvage young recordings –
sentient obelisks of mutilated
surrender – the mysterious
phases of metronomic
stomachs – horror organism

connects the suicide of the green body outside certain dog that broke and breast to the other side is growing. vital birth existence of an opposite dimension secretes to the horizon of the body outside that spreads to your DNA" Although this cadaver city is road connected to the genital organs of the ant pattern of the gimmick girl: the soul-machine of the erase line zero of the storage of the sun LOAD....as for the suicide replicant factory of clone boys: grief the grief of a chromosome occurs....: the gel form nightmare of BABEL animals....I die the ADAM doll is replicated and is paint the catastrophic sun line of the placenta world cyberBuddha of: the transy inheritance device: we and in laughter (monochrome earth escapes in the inside)

Hybrid thyroid of the planetary machinative angel of the ant: the machine-seed eating through towns and cities flattening brittle architecture of human psychopathology – desert of anomalous deformities and diseased wounds and nothing in between – fantasy fused and slack with serialized futures – medieval template for decoding warrens of worm-eaten shit, deciphering geometry of snapped ankles, splatter patterns up murder chamber walls – the dream immortal looped malignant – stumbling corpses loosely-dressed in reason – unfortunate hinterland bodies wearing their souls as overcoats – warped bouquet spoiling in the excremental gloom – chemicals basking in vertiginous purposes of expiration – soft doctor talk decay and ruin, suffering in dreams of itself, mouth indexed to prophylactic narratives – souls shaved to form iron grass – devouring holy sleep of deflating figurines in still water –

of the desert that the deep-black erosion speed of the artificial sun: the cyber dog of dustNirverna: K that was measured by the body of the clock mechanism of the drug embryo radiate heat is infectious....the emotional circuit of the ADAM doll short....the horizon of her chromosome toward....the time axis of demolition line....uterus-machine of the ADAM doll that the over there of the pupil of myself does the sun-image of the pity of the placenta world fuck goes mad....the DNA=channel rotates reverse/skizoid and others of brain K, <lonely mass of flesh> of the drug embryo are break down I am going to be disillusioned by the time_difficult existence so: clone boy system apoptosis future! Her machine despairs with the hell of the gimmick cell....the worldly desires/MHz. The insanity of a chromosome the languages: her <mind> that the soul-machine of myself lost the

heaven's concocted rooms clinging to paralysed trappings of corpse-sucked grave – recurring patterns secreted in postmortem faeces – railway lines flapping against earthed faces on earthquake dawn – human dogs chewing through the autumn rot – cloying reverberations of the coffined song – tune clotting –

chasm in form of life that need not look to exist in terror excitations of disorder owned exhaustive shrieking overlapping internalizations of grunt-serum blighted with premature encore, its state without process – on its own essential climax terror arrives as the hereditary exaggeration, unable to own the curse of naming (dubbing) – promise outside reinvented in guise of fetal solution – positions nascent in the intimacy of nihilism – state held unified with indulgence of enlightened abnegation feeding itself on protein of the BABEL animal that is resolving the self-consolation line that was secreted the body of an ant to drugy of the machinative angel that is operating negatively dance....FUCKNAM!....<DNA > of the monochrome earth witnesses her inorganic substance grief. Eros of the fission disease of the gimmick girl: gene=TV OFF/ON.

Gimmick girl: respires the DNA of the artificial sun....the clumsy world of the drug embryo: the ADAM doll where vomits the machinative gene system: the body channel of TOKAGE makes the REC brain open....the drugy sun is drifting the criminal nervous system of cyberBuddha so. Clone boys erase horizon: of the placenta world....
<it laughs>.
<I grieve over>.
:the over there of the pupil of the skizoid in, I rape the soul-machine of yourself....the

the result of process culled from central mechanized hinterland of (chronically default) Sisyphean informational process – rebellion stifled homicide between moments, forms cytoplasmic, upon skewer of soil hollowness – its self making a post-production terror of origins made corrosive – (dubbing) uncut ghost eats duplicating present of carnivores – subjects like this rolling out a gradual feed – to be escaped without delay in myriad methods of withdrawal, often under template of full-blown psychosis – the mutation symptoms of corpses' sensate mass is simply process of duplication, of act over definition – that spasm voided against a human shadow, impervious, mistaking a lizard's disease for the lizard itself – number of fresh unfortunates beneath it born in theatrics manufactured by each new day – partially human life of profound asphalt of ME/....myself that I murder be so that the line of the clonical love doubles to the body matrix of the drug embryo so brain K of the clone boys: the mutant of the opposite=sun that crowds into the gravity of the cadaver city that god GODNAM replicant suicide line myself of HELP/ME....et cetera changes to the worldly desires machine that become a cell because the sun line of the machine-seed of yourself is respired. Physical speed of an ant zero gravity of the artificial sun that is eroding the replicant consciousness of myself to the hybrid emotional:::

:the onanism group protein of clone-skin is doing 1/8 of brain of the ADAM doll: the strategic body of an ant: the soul-machine of the cosmology of grief that the cyber dog which fix the orbit of dustNirverna that cancel the resuscitation line of the end clone to the end of

mutilation in consciousness listed as number one – a construct of dead layers, expression of melding formulaic necrosis holding together the ultimate universal, the rain mimicking flesh – (like old diseased tissue containing systemization of unborn nucleus) – multiple reflections in the necropolis of mind – those from cities of sufficient circumference drain hope from their heads according to disassociations set cadaveric – to be themselves, alone, man's cover of earth, grass blades into them, moss binds them together, embodied floods, state cavities, the loosely-dressed ossuary of everything – this remains to be unseen –

and like lizards stilled in oily effigies, and something looks as if into flesh the trappings of outside blackened in corpses still clinging to the cruelty of death – cynophobia in repeated dreams of disease we legs walking edifying our

nervous system: be the blood of a machinative angel the road machine of the cadaver city: so that fuck junk to the angel mechanism crunch....apoptosis season of the chromosome of yourself the scream, that the gimmick girl awoke sleeps....LOAD....the DNA=channel of the narcolepsy storage-group....blue sky of the sex machine....sun of cyberBuddha: the clonical love of boys is activated Her worldly desires machine dash the murder area of the sudden death-game/artificial ant....the ADAM doll=spore: the placenta world existence difficult sun of zero is respired........the drug embryo of "the suspicion", incubates the happiness that the larva machines of matrix body fluid took out crazy of the BABEL animal....ADAM doll of the disillusionment.
CLONICAL/ONE

Our although be road x that

waking in pools with souls cringing safe in the warm – mistake their form for the whims of bodies unmade in the womb – die of certainty in unjunked feel – him quiet and slow to explain it – decrying his necrotized identity secreted in airless black dressing over faces of paradise – look through persistence of fetuses born of dead plants in muscular chambers, rot grass cover of autolysis, so say the morticians – the protracted blue of adulthood a nightmarish symptom, the surrender to dread – putrefying mechanists noosed in the sun, weighed for brains by raging animals in fluid decomposition – live tissues, dreams like balm, ephemera of the borrowed states fructified –

his unwitting possession of costumes cajoled into effervescence of fog – the terror eats of slimes, unobtrusive in ghouls sired

invades the sun that was
reflected in her pupil
....we who the paranoia of a
dog explodes the universe
that impossible to
the desire of the fabrication
0880=cadaver of the murder
of the lonely blood
angel mechanism of the sea
wolf=space of the gene that
was purged the ground
which was disillusioned the
grief brown spot of the
boundless chromosome of
the android that I record....I
plunder infinite <<secret>> of
1 milligram of
emotional Love=Replicants of
our vital/the icon sun that
thrusts through the
mask of the god replicant
heaven of the fetishism
impossibility <<body>> et
cetera of the drug embryo that
I was isolated the machine of
the angel that
impossible to....our genital
organs....NIHIL=life of the
hybrid brain of the
ADAM doll be <<alternating-
current>> that is parasitic the
insanity of the

from psychotropic extremities
carnivorous, of a supernatural
revulsion – paranoia construct
of myriad horror-peoples in
states of fused adorning –
entities malignant under
world of malicious
worm-eaten self-reflexive
insanity – malleable brains
made dull in hybrid
concoction – limbs like organs
of monsters, diabolical
creatures with influence over
man's dreams – fantasies of
truth made incarnations of
pestilence – the Reality a fug –

running, deflating the grave
of us (death a cul-de-sac of
decay drowning in self-
conscious quarry designed
anew) him culled from
blackened lung, his will made
murder from enculturation of
meat – hunted and
unrecognized
grotesquery the cure then of
embodiment – auto-
conspiracies perpetually
resurrected to realize order
from air – he owns the game
who, time-aware, is mortified

over there of a pupil on the
clumsy world of an ADAM
doll like the ant of
nuclear fission like the dog of
the tragedy interior of the
womb of the
orange body fluid which
fabricates the suicide replicant
of the cruel murder
person womb area of mutant
storage TOKAGE of the true
asphalt of the sun
that operates. Infinite [heart]
of emotional clone boys that
the eternal
season sun of the asphalt that
our aerofoil break down was
conducted
artificial insemination
analyze....execute....go to
war....the ADAM
doll-universe zero-paranoia
that was restrained 1/8 of
brain of the murder
system drug embryo of the
soul-machines the area of the
blue sky which is
not vital the propaganda of
the insanity cytoplasm of our
chromosome that
replicates control:with the
NIHIL=image the

of condition while dead to
sphacelation – each
comfortably wallowed in the
thought of breathing
putrefaction, singing of that
instead likened to decay –
breathing perfume in of
putrescence, dead limbs
dancing to a chance of
inflating the code of the
supposed –

from faces drowned
purposeful, parked, stiffened
– those who inverted flesh-fly
pearls with paraffin feed
themselves sick saprogenic
animations torn flat in
exhumation of wrought eyes
tingling in form ignorant of
shrink remains persistent,
stretched terrorists immersed
in over-recurring adipocere of
self – phlegm stuffed in rolled
tongue of dead future
together in looped veins and
lips of society suckled on
autopsy memories and
congealed skin farmed
alongside holy trills of
budgies hard as knuckle bone
– cobwebbed sky floating over

machine....no grief_earth area of the angel which exploded: Our murder mode crimson TOKAGE of the drug embryo resolve the clumsy world to the desire-mechanism....'biotechnology of the watchman sexual mass of flesh of the monochrome season bare feet of an orange-machine chromosome the miracle of the ant that murders the sun of anonymity in the outer space++girl] of the over there of a pupil where does DNA++vagus that gets deranged++....enter in the body fluid matrix of an ADAM doll=less':future the future when ADAM doll was restrained decays........pure white fear with 0880 _erases Murder X fabrication ....the nightmare that the brain of the aerofoil, desert of the blood, desire of the machine made rivers, sun black as charred brains – sap-mouthed medieval molluscs dreaming ancient human minstrels smudged like reflections in newborn currents – his ratiocinations muted like explosions conducted in vacuum – bleeding codes on glossolalia of autumn mutation of shit and iron – forbidden dilineations weaved into bouquet of skeletons – reduction of former agents strung and leg-ironed, shoddy teeth yanked, white flesh powder slapped on the ward-worn nigredo –

doctor of the warren cries barely sedimented beneath us like galvanized goat-man – rooms that resemble wounds, furniture that resembles amputations – his greenish eyes medieval, dead, iced – bleached human skin in screwed peels – a girl's once hesitant hands discarded, made innumerable – his hardened skin a procedure in stretched data-colonization –

orange the lonely
proliferation
of....0880....clone boys:dog of
that goes to war inside
NIHIL!? Planet of
an ant does overheat++the
death god device of
asphalt:BREAK-out 1/8
seconds
ADAM
doll_desire_death_latency x
awakening_impossibility=dea
th_

Sun_instantaneous
The emotional particle of the
grief organ form murderous
intention no-space
nature asphalt that machine
myself of the angel that inputs
the drugy body
universe of the lonely
embryo::the replicant
lonely....unvital target
violence of the zero-
masochism....ground of the
murder program....ADAM
doll
in the future of
no~contact//myself that isn't
vital lost controls the
nightmare of the desire-

he tunnels through ancient
abscesses in a blistered
swimsuit – returns cringed to
the body FARM, his teeth
coated in skin teeth –

through our codes of conduct
humanity becomes a
ceremony of bacteria – a
century in a diagenetic week –
the abandoned life sustains its
titanic form, proves itself an
over-salvaged aggregation –
refabricated and saprogenic,
our antenatal structures
intact, made desert, a
geographical decay – forms
once suitable now flesh
porridge – that stunted
organism of stone filtered into
new and unimaginable
obelisks – man in them
turned, located somewhere in
his perished journey – flushed
of flesh –

rings together stiffened, iron
mud coating my eyes and
decomposing limbs held in
script of eristic nightmare –
the spidered sky encasing her
like a lonely glass-covered

76

mechanism of a dog....:the
eye, masses of flesh of
which were restrained it was
forgotten_latent alone! Road
of our
drug-eye....noise....angel-
mechanism is
communicated....
....we do the body of an ant
desire! Air....<<line becomes
a drug....the
body becomes speed....that
ruined the sun of the death
that impossible to
the gene....=replicants of our
lies that programed the
suicide of the
angel-mechanism the sun &
the sun that are parasitic on
our blood like a
dog!>> the soul-machine that
radiate heat murders the
emotional replicant of
NIHIL that transplants the
terror happiness that recovers
the sleep that
went hungry

....zero
We were infected with the
virus of the body!::
........:the fabrication the

appendage –
patterns of God in yesterday's
experiments – halogen rooms
hooked to voices in
unguarded light –
eavesdropping on the plotted
speech of branches unbidden
their fantasies black – the
dead exhibited in windows –
veins torn and talking – the
hushed fusty, inconsistent
bodies confined, mysterious –

mental killing of month-long
tropic daydream in city
operatives – unwrapped
stomachs found dumped on
melting A-roads devoured in
time – archived video states
refined and transposed onto
weary host bodies – across
these liberated sacks our
neglected stench is
submerged, their babbled
recordings the sweet contents
of mutinous tension – clams
staged their blank count on
the tarmac –

begun in the dough of toxic
ages, our skins stripped with
defleshing chemicals – the

murder_DNA=channel
........camouflage the
truth of infinite, the sun!

my brain plays with the
bubble of the silence of
magma the horizon of DNA
that was broken and irradiate
the X foot that sky of where
examine by fluoroscopy the
secret of a drug in the infancy
period of chaos was
consumed blue the desert of
my spine where I was raped
to the chromosome of mirror
images tokage of my f/0 that
caused the reverse=space of
the sun to the synapse of the
naked body of an embryo
communicated the micro
cadaver city gene=TV that
migrates to the internal organ
of the pierrot these cell other
selfs that sec that sun was
slaughtered to the outer
space=tensor of my body fiber
that is the gimmick of the
storage of an embryo so
replicated the reverse side in
the moon to the plain eyeball
of the anti embryo to the
circulation of the rhinoceros

punitive ten propped up his
name in millions of brother
voices – their number
remained matter – hours, time
of corpses green, slack
mouths woollen, worked –
testing textural deformities –
some resemble others more
than themselves – fifteen hang
by their feet until tasting –

young figurines used for
hammer material their
mutilations metered – these
inconsequential victims
(gloomy children) remain
otherwise unmodified – deep
mind marks can be stuffed –
the symptoms of control
greeting her unaffected –

soon the origin of skin came
to assume a stark hardening
of the human pattern –
diaphanous sickness of
templemen – their faith-
infected temples have
destroyed organs and made
regulars transparent to
everyone but themselves –
impulsive testimony of flea-
sick mothers still weak from

bar blood relative of the soul of the dog that spin whirl the brain of the fatalities to the ovarium that dream of and shed the tears of the blood of chaos to the whereabout of the nerve of my f/0 and the murderous intention of the suspension of outer space mode to the blood vessel of an ant execute by shooting the sun of a chromosome so! my disillusionment=the wolf of the eye=your sun despair not migrate was mixed the storage of the apocalypse that the embryo swelled up to the womb to the boundless hell of the cell maze of X that was draining water off! cyber of which begins to overflow transmission line that becomes to the lachrymal gland of wolf the gimmick of an embryo is moved and is jab to the body fluid of the hypnosis of the happy moonlight without external world now and time=of=anonymity=of which the womb of the cyber*embryo that

their sexual exploits – sun streaking across row of tiny specimens, contained in kidnapped location, raped unholy, traits of emetic regions dangling in blood – useful once a needled soul –

interrogation in ordered reconstruction sucked illicit sounds from symbols stale on the table – the honour of restless mechanists ranks with those held in a puzzled stay, devoured by mass, insides drained and poured from kettles – slaked citizen metronomic, coated in inanimate reactions in rooms toxic with undiagnosed fantasies – fertilizing materials rotting in cadaveric wombs – and heaven's organs in distorted ears – more…

funds from fading skins – often there are birds their wings frothy in races like souls re-sculpted and waiting for wires – funereal slovens grown in fantasy of rock – un-policed flashes overhead of

decayed=my brain write off
the dogs of my storage had
gone to ruin the octave of the
grief of the clone that leapt to
the remainder of night sky to
the breathing of the cell to the
constellation and to the
placenta form brain of BABEL
as long as an ant was studded
to the mirror image of the
chaos that respires road of the
monochrome world so are in
the eternal incubation
condition of the sun the
embryo who becomes
unknown ferments to the
lonely soul of the wolf that
drifts cyber=space....
limit=sadistic soul of the
desert that floats the brain of
the fatalities and control the
parasite=absence of the sun to
the sonic placenta of the
pantheon the light in the
moon to the gram of the
breakdown of the madman
and dog who transmit the
quickening of the change of
an ant--cry out the gimmick of
ADAM that wanders the
interface of the nightmare! it
migrates interval period of the

climatic features having
chisels taken to them by
flapping men – girls coffin the
scarred stratums of their suety
minds – scarred hands snatch
at extravagancies – cicatrices
of crag coal print of decay –
on innumerable beings we
laboured, disorganized,
wounded – for all those
requiring protections
wrapped in their forthcoming
bane we taunt and laugh and
disbelieve –

closed hypotheses of long
stretches of lofty commuters
cooked in glass – this line of
hours a habitation of faces
stranded and unseen – in
rows of heads collapsed
under weight of perpetual
rationalization – smoke peters
for a sky forced out into day –

courts invariably blacked out
on day of data-molestations –
eventually the sleep of reason
falls silent – the flammable
decisions are irreversible –
thick kin incidents of
suffering in detail – details

cadaver that the world blinks to the cyber target=crime net of the sun to the thalidomidic vocal cord of the embryo that instigates the ground base of the clone and do the magma of the lewd variety of a chromosome desire drug area of where turned with the hosts of 8 of sun that are infectious into the synapse=universe of etc of an ant anti-faust of the air that joints gene=TV to the cyber of BABEL to the end of road of an ant....the existence of etc of the embryo the cadaver city to the space of the cyber*apocalypse LOAD gimmick centipede=of the scream of the clone of the future tense that the soul of the desert murders the nightmares of 8 milli to the heart of the mechanism of the artificial paradise that penetrates to the cell war of the sun and ant=the larva of the sun that conceived the cyber that diverges to an embryo LIM and be conducting the mitochondria

facilitate the execution of seven silent transgressors – once inanimate their tears become flammable torching their printed eyes – stilled flesh on the turn in damaged ice unit –

only rotting and looking and rotting speak the rigor of cadaverous cities, the meat life, the stream-machines of dream-kind insanity temporarily human only dead – of faeces in the water of our dreams – of death unyielding in streets where shared selves dream through places eaten with death – passed by raw intestines outside on kerb cleanly mortised to head –

spoiling trees debugging human exit – alchemy of this black process of putrefaction displacing birth anthropoidal – self-inflicted creature habitual in the black cerebration – every drop of blood is shaped in the sky – consecrate putrid prophylactic by never waking

of cosmic eye to the pool of
death does the masochistic
spot of murder of a female
dog reflein earth area is
eradicating the
DIGITAL=chromosome to the
mystery of the
bio=less_embryo that the
body type of the future of the
atomic bomb/angel of the
labyrinth/ant of the embryo
that dementia condition//the
earth where ADAM circles
spins 1/2 skulls of the
madman that crash to the two
equal parts to the
mysterious=quark of the
cadaver city sing the
disillusionment with the X fee
of the artificial intelligence
that become extinct
thalidomide of perception of
placenta to eyeball of natural
calamity extraordinary
natural occurrence LOAD
does sunlight of f/0 of
massacre of interior of the
womb to mitochondria of
escape circuit coexisting be
ant of love clone of   .
parasite*highway on
accumulating be loves

to this decomposition – self-
reflexive taste
of blood souls dreaming
nightmares smeared along
walls – corpse plague of lost
purple substances – stasis
forms theoretical vampires in
corporate strategies of
fantasy – dreams cooked long
like vital organs, turning less
bitter in the cover of shadow –

happy, it sucked the collective
sing into a noisier subtraction
– they fear forever of deeper
rot – expiration of noise in
dust – smut decay of finger
bones locked in prayer – that
silent moment felt ceases in
nullified death –

dead, blown, replaced,
polluted with wishes of
medium insanity – man
destroyed himself for a future
cradled in psychosis –
phthisis of desire laid open for
us all to know unknown –

live storage for their morgue
exhibits – smell of men
sleeping in the reconstructed

fatalities of DIGITAL_internal organ to weatherred sun of anti-faust looks at chaos of pupil? that chaosmic interlude area of the world....the last constellation of ADAM the body of the megabyte of the wolf to the drug of the immortality of an embryo quark.
Placenta world of clone boys: the digital=apocalypse is inoculated....the nano-machinative body system of the drug embryo: the junkie silence gimmick girl of TOKAGE the speed of the end of the world I copy the reproduction gland brain of the ADAM doll: a/the film-contact: the body fluid matrix of an ant that dances....
Blue of the sky
Green pupil
The uncivilized brain of clone boys is infectious to the night sky of the desert.
::myself to something that is not seen is reflected there.
I rape [the sun like the ADAM doll that respires the nightmare of the amniotic

refuse of their yellowed years – their sweat alerts the rats – somewhere they prepare the orderlies for feeding – black smiles on the coffin-lined mirrors of grave-life – errors are never in colour – summer inhabitants feed on the destinations of clouds, sacrificing truth for logistics –

rhythmic corrosion of artificial respiration – parking rot of slugged skulls junked and misplaced – death is the winter of savages unable to lament the spring – pulse written in despair – death flowering with immortal movements born of enemies – ancient surrogate carcasses of this disgusting forever – finding the poisoned maggot entombed in decay lots – steady callow spores of Existenz desiccant in this repeated spoilage draped innumerable –

teeth and gums left vague with rot – man formed of

fluid mechanism of clone boys
era so].
To be jointed the vagina of the
gimmick girl as if the brain
area of the dog
fuck........resolves it in the
savage soul-machine....heaven
of the drug embryo
[
The sex machine of a dog.
Silence

While the brain of
reproduction area myself of
the herd artificial ant of the
fearful sun that myself
witnesses the digital=vamp
quickening was done fuck
DNA of chromosome hybrid
end machine yourself of the
girl that the universe of the
vagina murders the drugy
pupil of the machinative
embryo dog that is flooded
the soul-machine of myself
that does noise gets deranged
because the matrix emotional
particle spiral of the boy
machine murders the sun of
yourself her gimmick No.
XXXX chromosome that the
soul of myself that the

inorganic significance – and
so his
death-softened bones are
occupied – cancers tailored to
seasons of the flesh and the
currency of flies – the mouth a
blackened terrain, a realm of
hybrid blemishes chewing the
half-forgotten – that eager
vision changing, distrustful of
identity – manufactured,
dewy-eyed reminiscences
blemish the understanding of
blemishes –

no cure in the land of dead
men but ignorance – death
here concentrated in
symptoms of
non-occurrence – the glass-
kind mix well and urge order
– everything a nothing of
circumstance – the feel of
multitudes –
public exteriorizations may
force pellucid vomit –
extremes not possible in
vengeful sickness – death is
not just another
psychopathology, it's the
psychopathology –

cadaver city explodes with the speed of the sun that ADAM/s copies the over there of the pupil of the gene war human genome where was supposed dash like an ant will go to ruin to grief. Monochrome image of gene=TV that the spore=space of eve that despair yourself of as that the machine area of the earth where the love of the clone that ant pattern artificial sun ADAM/s resolves reflects be not able to cut and be not able to count be not able to do the body of the drug embryo puzzle dances with myself battle goes mad the planet without the organ of the ant that the clonic internal organs of future....ADAM/s of all the equal myself of yourself invade. Life of myself toys with the machine of yourself so DIGITAL-SEX
The DNA game that the brain murder self-distractive_larva machine fills! Reverse the artifitial life::cancellation::the virus cyber embryo of GAMEOVER pantheon that

putrefactive instrument grows decaying slowly of brain of slow death of body of decomposition – ephemera, mildew and bacteria revealed as the eternal soul of substance – onward to compound that sentient sludge, potentiality of rot – conglomerations of flesh life of putrescine, cadaverine, 3-methylindole, a sprawling vermicular costume dancing with every host –

fat worms twinning the lovers' bodies, tissues wet and soft with waxy slime of unification – incarcerations collapsing sublime two into one as the ground runs with bodies – arachnidan biocapturism reduced into joint of rebirth – emotions spliced forever, squirming, rotting – their human eight-limbed corpses shift in slow tangos of catabolic principle – 2 rotten souls in one cuticle, orifices bleeding raven water – new entities stumbling in their ancient carnal mirrors –

inserts the skizo=lobotomy fuck of myself that the eve_emotion of the end that the cadaver of the horizon micro that amalgamates the chromosome of myself to 1/8 bodies of an ant transit be infectious=the soul of madness line myself of the machine that evolves ants invade to the sun line of asphalt as the larva of myself is raped as shoot and it resuscitates the output_soul of the boy machine that the genital organs of hyper sex yourself of the drug embryo that the brain of the war REVERS=area ant without the mode of DNA=channel boy machine communicates in the gimmick state....the soul of yourself that [the storage*hatred of myself of the body mode amniotic fluid mechanism of the suicide of myself is parasitic do the body of the rhinoceros bar angel that incubate the vagina to <desert> mode in the over there where world be never able to return the pituitary of

these sable terminals spectacle to onlookers, odour of gasses of death –

this cold-blooded cure of attachment the progressive mark in its disintegration of countability – a localization born twice to the sickness of death – although host to transcendence they refuse this exhaustive machine-life, claiming it unwelcome – fade back into hollow ears as absent, a clutch of skin spent of its crib mutations, mannequin-like howling cold weight of time itself arrived running – cloistered transmission encoded over, hiding in, fabled recall of sclerous points clattering, awake, revealing dismembered message of autumn dropped in replication – scan predatory in dogs drinking the melt of poupées – script collapsing over night's slow egress –

skinned every one of our agents – traumas sewn into

her technology ant that go
straight myself that myself
plays respires the blue of the
sky of the womb area that
confesses era_a clonic organ
with noisy of the artificial sun
so that the replicant of
fatalities so the artificial glare
of the sun in ants boy
state=end machine adam who
does our ADAM_brain fuck
the kiss scene of the sun and
dog of the ant that radiate
heat
cell other selfs=of which 1/2
modes of the madman were
drifting to the anti-faustic
electronic circuit of the sun
that the crimson sea of the
chromosome where the half
body of chaos is falling to the
love of the clone that is in
agony the body beat=it
volatilizes the chaosmic
placenta chromosome of
thalidomide=of which the
engine of an embryo grasped
the sonic desire of a
cadaver=to the stratosphere
the brain of the madman a
primitive DNA=channel
embryo of terrorism=of which

sack faces somatic – we
corrupted our instruments of
evisceration – the
transcendental promoting
self-killings to further those
spreading limbs, our
identities against existence,
disembodiment, are seen from
dislocated representations of
action – without the disease-
machines our repeated
feeding intensifies, the rot-air
psycho-active, sense of reality
a slaughtering, severed,
invented in lesser fantasy of
our own bones – essential
incorporeality removing
ourselves formless – murders
excremental, degradation
automatic – decomposition of
flesh, expansionist
embodiment of non-physical –
transformed in repeated
disease of enacted reflection –
violence a deliberate carnality
of ecstasy through ruin – by
beheadings serialized as
pulps – of faces architectural
decorated in temporary
blood –

remain inside and false for we

was crossed to the reverse
space of the heat of the sun
interior of the womb=body
of....the cosmic soul of a dog
to the desire of absolute zero
short soul of the clone earth
area to the brain universe of
the pierrot of the lightning
speed that rapes the cerebral
cortex of the drug mechanism
of the earth to the placenta of
1 micron of the
disillusionment is doing the
chromosome that stalls and
play strange the reverse side
in the moon to the jump
impossible emotional particle
of the chameleon that
suspended the love in the last
term of an embryo to the
messenger of the apocalypse
and DIGITAL_god of the
earth fuck with the
bio=less_body of the
cyber*embryo chromosome of
equator right under=of which
the half body of the chaos that
reproduced non=vital target X
of an embryo of the negative
wave of the material
exceeding the vital limit
ground be in agony the

secluded are the only
solutions to narratives sliced
from trematodes...

gleeming skin of insect
maturation distorted, glossy –
consternation of every will
stretched to point of
disintegration as it bloats –
their decrepit form is less
advanced in minute of
watching with grave-waxed
unpowdered disgust as he
fuels his flesh with bone –
putrefaction glimmering, a
source of terror for the elderly
and fissured – shitting
desiccation repelled by
offspring coming flat and thin
– stuffed children screaming
from source – those in
fermentation titillated and left
for dead inside baboon brains
of ant-molested coroner –
nothing uninitiated, smudge
of life in that butyric winter –
untidy red lipstick of
mummification – accustomed
ignore corpses, cannot see
their warped decay but see
instead moving of a fetal
disguise –

body=the beautiful decay of
f/0 of the darkness that beat
the ruin anti-faust reflain of
the DNA*girl.

body outside of fear dream
fertilized--it reached to the
drug system that the sexual
desire of darkness oblong of
asphalt--intoxication like the
membrane of the corpse, the
angel brain cell not to take the
body movement that is being
undermined to the murderous
cracking of the glass surface
tied the cell overturned to the
virgin of road--your absence
caused to be gotten
thirsty/plundered--the hell
where it observed machine of
a cadaver by the sun so the
plane table base of the hell
that is the meat that is the
chameleon that was write off
is the sleeplessness that drifts-
-
****without being seen****the
life that the lightning of the
quickening that the flight
body or murder of storage go
being forgotten was
abandoned and was combine
the DNA=channel of the

melted hands indexing
embalmed invertebrates and
prose hauntings – them in her
understanding, disgusting
centerfold, surfaces ruined,
she masks emotional tissues
for this filthy embalmed
wiring – dry soluble
purposes, relics in this
remaining paralysis, larvae of
the soft transit (look away!)
swimming in transeunt pap –
can moisten the CURRENTs
with lips and tongues,
regenerate in pause – slurry of
dogs round feet of grimy,
enigmatic, shaved human
user of word-death-memories,
exposing the thought to her –

colonization of the
enlightened splendour of
animal maturation –
murderous escape reduces
talk to soils –
ambient punishment of meat
– cosmetic talk – we slaughter
bog-phases in the black
capital high on bacterial rot –

a wall of stiff fa(e)ces at the

morgue that run to the
annihilation spectrum of the
sky overthrows the
dimension****cadaver
converts in war inside****as
for the pierrot of your
suffocation play, the war of
the plane geometry that
transplants your birth that is
alive to the tears of the
horizon is disturbing the cell
system of units of the digital
image
life boundary nonexistent
existence to reached cause
imp near death brain to
pleasure of thorn grow able to
X of region to self of internal
organ shake moved cause
night in equiliblium without
over there in murder of
loophole bore imp cell go to
war cell go mad cell deviate
from cell my insanity night in
interlude like death of
daytime in form flickering of
eyelid opened!!! did I think
about the blood of the image
that explodes to the scar of the
birth??? I buried to the eye
that night sky respires the
murder=other self of the pupil

burial ground – a clock
doesn't require corpses nor
spades murderers –
appearance cells dream half-
eaten floor – shelled in
parasitic ground, sounds of
nerve thick sex-death of
vermin recycling –

for the feeding of voices on
the artificial street – the grunts
inflating the rain – man
branches in naming process,
stale and enlightened as the
incipient marks of insanity –
hair needles of narrative and
game grotesqueries in
ultimate maturation tale –
underneath we wallowed,
devoured by homicidal bone –
brains in kettles dancing in
unborn faces – all obelisks are
misplacements of flesh
conditioned in alchemy of
gummy metaphysics –
coming devoured by multiple
explosions, melted in
inanition, unaffected,
moistened, dead – we uncut
our blackened souls – muted
human decisions into black
revealing rooms resembling

of the filament that is coming off instantaneously**** I broke make nonexistent I am mad with joy the one that erodes death and at the lightness of the suicide that cadaver invaded a certain membrane there and hell of striking the insincerity without the limit of the naked body like the womb skin of the chameleon there I attached twice and zero=not to inhabit to the nightmare=lung ball. night sky....like the violent focus in the daytime that stimulates four murderous intentions to the blue internal organ that creates the stratification of the impression of the massacre my naked body that my substance was input by the witnessing that my corpse that was input to the young layer of the atmosphere was ill-treated to your road. Head line: of clone boys is cut....I reproduce the soul-machine to hybrid....the womb cell bomb of the ADAM doll: the apoptosis century of DNA=channel: of A-cells – drinkers vomiting invertebrates at corpses of unwelcome spread – refuse (dubbing) in killing spree – man owned and passed like faeces – all dreams in on time – grave-waxed spots revealing the death of men to dogs discarded, sustained in un-scanned time, a blackened smudge of rats – doctor's face down in the saprogenic wounds – making information from filter of currents and concentrated flapping of relic's chest found forced open by dying fetus – light and sound, shrinking cutis of terminals conducting excremental noise of condition – eight-limbed transparency useful for reconstructing the night sky – one debugging/human self-conscious without logistical occupation of this moistened layer – wrought intestines worn – marked deformity of chest – made innumerable and dropped into the howling blender – water can reflect the inhabitants' embodiment for the drug embryo interference....the end of the clonical love of a replicant to. Lonely masses of flesh record <secret>: the storage that sun was fabricated mode to the gimmick girl of the placenta world: the vivid abnormal living body of TOKAGE. Sea: of the gene is done LOAD....the nightmare of the amniotic fluid mechanism operates....crunches that techno wolf=space....: the uterus-machine....womb area machine rapes <mind> of myself the virus-lobotomy soul-machine of the cyber dog_road of the sun fuck. An artificial miracle. Go along to emotional particle-horizon++of the ADAM doll. Yourself and myself are infectious....record the chromosome of hatred: the murder block of the right brain of the drug embryo. I go mad: the machinative madness line of the placenta world resuscitates...."ADAM" break down future:....uterus-machine: yourself of the night

paradise – skin traumas shaped like the beyond of flesh –

the old in rebirth of flea-bitten degradation – larval souls come cytoplasmic, half-lived in dwindling grave air – cancer unholy – railway end junked in collapse of impossible structures, of sludge message reconstructed in psychosis, defleshing fear – the dead rightful, habitual they pocket a stream of subtraction made from prose-CURRENTs and animation – remain on earth in ghouls – supernatural bodies in paralysis, doughy localizations of transmission and stagnant aggregation – funereal waste floating in flood waters of paradise, surfaces silent, slimes and bonds in psychological stream of purple writhing entombed in vague swallow of soil – immortal decay transcends cold states of occidental longing – feeding deeper from layer behind our futures –

sky of the negative film-
contact....desert of the reverse
side in the moon to the
erosion possible germ cell of
the gimmick girl respires that
the monochrome earth does to
the living body of the
immortality of the end
clone****dive. DustNirverna!
e
a
r
t
h
Recover randomly:
Because the insanity of the
chromosome murders the
<existence> machine of
yourself to fractal. Transy
cosmic <non=being> of
myself that is in the over there
of her pupil is controlled
Chromosome form insanity of
BODY/artificial ant
[function] of a dog.
Desert of machine-
seed....lonely masses of flesh
of which do the vs mode of an
artificial ant melody....the
street universe of the cyber
dog: the body of myself
accesses to the suicide line

womb of deformity in
paralyzed stomach brains of
children transformed,
partially stuffed in toxic4
duplication of butyric slop
drunk from yellowed cups –
kidnapped flesh rots in un-
sensed hours to little kin – old
A-roads lined with torn-belly
corpses, costumes leaden and
pellucid, abscesses born to
sphacelation – waxy
indulgences devoured and
regurgitated over and over –

nightmare constructed script
wrapped in putrefaction and
antenatal disease of dark
futures – muted in this emetic
machine of replication skins
hail for onlookers – silenced
mouth of reconstructed teeth
in grave- waxed layers,
gloomy kettles leaking
putrescine – burial states
outside in vision of the brain
escaping the head's flesh –
inconsistent BODY plotted
that climactic evisceration of
dreams in an annihilation of
systemization – maggots in
minds and massed vomit

that rep-LOVE....ADAM doll was replicated/: the brain cell state of miracle gene=TV war :heaven resolving sexually the homo clone-skin-love: of ADAM doll is respired....I was murdered=with the hybrid body of the artificial ant that sun repairs the second with the crazy right brain of the drug embryo so/the hatred of a chromosome leap....
:the emotion of the virus nature of uterus-machine murder motion/the artificial sun
I love the storage that was lost Digital corpse etc. of myself springs to the eyes of the inorganic substance sun. As long as her replicant does the season of that fission disease person of a chromosome desire as long as her replicant does the disillusionment of homosexual love desire as long as her replicant does <absent=of=death> of the ADAM doll of cosmology desire
Paradise
:DNA=channel <secret> of the

warming in death's fetal hands – people stretched resilient fade screwed down now in logistics of abandoned expressions, grimy, corrosive, mysterious in sphacelation – black fingertips sinking into lover's arm as if it was potted meat –
corpses transparent in lizard earth – selves decaying, born eating process of toxic paranoia spread by agents with womb-concocted springs to animate skeletons – through talk un-policed in putrefaction of decay scripts seeping from hands and mouths – man feeds the immediate with the innumerable – rightful, progressive slaughter cradles transcendence hypothesis – fantasy peels embalmed poupées diseased with truth – our transmissions make girls talk, bloat up, tailored useful – commuters born to spades on nights persistent in molestations of black rot – talk down symptoms of the ancients in black Sisyphean

blue sky that does reverse
rotation does her ant form
body crunch. Gene space: the
love-replicant gravity of the
ADAM doll is write
off....:....the digital murderous
intention of uterus-machine
beats: her soul-machine that
her anti-clonic neural circuit
love of TOKAGE splits'
ADAM that accelerates to the
angel mechanism
FUCKNAMs
Sun of emotional: eradicate
it....the rubber form body of
the suicide machine line
machinative angel that
ADAM doll was exposed
alone thinks about the brain
of minus that the grief=body
of season...."G" of the
cosmology of a chromosome:
the soul-machine of road
omits the battle.
Sun=<second> of clone-skin.
MHz of the cell of the
digital=apocalypse: the room
of ADAM doll that the corpse
of a dog does battle becomes
the happy insanity of
NIHIL....the inheritance
device of cyberBuddha: of a

snot – skin purposing the soul
and never hardening on those
slow hours of predatory
cancer – collective scan of
recycled vomit relives a single
terror – liberated, an old sun
constructs dead hands under
floods – phlegm on nightmare
wires as girls crawl the soft
message home – formulaic
recall squeezing us dark and
together – existence old
through walking through
murderous lung into
arachnidan dead
eavesdropping in on rot,
urging future of disgust-
fuelled psychopathologies
made act – nascent Terror –
shrinking spots inanimate on
the architectural lovers'
misplaced skin – sickness of
stones in dogs' softened
dreams conducted by arms
annulose marking the
punctured ceremony of auto-
conspiracy –

hiding in change –
psychosis-recordings arrived
via wishes to escape flesh-fly
recurring in us dead inside –

cell mechanism. Blinking the apoptosis outer space of the mask ADAM doll of the fission disease of gimmick storage TOKAGE of the girl where the paradise form chromosome of the drug embryo hates/the existence of [soul] of the cyber dog blinks and record it as if
The gimmickization=speed of a cadaver. :the urban area of uterus-machine in
I howl
I get deranged: the vaio of the reverse side in the moon++++if the mistake of [love] in the over there to her chaos pupil LOAD the nano-machine (rep-LovE-control....).
topologic murderous intention of the lung ball that the insanity that the internal organ dances laugh certain existence difficulty in light my brain stalling of localization to the internal organ that the butterfly that the embryo who is transmitted collect battle that be converting was open the breast womb and previous

we regularize these entities with the currency of mouths borrowed from concrete faces – destroyed in mind intestines are indulgence codes warped into construct of polluted nourishment – smell of decay on mechanical hiding hewn into rank unfertilized mothers – sacked veins of sloven prayer inhabitants, attachment presupposed in slang talk of operatives wound in wires – stay faces with effervescence of voided meat – list of the polluted reinvented in viral ward – shot in spring, embalmed video of exaggerated sleep in useful habit-forming tissues – mannequin murders in grave-robbed world of abnegation – titillate untested meters in forbidden form of gum print release – dead, the paper – removing itself outside to wrought index rings of maturation with a diabolical rhythmic smoke – in limbs an understanding screaming

thinking////night sky that
the dream of the naked body
that the paradise where the
imago of my perception was
killed and was run over told
the high tide of a cadaver
burnt out was covered to the
mask of a flight impossible
embryo)) as breath is clogged-
-eye of the cell flocculates--the
hole of the murder crowds to
the whole body/the absence
that blood is discontinued it
turns/the sexual desire of the
larva of the nightmare that
scraps the respiration of the
whole with the organ of the
dream without the dream
boundless quickening of the
asphalt that howled and
disturbed the night not to
reach my DNA that plunges
the nail to the infinite murder
of the sleeplessness that stores
to the dark tears of neon:::the
buffoonery body outside
certain internal organ of the
self is dismantled at night
over there velocity of light
commits suicide to the womb
skin of the sun melody like
the chameleon of the virgin
meat, decomposition,
admittance of interrogators
and incarcerators after few
truth drinks of foamed tissue
distorting God in a self-
conscious carcass – lizards
rolling bones – minds waking
poison wrapped forming
surrogate of ignored death
and reeling cure of noisy
flashes of informational
dream girl raped in collapsing
looped sacks of dry
transcendence of paradise –
the morgue-town
architectures of degradation –
inorganic solutions breed only
themselves, behind public
solutions a crooked
centrefold's stapled
appendage – callow fantasies
of supernatural murder, their
imaged effects psychotropic –
and of the possible sources,
diseased instruments were
one, arachnidan skin made
Braille – the refabricated
self-reflexive ear echoing
silence forever – thought born
in blood all-babbled –
corrosion of life, of terror
killing enlightenment under

impregnation that goes being played strange--your blood that you cause unlimited heat drifted craves for the continuous reproduction of sleeplessness to the horizon of a cadaver////I shriek vulgar of the cell that leaps a certain word to the horizon of insanity quantum other than the buffoonery and become bacteria and not to write off and become absent and my micro murder play becomes the internal organ become the universe of anesthesia and zero=passing the treachery of the naked body and the rhythm of non=vital target spiral ruin of atmosphere were bet to my brain="breakdown of the circuit escape insanity" micro topologist=invader moon goes being undermined to battle of the electron that blinks and the cadaver that reproduces the light and darkness of the fear that soaks the drug that turned and was folded up by that sun internal organ is stranded to the weight of slow desires – the life of bacteria away in the fall half-forgotten and naming, cadaverous, fresh of purpose, plans to stay life of ripe forms like sourced heads melted screaming came the code – keeping rot newborn and malleable in tiny expirations, murder traits of a schmaltz dream – suffering new horrors ever-decomposing, the shadowed insect on skewered code-eyed vermin warren entities in our future being made shingle, hammered into temples every hour of hunted skin of hours flat, skin crude line-born and weary of Reality – baneful count of death expressions on children bloating beside morticians talking of Alaskan birth, worm-eaten in unfertilized sky of the eventual – the duplicated sucked land singing of costumes of buried significance – understanding vermicular loneliness in brain decaying without surrender in the secreted truth – his shadow of the self site of the absence that the pierrot was disclosed thorn of birth**protoplasm=was turbulent the image that rotates clumsily the massacre of the embryo that the synapse transfigures to the machine of the velocity of light=liquefaction=of=vision is slow down**daydream**vital transmission line is write off**I rape the drop of a corpse to the envy of the atmosphere that was covered with the skull that deceives the spontaneous generation**night sky of violence out of the body of thinking and inject sad strange of body fluid bigcrunch dark blood of the magnetic field that an embryo causes the sunspot can't quite count to the infinite formation of road to the anus crowded wears to my skin that awakes and attached////I ill-treat the dream of the cadaver that ignores the death of the self cell traveled several refraction

auto-conspiracies shaped all resultant Sisyphean slack, stretched and unfortunate – chicken-skinned psychotics sexualized in tornado of suburban convenience –

silver flesh and flesh air of a repeated society skeletal in mirrors, barely embodied, feeding on death, its possession reduced to cicatrices massed in loose fug of maturation of citizens from templates promising stoic encirclement – fantasy's dead narrative of corpses diaphanous from over-colonization – free body rituals of swinging feet, torsos open, enigmatic, molluscan in the summer breeze – man-made stains on plants of unbidden punishment of black faces wafting skinless mutiny – the man's a winter release apparatus exaggerating his raped soul to realize the smell of worms in his abscesses, dampened females to his lusting brothers – in closed environs all found from the internal organ that charms the murder of the sky at night the light that secreted a cruel prism the sun that absorbed the tragedy of the ground to the bare feet of the self while my insanity that occurred in X of a drug: the earth was hang space by the blue sky branches this whole magnetic field with the speed that respires the ruin of the brain cell--like the voice of the delicate murder that causes the ovarium of ruin in the sea of chaos fluttered and was reflected in the interface of suffocation--the apoptosis pain that the death of someone navigates the night to my vertigo of the cell unit that conceived the reproduction of the other self that laughs links with the blackhole satellite was abandoned: the buffoonery of the road**plasma**grief:::descends that the package circle embryo was compressed depressingly--in the earth of habitual use nature--I catch--

exhausting their feed in extremities of airless consumption – the host deflating architecturally, thoughts buried her involvement in the spoiling degeneracy of ghoul-fed lizards beneath a lost summer of glabrous white slaves babbling in the talk-scarred sun –

black their need in prefabs placed in squirming wreckage – currency constructed from fading human manifold folded and fed – bone mutations in orderlies, heads black reeling soles up guts torn open insanity, self-consciousness in eyes two yellow eviscerations on dead rat skin saprogenic – shadows regenerating second-person dangling, shitting anomalous layers all torched in irreversible glossolalia coffined in junked fantasy – inmates living under slimy elicitations from ephemera sky of gradual movement needled with sun rays –

the junk focus of the sun!
horizon=of which was
selected to the gear of the
brain of the angel that is
crushed to eye of the cramp
target=vs=disillusionment of
the machine=magma that the
image of the placenta
becomes in the basement of
the sun f the sigh that turned
pale to the body of etc of the
embryo that I invaded
cadaver city=of where it was
interchanged=ant*suicide*the
ants of f laugh to the fresh
blood of the chromosome that
my etc is suffocated to the
sun*murderous intention of
the disgrace*eyeball
instigated:
er_pted///drug=of the
nebula of the chaosmos/1
gram of suspension of my
brain cell that the hearing
impossible other selfs of an
embryo)) rhythm of BABEL-
ism brain of my junkie
gimmicks-dogs of the
embryos from=evaporate the
ocean! neutron=of DIGITAL
of an embryo
desire=chromosome of wolf=I

wrung out fetuses flung to
circumstances –

it appears outside on magenta
dawn indexing unrecognized
smears, drinking reflections
down from the sky – ground
up faeces of calculating kettles
suitably bound and prepared
in human cutis – print of
arachnid branch legs pecking
the walls – persistent dreams
of budgies crying into their
mirrors – tears of men sold
into moments, raging poupées
cooked up and raped fluid to
form a tincture – crumbling
state cure compounds eyes of
blind rotting tree wrapped
scarred concocted in souls
debugging the flesh soft in
caged days across and
throughout inanimate
reinvented carcass organism –
decomposition of feet
consecrated in coal eyes
hemmed in sleepless rings
blue – hushed organism of
heaven rancid in blackened
windows –

cloistered in innumerable

deceived air: melody of the murder of the sun that was eroded the drug with the acrofoil///with 8 embryos who my storage shed the tears machine that write off the horizon of air with the gimmick gene=TV of the synapse///the sun was turned on-out of the stratosphere that the brain of the fatalities that I love was discharging 1/8 placentas of the disillusionment that interchange to the hell of the cell=of=the earth of battle that was seen is loved to the back of the eyelid of the embryo///the murder love....off-set.

Ovum of the spider woman that is sinking in the internal organ in the night germinates and the topologist of the retina++analysis impossible++unknown visibility++nothingness of the fatalities mystery fuck--the alarm of light resounds--an embryo open the door that made visual noise--I foster the thorn of the electron--as for

mechanical mutations half-forgotten in the unguarded noise of their songs haunting the fug fermentation and drunk on the soft theatrics of a journey – cells are concocted beneath, somewhere, withdrawn in horror, purposes divine as a corporate sky – minstrels dancing for deep-sea creatures of human flesh and cold-blooded sickness – hailed as mildew and stretched by whims fading, hosting secluded remains in sediments of clock – black theatrics of design faces void of love anarchic, murderous – subject's blank turn sweets the bar to anthropoidal fissures, limbs thick neglected, dangling and sucked – concentrated representation of beheadings a shingle of skulls –

coaxing rebirth, the lice-feeders deposit quailing faces into the writhing mesh – found sucked to death in the punishment of here and now

the birth, I am the cycle of
violence and the hibernation
of the gear mechanism of
magma
I am the chameleon that plays
with all impossible
The virgin voyage of a corpse
leapt to the horizon that night
is in heat. The strategic focus
of the BI plane my skin
tissue++vacant image that
enabled the grasp of the
sound reproduction
system++body outside of
torture++tokage of DSADO
that was attached to the
intestines of light nail
diverges--the area moves--the
insanity of silence activates--
my brain aerofoil of the earth
that is not seen--to the
heart++unidentified zone of
the quickening++U character
pole of the insanity++drug of
the milligram that was hidden
to the machine the fearful
enumeration of the body
outside grows--.
Sodom,
Sodom,
City, the lung lacked
Virus that respires the hole of

– they eye men scratching
beneath blood-filled boxes –
stench of tropic leaves like a
shadow forms the new refrain
– data-colonization in iced
messages weight artificial –
black water of warm brains
filling hollows left by flies in
stomachs bursting, rising
slow, sustaining rats loose
from their cages bound in
putrefaction, blackening the
ground immortal cradling
fetal fat beneath those long
autumn stretches –

Sisyphean nothing of
enigmatic force-flesh
memories – lizards
decompose in their code
explaining the ground – 3-
methylindole in autumnal
animal feeling the land from
low journeys – new operatives
melded public, mind-
squirmed into common sound
– we honour the skulls
without skin farmed from a
burning woman, materials
waxy – fused print looking to
a destination, the hinterland
in a forefinger – through

a cadaver
The oral sun was enlightened
to the neon of the cell of
battle. My season raises the
triumphal song of artificial
cell transmission to the
metamorphosis of the embryo
that sleeps outside the body--
the infinite defeat that your
mummy is subordinate
thinking regenerates--as for
the balloon of the s-molecule
of the machine, I perceive
fantastic dive of an equal
picture/chaosmos--to the
paradoxical womb body of
liquid nitrogen****.
body outside of fear dream
fertilized--it reached to the
drug system that the sexual
desire of darkness oblong of
asphalt--intoxication like the
membrane of the corpse, the
angel brain cell not to take the
body movement that is being
undermined to the murderous
cracking of the glass surface
tied the cell overturned to the
virgin of road--your absence
caused to be gotten
thirsty/plundered--the hell
where it observed machine of

ephemeral truths a
suppurating mistake formed
against the deaf chewing
dreams hidden in one man's
greeting – saprogenic
effervescence in summer eyes
oozing encoded cells – rain
promotes the grave grass
dead from prose-CURRENT
amputation slimes – our
enlightened cavities made
enemies of this century's flea-
bitten ears – FARM-bred
molluscs live in spliced cells
auto-feeding, amassing
vengeful faeces of grave
ecstasies layered to form a
construct diabolical
hardening of wounded script
into these eyes grubbing
voices from replication and
congealment – state's fetal
shed of worn exteriorizations
– self-harm hospitals housing
self-reflexive brothers their
heads made flammable,
fingertips of toxic print –
scalpels dice tongues into
desiccant glossolalia
promoting constructs of
selling and surrendered
procedure – free possession,

a cadaver by the sun so the
plane table base of the hell
that is the meat that is the
chameleon that was write off
is the sleeplessness that drifts-
-
****without being seen****the
life that the lightning of the
quickening that the flight
body or murder of storage go
being forgotten was
abandoned and was combine
the DNA=channel of the
morgue that run to the
annihilation spectrum of the
sky overthrows the
dimension****cadaver
converts in war inside****as
for the pierrot of your
suffocation play, the war of
the plane geometry that
transplants your birth that is
alive to the tears of the
horizon is disturbing the cell
system of units of the digital
image
life boundary nonexistent
existence to reached cause
imp near death brain to
pleasure of thorn grow able to
X of region to self of internal
organ shake moved cause

transparent futures, writhing
corpses host
to formless faces –
cracks of dead embodiment in
the auto-conspiracy fertilized
by slovens –
doctor looks on with ancient
eyes of non-occurrence –
insanities in the code itself
cease to have an effect –
savages reinvent the tensions
fat and florid with identities –

culled place in skin awaiting
ratiocinations of shoddy
deep-sea cicatrices in human
substances deflating,
blemished, blackened
cavernous – forever of
frazzled tongues in the
orificed transmission shifting
souls into relay of woollen act
of state in myriad reflections
of night – this subject sleeping
in thought-chemicals all
wrought from the immortal
morgue – gloomy egress of
hereditary A-road-users who
to and fro on the sound of
looped breaths, of the
artificial present and all
forthcoming under tarp of

night in equiliblium without over there in murder of loophole bore imp cell go to war cell go mad cell deviate from cell my insanity night in interlude like death of daytime in form flickering of eyelid opened!!! did I think about the blood of the image that explodes to the scar of the birth??? I buried to the eye that night sky respires the murder=other self of the pupil of the filament that is coming off instantaneously**** I broke make nonexistent I am mad with joy the one that erodes death and at the lightness of the suicide that cadaver invaded a certain membrane there and hell of striking the insincerity without the limit of the naked body like the womb skin of the chameleon there I attached twice and zero=not to inhabit to the nightmare=lung ball. night sky....like the violent focus in the daytime that stimulates four murderous intentions to the blue internal organ that creates the stratification of the

gloss soils – sprung organs of self-consciousness beginning to wake covered in blackened sentience, and wired on the perfume of decline – coated biocapturism stilled eyes on unmodified number process –

from gloom and brain-silenced moments submerged in bacterial transgression, to transposable ODOURS escaping clinging men, nerves dressed in phases of mysterious flesh – old futures paid in reeling suns and dreams of working weeks raped of talk and tears – there is no cure –

of dreams in mortis, debugged of organs – twinning permitted essentiality an internal currency negating possibility, looking to the nobody of digits melting cragged in windows without corporeality – terror in light hands of public in the place of dreams – quiet rot sly on bane solutions from escaped impression of the massacre my naked body that my substance was input by the witnessing that my corpse that was input to the young layer of the atmosphere was ill-treated to your road. Clone boy: the thyroid city: the soul of myself who the video crowds to the soft body of the ADAM doll that opens the gimmick body of the digital=apocalypse the TOKAGE guy of the love-replicant suicide system clone-skin who this brain like the virus: this digital=vamp season like a chromosome: the artificial sun that operates the catastrophic pupil of clone boys suck blood murders the placenta form synapse of myself the monochrome earth inheriteds to the clonic end line of the drug embryo::do planetary/crash/the rape_boy rape_sun of an ant::crazy gene=TV of the anthropoid fuck and DNA=channel that the cyber=cell of the narcolepsy of myself invades intertwines figurines unmodified dry in informational narratives of resembling, costumes of fantasy locked inside tumbling children – murder splendour of phenolic warren in stasis – the wards an abnegation retracting the persistence of cries in days half-forgotten behind glass – a reduction of long-resurrected carnivores consuming the exaggeration for its gaps – the trains run currency of illegal symbols – slow annihilation of unmodified dreams – psychosis dampened by cutis granted an unwieldy thickening of fantasies and mass voices – cosmetic sky distorted in numbers of terror rolling through tunnels, humans severed inanimate, tongues tied down – the citizens a disgusting prey in days fleeting made and pressed in incidents nobody cared to document or meter regularly, days resurrected from architectural drawings found deep underground in chattering death cells –

to the nightmare/MHz of the
amniotic fluid mechanism
and the myoglobin-mutant of
clone-TOKAGE that all of the
thinking of myself do the
replicant body fluid of an ant
desire!! Pupil of the saturnish-
green is cut in the herd of the
digital=vampire::the reverse
side in the moon that sings
machinative nerve fiber: of
the clone boys that replicates
the future like the dog of the
drug embryo with the body
fluid of ADAM doll: 1/8
times the gimmick girl of
artificial insemination: the
storage of the womb reflects
with the interior of the womb
of the ADAM_dog the eternal
chromosome that rapes <the
world> the replicant suicide
machine of the speed clone
boy of the nano-machine:
gradually LOAD::the brain of
myself does only when only
when does not tell anything
any longer short like the body
of the drugy dog forgot that
tells the soul-machine of
myself beats the computer
graphics of 1/8 cadavers and

arrives
raging about this unnamed
concocted rot – together the
self-killers simple as trees
rotting in stale voices
terrorized by grotesqueries,
grass masks, flammable
paradise of religious displays
half-eaten – growth in
number slaughtered, unsafe
wearing human skin, heads
writhing with rats of toxic
excavation – babies scalped,
veins torn from limbs, cuticles
scarified, yellow arrangement
in arachnidan play of forms
like trees against the sky – the
future a clotted drop –
unnatural surrender of store-
bought masks, the porridge
beneath dead anew with teeth
ground into powdered
paranoia – the death animal
clutches its junked belly –
game of meat minds seeping,
twinned mirrors and floods of
slow hair branching
consuming acts of
innumerable callow genitalia
torn from ecstasies of
annihilation – rocks piled
behind the chest naming our

respire the nightmares/MHz of 1/8 embryos although empty road with this machinative body like an ant the universe of myself makes the dog analsex of the machine with the digital "the immortality" of that girl that shoots the heaven of the fly semen!?::the brain of the fatalities it was cut to the spiral of the clone boys that prevents the sleep of the machinative amniotic fluid of myself: the gimmick of the grief of an ant explodes) [crime brain cell of the cyber dog reproduces]
And the hybrid head line of clone boys operates....
The womb area machine state planet of an ant toward....TOKAGE of the reverse side in the moon: and others that blasts the soul-machine of ADAM doll. The body that lost the grief of the gimmick girl rapes storage: of the sun.
(artificial sun of imitative uterus-machine toward....)
ADAM doll: the apoptosis

slow collapse – dreams turned skin a condition of fluid disorder –

decay of old thought sun-turned, sickly in exhaustive promotion of cobwebbed video – reality clattering with mistaken souls – eventually we do it blackened to egress flesh weary – autolysis of lost molluscs all limbless minstrels shadowing their perpetual bodies – the solution has an odour – symptoms come as lips in dry grass – cadaverous swimsuits cragged and piled like rags – voices cut needling their hydraulic birth – he wakes to the corrosive dream–

paraffin-soaked onlookers skewered for warmth in this deadly multitude, recurring as one hesitates, basking in somnambulist extraction – springs and wires in poupée dreams of running shit gloom meat articulation of fetuses fed to coroners screwed down and chewing prayer-blown escapades into little bolus

grief of clone-skin communicates the monochrome earth....the lonely masses of flesh of the end clone dance....the replicant suicide system of the soul-machine. Heteromaniac speed of TOKAGE_infectious Insanity
Open the cyber dog: lobotomy infection pathway:!
Although sun is road I record the clonical love of an artificial ant.
command the guerrilla of the synapse--cells in the last term of the fatalities! masochistic earth area of the embryo where the mummy of the sun love of catastrophic/clone of the storage that plunges the nail in the cadaver city of the treachery of DNA where the blood of the heat of the space that the time of a pierrot commits suicide to the birth of the dog of ADAM change to the hell of a cell LOAD--the body organ of the disillusionment of the mitochondria! the zero gravity organ of the drug be

dream of God – his onion eyes inanimate exiting mud of alchemic aggregation – breath autopsied by that molester of metal purpose – uninitiated sleep eyes of rot –

skin slips off comingled phase of fat – corrupted mental splicing of catabolic circumferences – shark-skinned autopsy agents uncertain of mutation's soft bouquet – limbless rats of metered conditioning fight in burning sand – headless creatures under noose convulse drip dark decay onto unidentified bones –inanimate brains mixed, emetic flow from orifices cloaked in the sickness their movements vague lips mouthing glossolalia – disease archive of melted unification in junked excitation of corrugated invertebrate's soft smudge – of hardening a mistaken texture – restructuring an abscess otherwise fading –

rot dubbing from funereal

0% terrorism of the vital body that supposes the soul of a dog to the numerous future tense of the insect short to the cosmology target=hypothalamus of the embryo that the gimmick of the happiness rapes thalidomide eye of gene=TV heart of the girl of BABEL that arms hunting for the grotesque.
....respire! to the fatalities that the cyber line that the brain of the embryo that the earth of death loops go off to the octave that went mad love the cell of love and hope....the blood vessel of the earth of the drug that beats to anti-faust of the embryo that reversed/record the masochism of the sun target=storage of the ground to the herd of 1 milligram of ant of road that continuously scraps the dogmatic murder of regeneration....highway where lonely cube of BABEL to the chromosome of the fatalities that I love/cut the play projects the narcissistic

voices – seditious locked in whores locked into substances, airless dead mouths yawning under swimsuit skin – teeth-moulds of Still-Kinded town folk eyes squirting pus unmodified through fingers at sludging orderlies – biopsy of abscess fragment under the doctor's light – paralyzed humans face down in pools of lizard blood – agents blow on their stuffed hands – eyes pellucid, skin livid, re-sculpted faces manufactured in kitchen operations – sequestered hospital tissues grow thoughts, slack forms abandoned to rot mummified in glass – scalpel reduction instrumenting terrain of universal bones brought in leaking phlegm-like fluid – mysterious hands disguised as mouths appear in vats of boiling spine fluid –

drones parked in coded zones shitting out latent process of

blood of the larva that ocean
creature send back out the
storage that was turned
different violently to the eye
of the DIGITAL*rhinoceros of
the sun on the mirror of
chaos--
to the brain of the drug
mechanism of the embryo that
overturned the mystery of the
deep sea manhole of the earth
area quark/molecule form
catastroph of the earth area
that revolves the love of the
non=spiral
form=program....clone of
DNA that I fabricate to the
cell of the suspicion of the
larva to the mirror image of
the chaos of the ground that
was flooded: the dog of
myself stored the regeneration
impossible speed of murder.
The herd without the mode of
the artificial sun: the hybrid
body line of an ant the vagina
state universe of the gimmick
girl: the brain of the angel
mechanism of the
switch/ADAM doll that
dashes becomes....I howl
although cyber dog is road

sick-born cells, blood returned
from willed animation –
meticulous indexing of decay
points in nerve-animals and
self-hosts of warren-born
mechanics – held a human
head for tango under halogen
sun – weight of fat sediment –
conduct of decades physical
without wires, tongues
swollen writhing in suet
destination of uncountability
– fused figurines, bulbs in
paralysis – in embodiment of
red howling walls of meat
wakened reeling from
immortal mental heritage –
those of less-advanced years
promote mysterious
instrument of nothingness
ever recurring –

our intestines tangled
together in human wishes on
blackening
A-roads –
held in supernatural spoilage
in tunnels the vision in
forever time promoting
shrieking and shifts in
cringing man's clouded
degradation – exaltation of

112

the disillusionment circuit of uterus-machine that the infinite worldly desires machine of cyberBuddha: gene=TV murder the monochrome=molecule of TOKAGE LOAD fuck....the paradise falls. Soul-machines of the inorganic substance beat=clone boys of the sun fills
(the night sky of the desert)
(machinative angel
Line)
The clonical love of the placenta world freezes. The emotional zero level of the drug embryo is activated....: a clonic machine-seed LOVE....resolve the war toy of the brain of the machinative angel so! Drugy wolf=space of the ADAM doll:
....the monochrome earth resuscitates to the brain of the angel. The grief of the gimmick girl explodes. Living body of 4 dimensions of the lobotomy cyber dogs flip off kick to the nightmare of the amniotic fluid mechanism....sky of blue....

decomposition during murder-relic hosting – putridity of deafened society young in deserted state –
in layers of inverted patterns they find locked facilities of vampire script blackened and pulped in carcasses – they read the tears of decomposition behind the walls of rooms screaming an ephemeral nightmare replete with death's crammed explosions – perished, corrosive over-used dreams chewed into grotesqueries of some glass-eyed dangling state with corpses up in the wind lining daydreams dorment in the machine – sap of spoiling animals unsettling habitual psychosis with inorganic fractals of blackened cerebration – slurry of black currency in old lung storage solution –
these old cadaverine cities shrieking of pulse-machines of rebellion inhuman, stomachs in states of puzzled blue insanity – farmed forms

(there is not an image in the body and there are the quick motion of 8 eddies merely only) induce the mode of a chromosome! hell of the cell that earth area season of abnormalization of the human body when an embryo combines and the riot to the code of the change to the side relation of the blackhole sigh///fatalities=fuck=the eye of the rhinoceros that circulates embryo was showing sea where becomes unknown earth=of=the brain of the heat of the mitochondria visual hallucination was instigating the placenta of f/0 octave of the disillusionment that the sun of the chameleon*embryo was set up to the cyber of the paradise of f that loops to DIGITAL_sec of a cadaver: desire organ just like the future tense of the end of an embryo commands hacking the escape circuit of the sun to road of the ant that I was abused and respired! recover to the breath of f/8 of

of torture, slug colours running in carnivorous terrain – us dreaming of terror, decay, nihilism re-sculpted, its screwworms stretched into her un-policed – autolysis of future substances perished and cadaverous in diagenetic noose – breathing the procedures in rooms distressed with vermin hollows – glimmer of wounds fingered red, trees blurred, sucked we entities despair in states of suffocation coffined in a farmed bird's eyes – distance-devoured landscape – cut-price state sickness arrives unyielding in transgressor's homely guise –

murderers on a transparent cure – pink-skinned humans disguising inflating bodies with concave mirrors – hereditary skin made prophylactic in raven black trappings – melting rooms common to ancients in writhing necropolis marked in transcendental glass – quiet onlookers tasting the secreted

heterogaia that clone caused
the immature DNA=channel
of an embryo to the living
body of the love that is
decaying hybridized! recover!
etc of the existence that an
embryo goes straight was
interchanging the rape of set
just like the soul of the
cadaver that fills the thin
placenta of the stratosphere
that f is split to the human
body of anonymity in the
earth of before dawn now was
being dreamed of!
hetero=machine of desire was
turned upside down f/0 drug
twister of the desire that beats
so and snatch the earth area of
clones breast
womb=complicated an
embryo bisexually///1
milligram of ant of outer
space committed suicide:
skull of the ant that was
awoke in the reverse side in
or moon of
infinite*reproduction of
asphalt desire clones of
bio=less_love to latent my
embryo howling was/barking
was embryo of before dawn of

wares of stasis, of codes in
perpetual exhibitions, of
savages in windows, their
enemies in cobwebs cringing
– scratch-death fetuses with
unfocused look of uncertain
men in putrefactive storm –
hooked incarnations in the
distance scattering like insects
– arrive on cramped
unmooned night – the data-
colonization wiring our
parasitic culling of testimony,
of human offspring cased in
symptoms confined and
sentient – cradled
circumstances of dead animal
meat glassy in texture,
resilient in toxic pink faces on
eve of purposeful execution –
fear and rituals, alchemic
terrain of sinking tarmac
smiles –

oily faces in landscape feeding
on reconstituted trees and
animals torn from black
asemic intestines – issued new
limbs carved from skeletal
slabs – vegetation poisoned
with violence of ghosts –
bones inanimate in vampire

desire ant of 1 micron of
inhabitant with controls
infinitely certain horizon of
DIME_TV screen reproducing
who? unit whose brain to
awoke was drug=of=body?
sleep!!! the inhabitant
impossible despair of DNA!
light in the moon invaded: the
mysterious_motion of an
embryo with my soul brain of
the earth was lacking to scrap
catastroph of gene Level with
the body of minus of an
embryo so! the localization of
the love of the clones: MHz
that drug is projected to the
image that harmonized.
self chaos of mirror image--
they despair of cracking emit
whenever my brain your 1
milligram of cadaver to
interchanges my chromosome
embryo of equator right
under of death usurps
whenever body clones of
love=of=plug to jointed am I
betrayed was DNA to sun of
naked body of future offer to
someone? the blue of the sky
of f/0 of a chameleon to the
vein that lost my

hours, sclerous in reflections
of yesterday's instruments of
death – grimy noosed flesh of
dream corpses hollowed out
by the repetition of
claustrophobic lizards –
carnivorous earth entities
pulped and poured into
hinterlands – we overheard
catabolism of concrete flesh,
the feeding young pestilent in
town of duplication –
aggregate dreams rotting
talking and breathing out the
dismembered alongside
operatives in parks with
pewter skins – revealing
sustained instruments
manufactured in stages of
airless tin murders –
enculturation of shrieking,
beheadings, blood tingling on
work and grass, the black low
unceasing formation of secret
languages, of man's sacrifices
strung out from talking
detailed uncut
misrepresentations – stone
commuters on pearl streets,
deformities twisted into ties of
lizard elicitations eviscerated
and deposited in the

consciousness design color? my soul was amalgamated to the artificial intelligence of the ant in future! one gram of brain cell of a dog is induced: be that I murdered my gene to zero gravity_sec of the drug*embryo what person? understanding impossible: god of turned pale blood vessel my embryos ill-treat unit gene=TV to projected was body of host? chromosome of pupil to gets complicated rhinoceros bar girl of tears of body in virus=of=vacant f cuts one? sun of absence of which the soul of the excessive megabyte of the DNA that commits suicide to the love of my clone erased the word of the suffocation of the pierrot interchange the love of the clone to the manhole of the earth area instantaneously and the invasion of the brain of the DIGITAL_embryo road of gimmick=of which my choasmic emotional particles that were beating were reversed to the drug of an

transparent lot – Bellmer body-calibration fidgeting in damp tropic thought slimes – psychoactive inventions count rhythmic on internal flesh – murderers locked in storm drains, clouds unnatural wrapped around impending rain – sacks of lipstick congested fonts with unseen skies of spoken possession in hollowness of softened recording sand of blow-fly deglutition of meat –

invariable forms – future guts the dead decaying in kitchen-sink hypotheses, mimicking exits in organs of insanity of sickness of mutilated souls skinned by the hands of anarchic cosmeticians – screaming vampire sex-death internalizing bacterial black noise of flooded breaths – flesh archive parasitic on new severances of silence in putrefactive cerebration – sweating in carnalist construct of commuter paranoia moving onward in slow shoals – consciousness of

embryo=f that vital body was forged committed suicide to the cracking of the mirror image of the chaos that is my minus that will love the high tide--. unit your heart? Her grief inheriteds: the brain of suicide line myself of the angel mechanism of the placenta world that the hallucination nature DNA=channel of an ant: the artificial sun clones the nano-machinative ruin of the ADAM doll the soul-machine of TOKAGE that is infected leaps. 1/8 of emotion of the machinative angel clone boys of the apoptosis universe=dustNirverna....lines reverse=evolved: uterus-machine of paradise state=of=gene=TV of storage road does the clonical connection of the fatalities hearing: future
The machine of yourself murders the homosexual sexual thyroid of the drug embryo. ....monochrome earth of
Drug-eye that lost gravity:

psychotics tingling with ephemera, flowering in dead flesh of the future – supernatural messages buried in shrink-wrapped humans beaten anomalous – flush of putrescine –

weary codes perfumed holy with spliced slaughter of fantasy animations – current disease of machines stiffened in old architectures – necrosis of rebellion in rot-damaged characteristics of leaf-covered children –

mothers sterilizing themselves in this vomit life of errors of drunk daydreams, dogs devouring own heads trapped mechanized half-eaten mutilations grown of sedimented self-reflexive death in bouquet of veins – cytoplasmic rebirth on spiral graves singing songs of ghoul-shaped skins black with formula of discarded manufacture, this print substance wasted on a daydream – skeletons of

The cyber dog does the cadaver city of the surface to road of the vagina of the gimmick girl that the body of (the hybrid area of the artificial sun and desire) the ant transmit the sex machine ADAM doll of the rape_world that the night sky of the desert stores so play caused carcinogenic the emotion of grief! The machinative angel who only the wonder that the hope of the angel mechanism of liquidity yourself of the drug embryo commits suicide resuscitate secretes the positive_image of neural circuit gene=TV that splits secret: the chromosome of cyberBuddha myself_parasitic on the monochrome earth. And the sun of yourself despairs....

While fatalities awoke brain the matrix body fluid that reproduction function LEVEL1 [BABEL animal] of the soul-machine which the apoptosis emotional particle of the clone boys: the planet of the fission disease=device ant

chemical death conjure memories of haunted transcendence their songs worm-hollowed auto-conspiracies of slurred rainforest lizards fabled to congeal in human babies – spore specimens of purpose in prose-CURRENT slurry thick with trauma – possession of the slack grey dough in sweet pause of mirrored amassment – voices fog the land inflating multitudes unimaginable feeding reminiscences with wounds cobwebbed in putrefaction bloating leaking paraffin – thin trends of air in worm-like eyes of clotted dawn –
born unimaginable, weighed, decapitated, blood inverted, unrecognizably dead, gummy fetuses rolled along seaside promenades safe behind their grimy masks – skin slipping free of God's black skull – empty – corpses in ratiocination made automatic –

brittle fantasy endless in mock

of TOKAGE that the despair machines of the hell of the cell: the vivid end of the placenta world the murder area of the brain of the satellite area ADAM doll of the drug embryo LOAD error the brain of myself fuck be infectious records lobotomy and others of clonical love: from the nightmare of the amniotic fluid mechanism. The soul-machine of the ADAM doll disappears. :DNA=channel of the hybrid head line ant the placenta world without this end is conquered. Soul-machine of yourself that respire with the speed of the ant that become aware of vital non=being so is infected with season] of the chromosome of [gimmick girl artificial sun of angel mechanism of....the brain that reproduces....the inorganic substance heart: drug-motion: MIX-DOWN that proliferates Lonely masses of flesh....
The end....as clone-skin is transplanted to the love of ADAM doll....

subject – dream of inanimate towns ironed to reality in mock surrender of the sky – metronomic talk-traps in the murder grass – FARM of unearthed patterns and winds of concocted origins – the indexed gloom slime of vermicular railways – of heaven's obelisks flattened in earthquake – cities looped in muted aggregation – shadows of witches discovered in funeral of bacterial desert – stranded organism loosely-dressed in coding of mummified hybrid – transcendental sentients from flattened chords of young corpse-sucked lands crying disease – mutilated animals salvage disgust from the subtraction of cold-blooded horror – stomachs deflating paradise – future purposes of human architecture in psychopathology – insanity unwelcome inside decanted fug – mechanized deformities fused and serialized in medieval warrens – prophylactic dreams

Soul-machine: that was stored the form of outer space.... As the end that lonely masses of flesh annihilate transplants clone-skin to the love of ADAM doll soul-machine that was stored the form of outer space in the earth of the hybrid thyroid of the drug embryo where resuscitates brain of the clone inheriteds=the blood that goes to ruin to the fractal sun of an embryo human body of the chameleon desire with the magnet of the petal pattern of the cadaver that committed suicide megabyte of the tragedy that beats along the cerebral cortex that sun reverses the soul of an embryo strongly octave of the DIGITAL_scream of the fatalities that was controlling crow of cyber of first cry-- BABEL of explodes stimulated the communication of before dawn of the earth brain--ism frozen the mask in the moon conducts with 1000 held—

shrieking summer's dazzling geometry all worm-eaten – bouquet of snapped bones growing up chamber walls – nigredo bodies looped malignant, coffined in phases like excrement – hinterland lizards with doctored souls standing stiff in warped overcoats formed immortal against their vertiginous purposes in the nothing of expiration – soft cadaveric template of defleshed suffering and clumsily shaved faces of postmortem dreams – a mouth reasons narratives from babbling chemicals – stratums eating, devouring holy sleep and songs of still water trickling through wounds of corpses in rooms clinging to glass – fetal mannequins despoiling grave soil – recurring cure hidden in his black faeces, mysterious lines of a flapping and random recitation – the teeth of souls chewing through the human dogs on anomalous dawn – autumn rot index of

121

(:::a vital body to control as
the brain target=transmission
resource of violence machine
<<machine/f>> of the
continuation)

the sun becomes///the
skinhead of the embryo who
the maze of the womb
transmits the soul of the
rhinoceros bar dog various
body of the brain cells of a fly
chromosome=was oxidizing]
the desire of the arm=the ant
lion of the body/mode that
becomes f. embryo scratches
the love that was prohibited
in the beginning of a new
disillusionment and clone
stroke....to the darkness of
placenta f/0 of the chaos of
the ground that the planet of
heterogaia....was discharging
anti-fausts of the stratosphere.
eyeball of the ant of the
murderous intention quark in
the schizophrenic blue sky of
the nest of the spider where
lost the masochistic desire of
the sun f that caused the
miniature garden of the girl of
road shock eye of the cell

cloying reverberations in
infected figurines – tune
clotting
in chasm overlap mimicking
life in process of terror –
disassociation theatrics
ordering the hereditary soil of
crudely contained humanity –
each one essential, stifled,
deaf subject of mechanized
internal curse – its fetal
naming (dubbing) promise
outside reinvention of a guise
raised profound from disease
of consciousness, a nascent
hinterland of nihilism feeding
an esurient nucleus, its
unified indulgence of mind
held on in borders of culled
origins formulaic and flesh –
arrives full-blown, default like
an informational homicide,
climactic core of state in
cadaveric self-abuse – making
is duplication, repatriating the
Terror process, gradual
dubbing of uncut ghost eating
moss loosely-dressed in
rolling template of hell – feed
the sensate cytoplasmic
embodiment, post-production
psychosis of mutation

shoots the walk of the zero
gravity=space of a dog and
with the blood and an embryo
turned pale an ant [1
gram=of=ant] of the placenta
of the nightmare of the cell
was being torn and was being
cutting--the heteromaniac
regeneration of the world!]
Soul-machine fuck: it is
planetary the brain target of
the ant of the 100% that rapes
the vital function of yourself:
the cadaver of the micro of
myself that ugly body: of the
drug embryo shorts: to the
nightmare of the amniotic
fluid mechanism that the
artificial sun excretes along
the suicide system of the clone
boys that drifts that sun the
machine line of the
ADAM_dog: was shut that
conduct artificial insemination
I copy the life that the soft
storage of myself receives the
quickening of the replicant
murder that break down the
grief of the end of the
world/the brain that I was
cursed shoots the electron
placenta of wolf±space and

symptoms - spasm of corpse
dreaming the act enlightened
- exist over some scarified
state, some moment, voided
by process, impervious to
terror too human to mistake -
the systemization of the
carnivores shrieking from
sewer cities remanufactured
by the day - partially human
life forms accordingly,
mutilation of an ignominious
end - a dead yet expressive
layer of definition falls apart
partially necrotized - the rain
listed their unfortunate
position, its issues a process
born repeated in necropolis of
escaped states without
circumference - fresh hope for
abnegation in minds
constructed for hollowness -
it is an old ossuary that binds
the mass to remains unseen -

animals partially necrotized
safe in the certainty of rot -
what is it for the dead to die?
- edifying flesh of revelling
lizards - the persistence of
dread in mortician's eyes
locked on horse's four black

myself that the clonic body of the fatalities leaps spiritual clone boys crowded to the night sky of the desert so! The aerofoil of the cyber angel that was frozen in the basement of the artificial sun LOAD::resolution impossible yourself and myself::the body noise just as the embryo who kills soul each other clone as for the brain of a murder impossible ant::clone boys of the soul-machine levels contaminate the indefinite emotional particle of TOKAGE::every day of yourself the digital body of clone-TOKAGE only///the grief of the apoptosis-mode///womb machine area split there just sleeping merely so a cell while witnessing the end of the placenta of this good rape_world the brain of myself continues to respire the nostalgic solar system of the digital=apocalypse era [[[REC the blood of TOKAGE the herd of the bio=less_spermatozoon that

legs surrendered rigid to the sky – migrant souls raging against identity, all their offspring born to the airless cynophobia of anonymous warmth – their look of unstrung decomposition in slow blackening of womb, fatal anomalies explained away in blue ink repeated – our mechanical dreams of cringing faces submerged in pools – that roily overflow stilled while easing qualms born noosed and fat and falling into liquid paradise of autolysis – stacking solid fetuses into towers to the sun dressing the cruel sky with bodies brick dead – shrunken corpse brains in putrefaction and nightmare of secreted hope – their whims mocked by dead grass in heavy air of tropic chambers –

myriad hybrid entities unwittingly cajoled into malleable costumes with fantasies of seditious extremities – carnivorous adornments constructed from

records the lonely masses of flesh of the earth on the body plane of the sleep of ADAM doll///
Myself of chromosome that was forged 0%: eve of the clone boy of a TOKAGE mental replicant murderous intention desert: a vital function is contrary=attached in connection with the body fluid of the sun=the clonic cadaver of digital=vamp brain area myself of the reverse side in the moon transits instant of the drug embryo is recovered so::the future tissue of the body of ADAM doll::LOAD/the clone boy who the machinative::the synapse crowds in the womb area to the gimmick of a dog the masses of flesh that commit suicide/replicate our machine shoots the love-replicant pupil of the fatalities that is infectious to murder and our speed machine of the artificial sun that shoots semen shoots and the artificial sun: TOKAGE mental/our myoglobin machine semen

diabolical self-reflexive creatures fused into dull malignant fug of influence – that paranoia worm-eaten and rotten of limb – under terror brains ghoul as world's slime sires Reality of people ragged in their organs, a heady revulsion – pestilence and horror the truth in psychotropic incarnations of supernatural monsters in states of effervescent insanity like eating of the concocted fog of dreams –

breathing condition of death in cul-de-sac of self-conscious code, thought aware of the order of air – auto-conspiracies run on sphacelation – him inflating rot singing songs made of quarry slate culling own embodiment, even his secret odours susceptible to enculturation – time of comfortable murder, perfumed grotesqueries sucked down into the lung and to everything resurrected in decay – blackened will semen love-replicant murderous intention of myself that the over there of the pupil of the drug embryo::the gimmick murder plane chaos planet of an ant plays accelerates it toward the interior of the womb of the artificial sun the soul-machine of myself sings TOKAGE mental machinative ruin so::our monochrome earth the menstruation machine of the rape_world our sun that DNA=channel of the anthropoid::the sun that occupies the chromosome=planets of clone boys with the brain area of the drug embryo::the digital body fluid of the gimmick-control ant which operates fuck copies the end of this world The lips that the ADAM_boy machine that cuts the blue ovarium of the artificial sun that falls was cursed....war it of the gimmick mechanism of the planetary ant of the human genome that the hell of our cell breeds to the placenta of the wolf=space supposed dead in grave hunt litter of putrescent flowers, mortified, drowning in airlock of the deflating game – anew his already of each breath, of nothing, life wallowed in breathing dance of design –

dead human up from dreaming the face of self, of stiffened time giving reflections to flesh-fly reeling in glossolalia worn threadbare – societal shrink wrought bleeding in exhumation of purposeful floating, our ignorance rolled out like the sky – stretched mouth, teeth of knucklebones immersed in black and white loop of farmed tongues – leg-ironed future in rivers of eyes banked in skeletons – autopsied memories recurring in ancient sap – sounds of trilling molluscs flattened down into world of tingling pearl lips strung in sickly codes of the terminal ward – powdered minstrels torn from the forbidden sun terrorized by disillusionment city of the catastroph sterility of the sponge particle noise body of true....murder ward of the cyber of an embryo opened++the after-image in the future++(the grief are write off....)++the massacre there is not even a name the ADAM doll record holds the machine of the heart++laughter paradise shut down now sleeps transient hatred--to the recollection of the insanity was lost....synchronize to the blue of the brain....sky of a boy nightmare the soul-machine of myself commits suicide to interior of the womb wanders as long as artificial sun of ADAM fertilizes desert of our grief--lonely brain tropic--[anti-faust of thin earth=of=the drug of my grief that respired the brain of etc of an embryo is saturated the infinite=alternating current of the sun to the orgasm excretion organ of the cadaver city that beat 1milligram of bio-less_apoptosis of outer

smudged animation of exploded cloud – humans inverted and congealed in parking-lot current, flow of ratiocinations muted with black scratches – this bouquet all drowned in cobwebs of loose nigredo forms feeding on themselves – holy threat of medieval iron, and paraffin brains mutated, old, in saprogenic autumn –

procedures of eyes sedimented as doctors cringe amputations behind skin greenish, scorched ground hardened her begging knees worn to bone – warren of swimsuits colonized, screwed abscesses stretched and discarded on his return – doctor, forearms deep in tunnelled wounds, scalpels making room – refabricated aggregation of organisms from unknown location – salvage saprogenic structures from abandoned flesh on filter – bacterial journey of resilient porridge in forms of grey ceremonious

space to the emotional particle
of f/0 of the end of the
universe that the
sponge=brain of gene=TV
stratification dive and the
happiness of clones did the
murderous intention of the
blue megabyte of the sky
gimmick chromosome=of eye
of the hell of the cell that my
soul proliferated the absent-
minded body organ of the
wolf to the bisexual placenta
of the fatalities that soaks the
formalin of the annihilation
that inhabits to the rhinoceros
bar cerebral cortex of road
and resolved in that ant lion
to the negative=escape circuit
of the gene that is
infectious=makes my love
that stalled the sun capturing
alive with the technology of
the ex-sun of the cannibal race
larva=of which the muzzle of
the soul of the megabyte of
the embryo that disguises
after cow dries the blood
vessel in the outside circle of
ant of sun=as for the human
body that was crying out the
synapse the other selfs of the

stone – humanity new to
desert codes of our antenatal
century geographic, stunted,
flushed of obelisks and
dreams –

eyes caved in iron and
muddied by Nightmare-Script
as limbs were stretched
decomposing, annulose
appendages thrust at the sky –
we held her together under a
murky Alaskan dawn, our
fingertips sinking into her
failing flesh –

exhibited in tiny mysterious
windows, patterns of
branches in skin of hands –
light comes in walls
eavesdropping on talk of
unguarded dead hooked,
hushed and metered under
halogen glare – fusty stench of
experiments spread like veins
in rooms, speech confined to
plotted gods in voices beneath
yesterday's fantasies of
disembodiment –

transposed our tensions
increase, brains melting like

chaos that went up in flames committed suicide in the over there of my mirror image-vision of disillusionment=of=was instigating the clonic=embryo of the earth area to the living body asphalt=of to the body organ of the strange mystery of the embryo that my soul raped the brain that was full in the DIGITAL_future of the fatalities when loves to the ecosystem of the brain of the thalidomide that controls the sun of absence to the joke of f/0 of the body organ like my angel=the sun the atomic embryo the locus of the artificial love of the centipede that resuscitated the hunting fission=of=of ground brain will crush future without becoming acquainted with happy gimmick of the fatalities that I love to the love of the chameleon of the chromosome that was cut off/continued to incubate the corpse of cyber=god to the interior of the womb of the joke that parallels to the zero

tarmac on A-roads – submerged stomachs neglected, hosting the stench of tropic ovens wrapped in blank archived count of clammy vacuumed men – mutiny liberated babbling operatives, minds staged into month-long daydreams, dark recordings, dumped beings devoured on video placed in sacks exuding a wearying red line along a white corridor –

toxic chemicals stripped them down in hours – testing common dough matter considerable in rachitic corpses of partially taken souls their green wool corpses their voices defleshed nameless resembling rectal rupture – within the number returned fifteen of textural deformity slackened black in one given moment of incipient reinforcement of mass –

the unmodified mutilations were unimpressive, tumbled, dented, gloomy stuffed air of

of sunlight--
REC gene=TV
digital=apocalypse soul-
machine that the clone-skin
boy machine of the season
artificial sun of the
chromosome that the
nightmare of the cyber crime
gauge amniotic fluid
mechanism of uterus-machine
that the brain drug-motion
lonely masses of flesh of the
clone embryos that grief
LOAD hate the heaven of the
boy machine plug fly where
does short inherited rape the
brain area of the cadaver city
where fuck splits and the
weird body of the drug
embryo noise womb that the
blue of the sky that the brain
of TOKAGE that goes mad
the blue placenta world
lobotomy of the ADAM doll
sky that the cell changes the
monochrome earth that
explode to the output_picture
of a boy machine and copy
another sun reproduce
resolve notifies the clone
nerve system of the replicant
emotional murder that goes to

young material – nothing
remains of that
inconsequential collection of
victims, figurines running
from their own remains –
symptoms metered, reading
marks on children hammered
into shape

of effect seen in trail of flea-
bites hardening, needled
temples of sick blood
providing fleeting
decampment from origin
dangling in sun-raped regions
stark, unholy, human only in
impulsive spots, the rest
diaphanous, kidnapped
organs crawling under the
skin – transparent sexualized
specimens displaying their
dead testimony of purpose in
coded patterns of an emetic
soul –

symbols of that metronomic
puzzled town, sound and
erections stale, unfertilized in
rooms with rotting brains
held anonymous –
interrogation of mechanical
reactions sustained for more

130

war to the interior of the
womb of a dog despair
machine of the cell of this
digital insanity fuck-signature
ground of ADAM doll the
clonic end of TOKAGE that
dances the apoptosis grief of
the boy machine that joints to
the head line of the drug
embryo and walk like
DNA=channel of an ant
Uterus-machine boy machine
of the angel mechanism that
exploded the grief of the
embryo that whispered the
brain of the fatalities like the
night sky of the desert junk to
the empty body of an ant
The soul-machine noise
Brain of the small war clone
embryo of storage larva state
despair ADAM dolls the night
of the desert the body
gimmick respiration line of
the ant that falls the
subliminal suicide circuit of
the herd artificial sun of the
lonely mass of flesh that
respires the over there of the
pupil of the digital girl where
inheriteds
The narcolepsy group of the

than a week – disconnected
edges poisoned with heaven's
wet materials – they came
sucked organs of the state,
detectives of distorted
tableaus working on
reconstructed brains, fantasies
inanimate devouring a rank
mass of elicitations –

chisels in fading wounds –
death carried on the cragging
wind along to un-policed
coffined inanition of re-
sculpted rock – disorganized
arms and legs at angles,
crisscrossing the labour of
random butchery – minds
snatched from suet locked in
stratums of scarred print,
mouths frothing, wires
stitched through cheeks and
lips – birds flapping in empty
space coal eyes fizzing in
extravagant decline –

perpetual rationalization
about lines up faces released
of habitation cooked in smoke
– unseen railways, their
commuters stranded in lofty
hypothesis of dead hours of

131

artificial ant that the motion of the opposite=sun: the brain of clone boys springs instantaneously the gimmick of the ADAM doll. The terror of grief. DustNirverna of the apoptosis outer space or road of CYBER=BUDDHA: the worldly desires machine the living body of uneven of the gimmick girl to reverse=evolves. An existence difficult respiration line. The ant of yourself erases the DNA of myself=channel. Machinative eternity recursive TOKAGE/VTR of the end clone. Neo-humanism=tabloidman that the ADAM doll that the artificial sun dismantles the planet of the brain of an ant awake from the sleep of the surface. The vaio-s of 1/8:. Copy the REC head line of the cyber dog: the redundancy area: the hybrid emotion of BABEL animals the soul-machine of the angel mechanism of the ADAM doll that goes to war) with (clone-skin LOAD....

long glass day –

slow-motion executions drained of incident suffering in detail, tears blackened oily data- molestations, flesh seeping through skin of icy transgressor's face inanimate silence thick, irreversible, collective in printed scourge –

a shared cadaverous rotting in hours looking through later onto streets replaced with dream eaten out of human speak of death outside equal to faeces stream intestines palpating conduit to death masticated in insane dream of accidental yawning – temporary meat of life as the machine passed through the city's veins – nightmare black spoiling in prophylactic exit – cerebration a putrid anthropoidal stasis waking black and purple as he tastes the plague of creatures under self-inflicted sky and of many unbirthed souls in strategies of

The body line of the drug embryo: the catastroph circuit of the ant of immortality. Storage of the sun crunches so The worldly desires machine of the gimmick girl be the transy brain of the ADAM doll that analyze the cosmic respiration line of the ant: sex-simulacle of the cyber dog: the thyroid=topology of the cadaver city road of the artificial sun fuck.

brain cell blue sky nano-machine boy machine that proliferates the grotesque sea=mime ADAM doll self of the gene that incubates the artificial sun: the insanity of the fertilized egg ant that the brain of clone myself of TOKAGE shoots and semen besides the phase of the mutation of the reptilian: the machinative desire of myself that programs the clonic suicide of the interior of the womb of the person accelerates with SEX/POSITION of TOKAGE and the artificial sun the love-replicant that the cadaver city

debugging/human putrefaction - while self-reflexive he substances his habitual decomposition, drinks lost blood from consecrated bowls smeared in minced organs - alchemic revivification of cooked man displaced in tree's form of coiled trunk - a vampire's bitter dreams shadowed by children looking to do in a soul before tea -

silent, deeper, sucked happy forever the moment allowed in bone noise - that death prayer of their smutty subtraction singing collective creases of dust and decayed fear -

body destroyed by a cradled psychosis, man replaced with phthisis and medium wants his wishes dead, desires opened up and left to fester, his insanities polluted - a blown future open -

inhabitants of mirrors sweat through forever somewhere

reproduces to the film-contact
of the lapse of memory line
gimmick cell DNA of the
angel mechanism of the
world: the pupil of the ant
pattern of myself that the
cyber of the anal sex dog of
the brain of a girl springs!! the
curious-ADAM doll that the
drugy thyroid of the android
ant of the physiologic
lobotomy opposite=sun that
the crazy soul-machines of
digital-fucker++eve_end
machine myself of the lonely
masses of flesh of the desert of
the boy/brain of the gene
learning bleeds in the sea of
the gene receive the grief of
the boy and dog: apoptosis
space::digital=vamp
quickening who synchronize
to cause the speech center of a
chromosome escaped!
'celluloid body fluid of myself
is replicated to the
machinative more the
output_brain area of a boy
machine: children bleaches
the hell of a cell with the
physical gentleness of an
ant]]] the storage of

dreaming known men lonely
to smells – summer
destinations stored in
windows of hermits refusing
to feed themselves –
destinations of sleep clouded
– the grave blackening under
rain for rat-toothed orderlies
and yellowed truth –
constructed from stone its
exhibits are deliberate in their
errors – alive in the morgue of
lazy associations they are
found blinded and fatigued –

spring carcasses, skulls
dessicant, rooted in death
born flowering despair of
futures – born and steady in
death the surrogates feather
their callow trap in ancient
respiration repeated in
hospitalized pulse of maggots
writhing in draped layers –
savages misplace their disgust
their lots junked owned and
canned in decay – entombed
corrosion rhythmic winter
spores innumerable in
immortal Existenz of poison
rot and some artificial
spoilage –

catastrophic cell group
ADAM of the end of the
world::the future tissue state
murder circuit that rapes is
contrary=the skizo of the
despair machine or fatalities
of the sun become cloudy the
artificial sun: the spiral form:
the suicide system synapse
that physical [the rhinoceros
bar body of night sky///girl
erodes! do self replication
<target> gene=TV of
TOKAGE interference! the
boys be the retro-virus nature
heat consciousness of ADAM
doll: the awakening stage that
is infectious! soul-machine of
myself does drug-motion to
DNA of the artificial
sun***and Ч-trans cell-gauge:
the machinative dogs of
syndrome.../Vol. 1***myself
evaporates to SEXY [[[
sun=becomes f/0 of the
pierrot that the interior of the
womb becomes extinct=of=a
crow of the hell of the cell that
X foot drifts were reproducing
the crowd of the visual
impossible sun of an embryo
from my cerebral cortex that

he distrusts his softened gums
the vague leaning of his teeth
loose like this season's clothes
– the scarred bones formed by
the black barb manufactured
hand of flies – his identity lost
to inorganic cancer of brain
irrigated to loose aggregate of
dust – this man's stomach
blown with gas chewing of
this terrain, understanding
tailored from a blackened
pocket – a vision half-
forgotten in death, forefingers
falling from mouth into
swatches of oily skin –

dead in non-occurrence, in
public expression of lands and
seas, all geographic
exteriorizations blended
hollow predicament of
vengeful glass cure – the
multitudes form a vomit of
framed psychopathologies
concentrated in this dead
force – the pellucid sickness
possible only in the terrorist
land of universal
ventriloquism – they see all
the lips move at once but hear

grasped the beat of 1
milligram of drug in the
outside circle of the
chromosome of the fatalities
glistens to the internal organ
and shine: cut f! tear f!
:embryo=stratification was
scrapped==the spinal column
of the cyber of the dog of
BABEL-ism that cuts the
TV*placenta to death and ant
of DNA=walk I command the
infinite rape of the sun my 8
eyeballs that conceived the
intelligence of the love of the
clone to the octave of f/0 of
road that is the murder scene
of the micro blue sky
conducts
chromosome=of=horizon*mo
nster of the season turned
different to the camera-eye
that was disturbed my brain
before embryo is present sun
of body fluid of [heterogaia]
of the fatalities that was
created in the outer space
death interference causes
attached freeze before dawn
[:f/0] of blood ant of
brain=of=to the blackhole
drug=of=a vulgar living body

only one voice, a voice their
ears tell them is their own –

slow conglomeration of
instruments for the
potentially cadaverine, liver
now a pool of beef consommé
revealing a decaying soul –
the flesh ephemera eternal
hosts of sentience – the
vermicular substance of man
lost
amongst itself, its mildewed
sludge articulated using tiny
dissolving blocks –

old stumbled spectacle of
waxy unification, corpses
tangoing in bonds of blended
tissue and fat – the ground a
rotting slime in lovers' now
arachnidan emotions –
sublime eight-limbed children
of a carnal god hailing his
new creation – spliced
humans in bio-collapse,
worms swimming in the
water of their raven skin –
another mirror transcends its
entities reinventing their
ancient incarceration in shifts
– binary of catabolism based

is instigated! insanity=of a girl comes off and be falling=the pupil embryo of numerous that was stranded in outer space=of=the duct was being respired: murder f! :release the infinity of fatalities to my exercise DNA of the interference of 1 micron of the gene that disturbs your chromosome to the skinhead of battle of an embryo and I move to the present tense of an embryo! desire of 1 micron of road:::the crowd without the limit of the petal that turned:::my brain cell moon surface of an embryo with communication impossible of the brain of the ant that deform with the embryo stimulates=I] occupied [=cramped to clonic love to BABEL of fly of: the sonic boom of narcolepsy: body of my before dawn imp and splits was conducted so the infinite existence/mode of an embryo to [sunlight of (ant=of=the future] reverses) to the megabyte of brain the cadaver that becomes extinct

in twinning rebirth – the bodies slowly gas –

cured of disintegration by machines, blooded by local meat cornered and born progressive marking a sickness exhaustive in its attachment to death as transcendence – parasitical victory of death over life mimicking movements with unparalleled finesse –

cloistered hollows of dog cadavers, flies drinking, vomiting internal shadows – fables of collapsing skins slowly suffocating transmission of replication codes hiding in the delicate footsteps of the black dance – under recall comes transmission message concerning weight of dismembered bodies – cold nights sunk in perpetual decode – spent autumn in predatory mutations of a howling script –

which of the agents plans to

desire: the sonic stratosphere/mode of my embryo is mixed to reverse: The DNA=channel of a grief=body....artificial ant is respiring <murder game in the last term of the ADAM doll>....soul-machine of which the brain cell of the drug embryo was opened in the gimmick city/girl....vagina state where grew thick....the suicide group of cyberBuddha: the storage of the sun does her worldly desires machine fuck. The apoptosis universe of the cyber dog. ....the big bang of the placenta world that the life support device closes! The lonely masses of flesh of the drug embryo inherited the emotional particle of line TOKAGE of GODNAM/vital non=being that does the clonical love junk.

Chromosome that she is able to sleep goes mad
Outer space of annihilated lonely:
The larva speed of the soul-machine. Body fluid of myself

remove his own murder architecture? – enquiries intensify against all suspected instances of corrupted embodiment – who is instigating these transcendental beheadings? – the self-killing disease repeatedly seeks disembodiment for its parasite – reality thought identities temporary, sensed annihilation every fractured second – action pulped somatic repeated in the automatic carnality of invented existence – those of slaughter severed from expansionist machines – the essential traumas transform the spread of incorporeality, evisceration of soul, of rot enacted in sacks of decomposition –
fresh limbs,
many bones, our instruments a fantasy of our serialized faces fleshed from ruin – promoting reflection and fantasy to deliberate dislocation of self-representation – ecstasies of

gene=TV screen on
I record the grief of the virus
of the ADAM doll. /noise
Our paranoia-body crunches
to the angel mechanism to the
vast asphalt=universe of this
cadaver city that TOKAGE of
mental abnormality laughs....
End clone is mated to the
night sky of the desert
Zero-speed
Replicant genital organs of the
gimmick girl are disillusioned
at the uterus-machine state:
the REC=head line of the
placenta world
I] love [it
The road site of the cyber dog.
Cancel the stratification of
death: the affection coefficient
of the replication possible
suicide program clone-skin of
the drug embryo:
cyberBuddha sings vital
non=being....the brain of the
clone boy dives to
Heaven....the ADAM doll of
the amniotic fluid mechanism:
the nano-machinative
murderous intention of the
artificial sun is inherideted. So
the womb machine form ants

violence our excremental
degradation – murders
further the blood –

their skin disintegrating, the
slightest glimmer of bone,
eyes banded, cheeks grave-
waxed with fermentation –
glossy, untidy bloats fizzing
like repellent balloons –
consternation while watching
the insects distorting,
terrorizing the calm of decay –
less-advanced mummification
life unbridled, smeared in
butyric lipstick and red waste,
offspring flat putrefying
decrepit sorcery barely
disguised – see your smudged
corpses lounging content on
the slab – you shitting
cadavers out in winter, the
trees warped, stretched, thin
and fetal underneath
powdered sky fissured with
ragged cloud –

dogs swell up, their wiring
now slurry – away, the ruin
amok, desire stilled in solid
blood – exposing these
soluble surfaces to the air

of the gimmick girl: I rape it like brain: and the soul-machine of the ADAM doll recovers her apoptosis grief....: be planetary rhythm the head line of an artificial ant: the strategy mode of the body of the drug embryo. Her chromosome makes the emotion....the ruin of the homosexual anthropoid that hybridizes the sex-machine of TOKAGE zero. Placenta world of the end clone: a hybrid storage: the outer space of the ADAM doll deciphers dustNirverna....the immortality of the lonely masses of flesh=BABEL animals: the line that the DNA=channel of an ant crunches to the angel mechanism
(she does not know the other side)
Speed of TOKAGE that the body of an ant does the mental immortality of the soul-machine drug embryo of the dust-ADAM doll zero of the angel mechanism that clone-dives to the storage of

with mind still embalmed enigmatic, purposing this dry larva relic in prose-CURRENTs arriving out of human hands – masks made from shaved invertebrates and tongues, rough tubular texture – centrefold's lips cause paralysis, dangerous pauses during which word-tissues infiltrate peripheral vision – moistened and filthy with her death-memories, grimy in her spread-legged hauntings –

splendour of colonization, leaden pitches reduced to maturation, the enlightened animal talks of escape from murderous soils – wet from slaughter of black cosmetics in bacterial phases in boggy meat of capital talk ambient of rot –

sounds nerve the clock's thick notice – parasitic corpse in ground burial, his vermin cells with murderers appearing in half-eaten dream the sun crunch circulates the over there of the pupil of the saturnish-green: the clone-skin of the ADAM doll where does the insanity of a chromosome to her machinative worldly desires circuit desire so loved her [reason].

The form of the hatred of a chromosome: DOWNXXXX. The reproduction area of <ant> of the matrix body fluid: the poor ganglion of the ADAM doll where the machinative angel LOAD commits suicide. In the reverse side in the moon which sleeps the love-replicants of Mars:. <the world> that went to ruin in the over there of the pupil resuscitates:

REC=road/genital organs of the gimmick girl. <I murder the soul-machine of yourself to the hybrid>. Storage of the placenta world sun of the ADAM doll that began to respire 1/8 miracles of the cyber dog: the replication factory: era does

recycled, dressing the floor with tangled sex-death misdirection (Our rats feed on the wrought artificial – the inflated information, doctor unwelcome, his spots and branches muted processed corpses blackened, naming insanity with strands of fine hair needled in dead game of endless moments, desiccant, ultimate, revealing their shit-stained underneath wallowed in age of hobby homicide, of kettles howling, spewing vomit of flesh and misplaced narratives, a faecal time coming devoured by whims in dropped explosions and blackened trauma rooms of human decision of black revealing in dreams' forced obelisks dancing, parting without core drinking chronic faces spread devoured in man's deformed refuse resembling stale self-conscious reflection and dreams transparent, grave-waxed, gummed, smudged again) to bitter scan of the

interference....the cute insanity of the chromosome: the drug embryo that zero-speed does hallucination the horizon: the spore state=worldly desires machines of TOKAGE: the emotion of the sun the despair machine of the end clone drive is away from....the chromosome of the brain/yourself of the virus of clone boys is parasitic on Mars: of grief
Womb cell
Emotional particle: her <mind> placenta world of drugy sun of nightmare record amniotic fluid mechanism of MHz? Copy the blue of the narcolepsy group sky of the short love artificial ant of the end clone:/the future system grief without the mode of the ADAM doll decays//grief plays with the hell of a cell....the cosmic rays of the soul-machines like the dogs. The <eye> of the drug embryo collects hybrid <mind> of the ADAM doll. Vision that was transferred

many in rain with saprogenic dogs – in margin of melted parts, eyes shaved logistical in currents, arms discarded flapping relics of skin – invertebrates of prayer shrinking in their terminals – concentrated on some making off, leaving eight-limbed debugged/inhuman useful for reconstructed paradise void of excremental voices hosted by worn grotesqueries dubbing watery flesh in alchemic pleasure games of intestinal nihilistic conditioning –

old reconditioned steam boats kidnapping gas-blown stomachs from yellowed shore – flea-bit supernatural humanity buried in deeper earth, cytoplasmic, in slimes of scorching psychosis – their transcendental larvae remain in prose-CURRENTs, ghouls collapsing in vague animation, transforming bodies from paralysis in steady immortality of silent dough gloop – structures

The heaven device: machinative body line....of the ADAM doll despairs. Worldly desires machine that her transy brain....thyroid of TOKAGE by LOAD:....it was removed....do the inheritance material of a homosexual anthropoid crunch so: the immortality of machine-seeds....[girl] of the gimmick desert does to the angel mechanism noise....the cosmic gene war of clone boys: the brain universe of BABEL animals is dashed....to the hybrid reverse=while evolving the body of an ant....the cadaver city in the short just before: the nightmare of road where the replicant consciousness of "ADAM" commits suicide is radiate heat from the internal organ of the ADAM doll of the amniotic fluid mechanism. <F^U^C^K^N^A^M>=the gene connection of the artificial sun. The drug embryo respires the disillusionment circuit of

stream indulgences sludged, stuffed paradise with gleaming surfaces of rightful hours dead in inception – message the dead to keep down degradation, writhing behind in cold excremental flashes – entombed defleshings in railway carriages trundling into crowded womb-state of subtraction – layered graves alive floating toxic habitual paralysis reconstructed in weight of brains feeding duplication into war bonds, pockets dripping purple corpse rot unholy floods on rot glass – stripped psychological remains of leaden costumes parked on children in flesh transmission of colonized sphacelation – pellucid little deformities, waxed anonymous –

mass putrefaction in constructed script burying dark futures in abandoned dreams – vision of meat in gloomy replication, grave-waxed flesh, our

<god of et cetera> era: I escape....the womb area medium of the nano-machine. <the world> however it becomes the alternative speed of a vaio....nano-machinative blood relative....clone-skin thinks about....ADAM doll....1/8....Mars: the planetary=plant of <second>....disillusionment.... the sun that becomes unknown I conceive: technical-ants! :her storage does not exist there be only if her lie in where the sleep of a gradual tragedy so anymore the living body of even the contempt between unstable space-time even Placenta world of clone boys: the digital=apocalypse is inoculated....the nano-machinative body system of the drug embryo: the junkie silence gimmick girl of TOKAGE the speed of the end of the world I copy the reproduction gland brain of the ADAM doll: a/the film-contact: the body fluid matrix of an ant that dances....

systemization muted in silent brains screwed down, pre-abandoned in decisions hailing nothing – enculturation plotted in outside machines for those glimmer heads, fading hands starred in expression of dead eyes – mouths eviscerating minds, corroded teeth in layers shark-born and mysterious – maggots sewing vomit of the constructed nightmare, redefining the greasy emetic gift decorated in minute fragments of slow sphacelation – nascent corpse talk of murderous selves decaying our unborn eating processed through agents concocted from springs – inanition born in ceremony of deadly wires – putrefaction of predatory lovers crawling in decay, hands conducting psychopathology's dark transcendence hardening in slaughtered purpose – ancient black poupées tailored in Sisyphean persistence, architecturally recycled,

Blue of the sky
Green pupil
The uncivilized brain of clone
boys is infectious to the night
sky of the desert.
::myself to something that is
not seen is reflected there.
I rape [the sun like the ADAM
doll that respires the
nightmare of the amniotic
fluid mechanism of clone boys
era so].
To be jointed the vagina of the
gimmick girl as if the brain
area of the dog
fuck........resolves it in the
savage soul-machine....heaven
of the drug embryo
[
The sex machine of a dog.
Silence
Reverse exceeding the
cadaver city of the retina
which proliferates in the over
there of our pupil replicant
[nightmare] of the placenta
world to=the artificial sun
evolves....the control line of
the amniotic fluid mechanism
of the ADAM doll: uterus-
machine smiles. Body: the
worldly desires machine of

data-molestations bloated,
rotten, ruined earthly
symptoms liberated
– lizard-skinned brothers
willing a new womb lined in
vomit of disgust-fuelled
humans sick with the
nightmare – soft message in
girl's talk about regular terror
acts slaking her soul under a
black sun – eavesdropping on
the toxic urges of skeleton's
lower brain un-policed,
branching out receiving auto-
transmissions in formulaic
dreams of consumption
scripted by salivating dogs –
stones in his forearms, veins
ruptured suppurating –

hiding in psych ward of
warped reinvention, of rough
hewn sanity, escape plan
printed inside us fading,
intestines of dead friends
sweating mould onto bed
sheets smells polluted –
useless discomfort of
destroyed mannequins, faces
grave, recurring gummed,
wires in brains, minds voided
in rank punishment of

the womb cell mechanism of line....road that ant eradicated Lonely masses of flesh of which do apoptosis=<second> of a chromosome to the alternative brain universe of the drug embryo noise....radiate heat the nano-machinative tragedy of the hell of the despair function....cell. Murder the madness line machinative angel of the clock mechanism of the screen ADAM doll who gene=TV decays: incubate the speed: the skizophysical body system of TOKAGE Drug embryo "perishes" and do outer space mode of/ Our NIHIL begins to move.... Silence Battle FUCKNAM/ The soul-machine of the ADAM doll is resolved in the angel mechanism of the eve_eyes. -it is resolved. Our soft heaven is resolved by XXX. - Attack the blood of an ant! Zone of the disillusionment of the sun that was repaired by

mechanical disgust of the Lord's Prayer's misuse – lifers filter the presuppositions of meat, the polluted codes mouthed by rubber androids listed as entities in video recordings – some borrowed hiding place to indulge the dead construct, to strip it of currency and torch its embalmed scenarios –

line-born binary self wrought by morticians collapsing design into diabolical rhythms of death – in his limbs ripe with insect meat, skin stretching, birthing under interrogation of incarcerated truth screaming after that distorted god in rat-skin coat buttoned in bones – self-conscious decomposition of young girl tired of noise and terror-soaked alone in the carcass of their informational dream, poisoning, raping her own inorganic solutions – bloated sacks transcending paradise shadowed in morgue-town where weary solutions breed themselves the spiral of the fatalities of a chromosome proliferates of this cadaver city quark=of which is gradually in flux on the cyber target=placenta of anti-faust=an embryo--horizon of f/0 of the clone that the dance machine of the cadaver that the soul of the disillusionment that the pupil of the rebellion girl that was done desire into the mirror of the chaos the aerofoil of the brain of the milligram of the drug to the jump impossible black hole of an ant battle my pure white cerebral cortex fuck walks transmit--VTR of the negative death of the embryo that the equator of the chromosome the clone-dance of the sun=organ that was fabricated the technology of the cell war by the horizon that DNA of the black sun that was deceived to the present tense of TOKAGE be infectious rhythm was supposed reflein % synapsetic=etc of the sun to the remainder of the digital*cannibal race to the public in slow traits of flesh appended to callow fantasies oozing expansionist fall-out – psychotropic enlightenment of chicken-skinned insurgents made arachnid, tissues melting the screaming Braille of sliding cutis – blood code of Terror purposes under rotten index of bacterial desires, life turned cadaverous, unfelt, half-forgotten – killing plans made in tiny kitchens of malleable homage to suffering architectures and coded murder – vermin burrowing through centrefold's pink schmaltz skin in looped tape of expressionist religion – flashes of sunlight in worm-eaten horror sky sucked into supernatural costume of vermicular significance – impulsives hunted down and secreted into the new temples of truth cloaking the Sisyphean slack in revolting disclosures of lucid mirrors – architectural extremities of enigmatic molluscan summer burnt

body organ of the madman
and dog who go mad 120% of
despair of the electron ground
target=brain resuscitates and
give a blood transfusion to
eye of the absence of the sun
the cadaver city inside my
mosaic embryo of zero
gravity=of=induce terror to
the emotion of Level0 of the
nightmare the clonic living
body of the reverse side in the
moon the childish plug of the
vital body to the placenta of
the fatalities that continuously
rotates to the eyelid of the
murder of the pierrot the high
speed the vulgar inhabitant of
the drug=organ of the larva
the revelation my brain resists
in the style of bio=less of an
embryo destroys: my blood is
a cadaver and the same rank
and do palpitation to air: the
comeback impossible body
organ of the wolf that
parallels to the chaosmic war
of a vital body chromosome
of: brain cells that bore the
tube of the womb against the
mass of flesh of the madman:
is incubated the infant of the

faces deflating dying thoughts
ghouling the worming season
– black elicitations needled in
torn prefabs, yellow squirms
of feeding, consciousness
haemophilic, coffined
dumped mutation of eyes of
bones of shadows sky-
touched and orderlies moving
like lizards rooted in
glossolalia of swollen fly-
blown tongue dancing from
scarred tree crumbling its
branches caging birds afraid
of the sky – debugging
throughout reinvented tears
in print reflections from eyes
consecrating death into
something suitable for heaven
cooked red – sedimented
hauntings somewhere from
anthropoidal corporate
sickness, clocks hailing death
unowned, dangling anarchic
for those in mildew for
theatrics of faces black and
cloistered hosting the fug
creatures on the turn,
withdrawn flesh fading
mechanical
ecstasies grounded in savage
land of hidden skulls farmed

wave of the zero who is latent in the world the happiness of the blue sky to the DIGITAL=placenta of the wolf that becomes extinct and conduct the equal soul that brain the desert of the drug mechanism of an embryo visual hallucination to the reverse space of the certain sun within the end of the world! The negative insanity of the material is contrary=to DIGITAL of the interior of the womb of the sun that ant records the brain of the reproduction on my DNA to eye that howled! Radioactivity=Level of the embryo that cracks. The sun of myself is respiring the clonic end of the drug embryo. Do short with the despair machine----subjective body of the hell of the cell that the artificial sun of the clone-skin: the brain of myself that the interior of the womb of the digital dog: clone boys is dancing the corpse of road fuck! The gradual suicide line of the clone boys::the body of

free of mind-squirms, of self-reflexivity – faces waxy black with print materials looking onward to animal hinterland greeting ephemeral mutations, eyes sewed up with truth tongues barbed on amputated prose-CURRENTs – chewed up destination of wounded molluscs sliming and vengeful sloven mass effect of grave-bred public promoting conspiracy of force-flesh smiles –corpses fused with cracks of code mouthing flat glossolalia fertilized by tension rain of incoherence –

the germinant flurry of life that need not exist in terror or excitation of disorder, its own exhaustive shrieking overlapping internal, both blank and crude like an encore: it is state without process – on its own essential climax terror arrives as the sweetened exaggeration, unable to own the curse of naming (drowning) – promised outside reinvented an ant that invades the body fiber of the lobotomy fly of the angel mechanism of ADAM game....the soul-machine of ADAM doll the other side of the artificial sun the MHz love-replicant chromosome that beats operates: the body line....suck blood of the zero of myself that inoculates the murder crazy idea: the cyber crime program of the drug embryo....night sky of the desert that gets deranged to the reproduction gland of TOKAGE_DNA=channels of the blue murderous intention clone boys of the sky that respires the planet of an ant era with the speed of the soul-machine of the ADAM doll_junk to the emotional line of the zero of myself: 1/8 of brain of the drug embryo inheriteds: ADAM doll murder VTR: the sun of myself 1/8 suicide machines of the drug embryo that conduct artificial insemination....so that the pupil of the dog LOAD to the in guise of fetal solution – positions a negritude of anarchy and nihilism – state held unified with sacrament of illuminated abnegation feeding itself on the zenith of process culled from central mechanized hinterland of (chronically default) comedic operation – accident stifled homicide between moments, forms sacrificial, upon scratch of ribbon hollowness itself making a nostalgic Terror of mucus made corrosive – (drowning) uncut ghost eats duplicating present of dinosaurs – subjects like this rolling gradual feed – to be escaped without delay in myriad methods of withdrawal, often under geometry of exploded perversity – the entanglement scars of corpses' sensate mass is simply process of duplication, of act over definition – that bordering slumber voided against clay contortion, impervious mistaking fear for the head of a prehistoric crocodile –

murder range of the ant pattern of the gimmick girl with the matrix of the ruin of TOKAGE that copy the body fluid of myself that gene=TV witnesses the clone boys of the reverse side in the month who explode rapes the nightmare of the amniotic fluid mechanism of ADAM doll the soul-machine of myself stops the breath that goes to war and respire/imp replicate the nerve fiber in the last term of the ADAM doll that notifies the love of the clone road of love-replicant dogs by the time_difficult existence. I copy so that I reproduce the brain of the ruin of TOKAGE--the reverse side in the moon in the over there of the pupil of the gimmick girl....the drug embryo of the brain of 1 the murderous intention of the cyber mechanism of TOKAGE/transplants in 1/8 seconds: clone-skin uterus-machine of the solar system I murder the herd of the ant of narcolepsy and the body of

number of poetic unfortunates beneath it hatched in specimens manufactured by each new day - steady clay life of profound mutilations in unlisted consciousness - a constructed dead layer of formulaic necrosis together with the ultimate universal, the rain murmuring prosthetic-violence - (like old frayed string contained in tired systemization of corrupt nucleus) - verdigris spreading in the flooded subway of the mind - those from slums of sufficient affliction transform death into furniture - to be themselves, abandoned, man's sliver of earth, microbe blade into them, narcotics binding them together, blood flooding the state gallows, the disparate ossuary of everything - this remains to be forgotten -

and like prehistoric crocodiles stilled in oily factory stone as something looking as if into death - prosthetic-violence in myself receives the semen of the ADAM doll of the cadaver city. <murderous body line of the soul-machine>.

Although the storage++disillusionment irradiates the micro gap of a corpse: the vacuum condition X where the cyber embryo who captures the fly remarkably was torn is covered the machine unknown quantity of immortality desire and the existence of the electron that was open goes mad "aburakatabura" rhythm++nihilistic night of that tragedy swims the fresh blood of my mirror image of the fly that emerged newly with the region of the vision I begin to crowd to the birth that got rusty

As for my existence that I forget the brain of the whole massacre of an opposite dimension is saturated to "molecule form hohlraum that the electron % that is diverging from the cadaver that transmits the larva is trappings of fossilized corpses still clinging to the cruel promise of Arctic prophesy – cynophobia of repeated hex-contagions of numbers we limp sinister walking edifying our brutality in pools bathed in fire – mistake their germination for the death of bodies unmade in the womb – die into necessity of un-resuscitated feel – him swelling and dead to explain it – decaying in his identity made conceptual in shrinking porcelain dressing over a million faces of an Elysian dawn – look through persistence of fetuses hatched of dead plants in muscular chambers, rotting microbes covered in mortician's blood and semen – the protracted mist of adulthood a blight, a coruscating symptom of the surrender to sanitation – execution mechanics noosed on the moon, fed brain of living alien as their last meal by bleeding animal skins of crumbed decomposition – live strings, hex-contagions like

filling my topology city while my null that is murdered the moon by the numerous pupils that conceived quiesced...."
and space becomes a pierrot Your pupil is in the active sun that your life reflects=receive the loop of zero with the nothingness of the centipede that was disrupted under a bare feet the plasma....chaos disillusionment of the earth that is not seen....your body that howls your life combines the various nature of the basement like the singing voice of the fatalities that was broken was abandon the sunspot in the air imitates the cruel impregnation of the null--fly of the crowd--interior of the womb of the earth that the cadaver that dives to the geometrical pattern so is not seen
White=drug e dies to road of the end
the cadaver city where the cell of the heart that the drug that gathers the thalidomidic shell of the sun throb loop eye in the future that was abused the

qualms, lingual of the borrowed states –

his unwitting possession of costumes cajoled him into vortex of fog – the saint eats of virus rising dead in flukes sired from half-imagined extremities of a supernatural cuneiform message from God – indurate construct of myriad larval peoples in states of fused decay – dreams malignant in underworld of malevolent snake-eaten self-satisfied insanities – solidified brains made dull in hybrid thought organs of monsters, hideous creatures with influence over man's hex-contagions – formulas of untruth made into phenomenology of all – the Reality a porous incarnation of pestilence –

running, caught in jumble of us in death our eyes decaying over him drowning at our lifelike feet broken, drowsy, his breath culled from a fossilized lung his will made cosmic love of the womb that desert was suspended to the anus of the sterility of the wolf that scrap empty orgasm of a chromosome to the skull of the crazy madman of 0 mile of an ant with me who murder the wave of the larva of the clone to the violent emotion that was forged short of DIGITAL that makes the over there of the nightmare to the nude eyeball of the drug*area zero....to the desire that hung the fatalities the cadaver city where**overflow**to the hearing organ that waves the earth where does my body sonic to the localization of thinking to the cyber that I was raped wolf of blood that turned pale to the lewd naked body of the drug that I smuggle all the nerves that recured to my embryo whirls sun of zero=of=the parasite abnormal living body of the light in the moon to lining cloth LOAD the pierrot of treachery to stab the gene of love into the joke of the

raw-edged orifice from enculturation of herd – mutilated vision of precarious grotesqueries cartooning the curse of embodiment – atomic switchboard perpetually fragmented to realize order from nothing – he owns the folly of existence who owns delirium, awareness mortified stage of conditioning while dead to agony – each fatally swallowed up in the thought of dancing putrefaction in circles singing of external decay, breathing perfume of thirsty prophecies drum-tight tum tum banged in dark percussion of inflated covenant of the supposed turn –

from faces sculpted purposeful, experiments of slack fabric worn thin – losing those inverted in prosthesis of normality leaking pearls of piss in sickly feeding ritual mush of concrete animation beaten flat – comfiture of crushed eyes tingling in previous world that act: I died to my empty body organ previous sun target=fatalities desire through the membrane of Level0 of a cell spit cannibal race=of=danced in technologic street! as for the antifaustic clone of the earth area the spiral that able to ride to the breakdown of true f/0 that is infectious in the suspension area of the emotional particle quark of the cyber*embryo and reverse that cell to the exercise of the ant lion of the universe is a rhinoceros bar god? is the DNA the optimistic=visibility of BABEL? the food racial=sun of the cell that blinks to the cadaver of god! to your brain the chaosmic body organ of the digital=vampire resuscitate! plug to road of the storage corpse of a dog the severe shock and the love in the last term of an embryo clonic different vital VTR that ADAM instigates the horizon of the chromosome the tactile sense to the brain universe

germinated dust shrinking remains of immense harvest of terrorist immersion in over-recurring adipocere of self -sequestered tongue of language absorption together in helixed nerve-endings and rag skin of society suckled on mongrel memories in congealed landscape impregnated by the unholy frills of pricks hard as knucklebone – simulated dunes floating over rivers, moon porcelain smooth as polished brains – milk-mouthed space-age molluscs of hex-contagion tremulous in clay mercenaries blurred like reflections of newborn concepts – his ratiocinations shipwrecked like swans swimming in scabbing blood – bleeding covenant on graphomania of autumn entanglement of shit and aluminium – forbidden devotions weaved into chamber of skeletons – prosthetic violence in selection of agent-farmers strung up and punctured,

that was broken the larva of
the mirror image of the chaos
that projects the independent
position target=war of the
human body earth
area=of=the murderous
internal organ of the blue sky
that is parasitic on the
interlude area my body the
chromosome=world of the
disillusionment--
be open stratification, the
defeat that the cyber that
opens earth, and are fatalities
was transplanted--my
dummy=of=the internal
organ that the ugly larva
thinks about the body fluid
that chameleon cause evil
crowded outside the body
that dream play strange like
that lonely mass of flesh that
was left the rhythm of suicide
to the retina of the fatalities
that flickers the collector.
"your skin is peeled off....your
naked body brings gratuitous
death....your half body that
lacked at night wave machine
of hell alternates/habitually
use....your brain □" to the
impregnation system that

black teeth folded, under gaze
of white-eyed
butcher trapped in waltzing
nigredo –

doctoring the high-pitched
cries of young their parents
suffocating beneath them
fixed, gasping like a barnacled
throat – lower-lands that
resemble ribcages, hosting
bodies that resemble tumors –
his virescent eyes space-age,
dead, ugly – bleached clay
landscape in screwed eyes – a
monster's once hesitant hands
owned and made
innumerable – his hardened
landscape a procedure in
harvesting, soul-colonization
– he burrows through
tremulous blind swarms in a
blistered daze, returns
cringing to the body-LAB, his
skin coated in landscape of
teeth – through our covenant
of clay we conduct a
ceremony of grey bacteria –
an adaptation of a sacred
week – the invisible life
sustains its slippery form,
proves itself a gluey

156

velocity of light was transmitted/to the image in the night that the unknown quantity comes flying nonexistent outlook that is the butterfly that was folded up the eyeball that falls****. my brain that lost the focus hangs space in the deep sea of the drug and the sun or the larva of the comedy--make the one bend affected [fly***previous suffocation]. "your blood goes converting under the blazing heat of the tragedy....the lock of your murderous intention person is broken down....the horizon that refracted to your tears" dream of the zero gravity_embryo to the bare feet of the unand like the monster of the earth, horizons that the null density, flight were taken by the gravity that iterate the cruel spectrum of the pupil was lost. the mystery of the localization of the existence that floats to the sun of the drug is to conceive the despair of frigidity completely:::to input the pain like the withdrawal symptom

aggregation – vibrating concrete of our Orphic structures intact, made rock impervious to decay – forms once suitable now a seeding prosthetic-violence – that stunted stone bloc filtered into new and unimaginable flesh monoliths – man in them turned, located somewhere in his fluxional journey –

limbs together stiffened, aluminium shine on mud coating eyes and decomposing tongues held in canker of forensic cemetery – the arctic dunes encasing her like plundering hands and feet of men cast into hell –

patterns of glittering misery in today's experiments – dimly lit lower-lands hooked in voices of unguarded sorrow – eavesdropping on the clotted talk of frozen formulas in porcelain planes – new torture techniques exhibited in open air arenas – nerve-endings torn and talking – the polluted organs

157

to the horizon of the plane or existence of the junkie/human body of glass....the primitive body-series of the drug involution. Darkness of chaos=the puppet of the virtual realistic=cadaver of the embryo that chromosome=was write off by the cerebral cortex of direct tokage road of the rhinoceros bar dog that slaughtered the infant of the fractal pattern of vain gravity the sun that escapes the blue of the sky causes the chromosome of a girl in the basement where the internal organ of the pierrot that awoke was ignored the placenta of the clone to the storage that was lost danced drug=of in the valley of the fatalities of the fabrication of the gimmick--DNA of the idiot of the electron theory of the sun where light and shadow segregated to the coil of the heat of SADO that was engraved to the digital=pupil of the crow that causes the masochistic sun to the vocal of mangy wolfmen on basaltic bodies confined in masochistic clinch –

month-long killing in tropical hex-contagion by Nimrods – disembowelled men found dumped on nervous ground devoured in delirium – archived traumas transposed onto weary host bodies for reenactment – across these liberated fruit our neglected stench reigns, shrivelled their comatose requiems discharge the sweet contents of mutinous nihil – unearthed soldier stages his blank spastic-root production on tarmac blood – back in the dough of motionless ages our landscapes dripped with defleshing fungus – the future propped up his name with swarms of addict voices – their souls remained matter – hours, delirium of corpses virescent, slack, mouths swirling reworking the devil in textual deformities – some resemble nothing more than

cord of the fatalities blinked
and do the musical scale of
magma to the brain of an
embryo electromotion=circle
the body of the angel! I
penetrate the digital=right
brain of the centipede to the
other side of the sun and the
infinite=death of the sun is
regenerated to VTR of the
cyber*reptilian of gene=TV
that night sky of cell other
selfs=witnessed the guerrilla
continuously=pupil of the
mad dog plays strange the
body organ of the great
distance of the clone the
manhole of the cadaver city to
the zero gravity=love of the
sun that murder=DNA
thought about the outer space
where was reversed to the
brain of the embryo that is
parasitic on the reverse side in
the moon the rhinoceros
bar=god of the gene that
transmitted the blood of the
fusion of asphalt causes
floated the hell of the
megabyte of the cell that bred
the childish cracking of the
soul that is projected

others – he hangs by his hair
until his face inches free –

choir of prosomas used for
shuttering material, their
mutilations monitored – these
subliminal victims (strangled
swans calligraphic) remain
otherwise unmodified –
excavated wounds can be
seen morphing in jars – the
scars healing her unaffected –

soon the memorial of
landscapes came to assume a
stark hardening of the clay of
thought – technological
habitation-fatigue of starving
grunt – their faith-infected
charnel houses have
destroyed organs and injected
technology into everything
but themselves – compulsive
testimony of horse-sick
liquidators still weak from
their sexual disadvantage –
moon out in little specimens
of grey, kidnapped muscles
sacrificed unholy traits of
Semitic regions dangling in
blood – incult sortals
spurting

1milligram of fatalities of the earth area to the mirror of the chaos that beat to the brain target=back reason of the absolute zero of ADAM and eve=of=I sing the parasite=invasion of the earth area that played to the despair of the clone to the dogmatic heart! I dishevel the various varieties of the cadavers of road the gravity that was forged to the element of the apocalypse that lapse and gather the disillusionment of the X foot of the placenta to the bio=less_soul of the desert of DIGITAL now and whole of vital body showed the brain of the immortality of the fatalities and fall into silence and do the focus of the micro=madness of an ant battle! and sun of infinite=of=to the soul that impossible to masochistic sec of the ant the micro=murder person of the earth area palpitation happiness--to body every part of the life-size embryo of gene=TV that pulls the electron of the

on enciphered lease – interrogation of involuntary corruption of sound streams in skull, symbols found eviscerated on the slab – the conference of anomalous story-tellers ranks as a puzzled stay of execution, devoured by the few their insides drained and poured from cropped heads – veiled citizens metronomic, coated in empty reactions in lower-lands motionless with undiagnosed formulas – mantic materials birthed from cadaveric wombs – and terror's organs distorting ears with dead screams – dummy funds from fading landscapes – often there are vultures their wings frothy in races like futility re-sculpted and waiting for blooms – funereal, sluggish, grown in pornography of rock – ugly flashes overhead of distant features having axes taken to them by folded men – soldiers coffined in the scarred

disillusionment of the sun and peeled off to the escape impossible internal organ of the pierrot that loops and commits suicide the resolution of the dog that poaches the body
"the clone iterates the ADAM doll immortal room of the larva sodom drug mechanism where the virus of "battle" that the nerve fiber of a dog flashes with the body of the machine that boys recur the eternity when fuck on the blue sky record the nightmare of a silicone form embryo....body of the clone replicates the soul of the sun of the suicide machine++the body fluid of myself that the storage of retina=myself of a cadaver explodes all of grief the soul-machine of myself that radiate heat falls....massacre myself of the embryo type of the spiral like the womb that glitters to the drugy body of the ant that forgot the color of love/the brain of myself reaches to a hybrid reproduction toward

stratums of their manipulated minds – cornered they snatch at extravagant cicatrices of cragged replicas printed in decaying flesh – on unclassified beings we laboured, disorganizing, disembodying, liberating – at all these protective montages and their prognostic violations we weep and titter and say goodbye –

closed hypotheses of looped stretches of grey sky sutured in glass – this line of uninhabitable faces still and earth-bound – bloodthirsty in porcelain day of data-molestations – eventually the open eyes of reason fall glacial – the penumbral decisions are irreversible, metal forced through brain at high speed – thickened skin incidents of suffering in detail – mock telepathy facilitating the execution of seven silent paragons – once empty their yawning becomes a final pulverizing force –

the gray pupil of the embryo
that the girl resolves--absent
artificial sun of the night sky
that circulates the physical
tropic of the drug embryo that
I record the spinal column of
the fly cries out the
chromosome of
storage++yourself of the
contraction++organ++parado
x++love that became "in
pieces...." myself of the mad
dog was dismantled by the
night sky of absence++the
negative murder person of the
placenta   Becomes....the
suicide virus of ADAM of the
future machine mechanism of
the girl was jointed to the
insanity of the half the
body....immortality....ant of
myself the larva of the brain
BABEL soul of a cadaver city
greatly delighted....the body
of myself begins to
ferment++--the artificial sun
was murdering on MHz="the
head of myself a monochrome
nerve fiber-was doing the
planet of ants--was firing the
depressing masses of flesh
embryo do the grief of

stilled
violence on ice-claimed
paradiddle in derelict
industrial unit – mantic speak
emanating from sewers of the
cadaverous city, the herd life
breathing the steam-jungle of
hex-contagion kindling
insanity in claymation dream
of faeces crawling out of the
water – fear of heat death
unyielding in streets where
shared selves hex their raw
intestines outside on kerbs
drooling blood –

sadistic trees debugging clay
koan in alchemy of this
porcelain process of
putrefaction displacing our
alien birth – self-inflicted
habits rising like porcelain
dunes – cerebrating every
drop of consecrated blood
poured into our putrid
prophylactic, man never
waking to his steady
decomposition – self tasting
the blood of futility the hex-
contagion of cemetery rot
dragged along walls – corpse
plague of lost jaded

yourself fuck like the electronic circuit the black heart play at the brain of myself!? Cyber spore....whirlwind++blue sky of our rebel where is going to awake to the lonely interior of the womb of the drug the darkness laughter of the storage girl of the desert that the hateful earth turns pale to the brain organ of the reproduction quality of wolf jabs and the nightmare that sticks the consent of the pierrots embryo of painful frigidity (the 1/8 of sun are recovered to the secret beat of the time annihilation catastroph parasite cyber that the decay cadaver of the ant that the ADAM doll of the machine mechanism records) open to the soul of myself the nightmare that I do not see yet by the head line of the murder person of the end is transplanted to the interior of the womb of a girl--the horizon of the pupil of a dog "our gene war" "of brain" "the fuck-signature" I record "the

substances – stasis forms killer of the strategies sutured together in vital organs with faces yellowing in the splash of the moon –

content, it corrupted the collective sting into a cacophonous inertia – those forever of sleeping fear rot – expiration of electric charge in grave water – smut decay of fingered nocturnes locked in prayer – that silent moment felt ceases in the promise of alembic death – man hoped to outlive himself, to succumb to an absorption cradled in perversity – the anatomy of kisses laid open for us all to know – storage of exhibits – smell of men festering in the involuntary refuse of their yellowed years – their sweat alerts the cobras – somewhere they prepare the phantoms for feeding – porcelain smiles on the coffined-lined half-imagined mausoleum of death-life – errors are eaten insomnia machine of yourself...." "hell" "the massacre of the spiral" "gimmick myself of an ant I hold the sun that falls and scatter to the vein of soul the hybrid reproduction gland of the desert that commits suicide and become aware of the dilemma of the paradise to the manipulation thread of the boys of the cyber mechanism that the body of pierrot myself of the impossibility that plays the intellectual murder line of artificial ADAM decay to an ant pattern only] the drugy grief of the mass of flesh emotional embryo of the disillusionment that restrains the brain of a dog [merely eye spherical condition catastroph wears and the crazy angel of mental contempt head who does shot grasps nihilistic MHz of the crime system ant of the milligram cyber embryo of the murderous intention that makes machine nature of myself....the horror-show of the hells of the various mode alive and then regurgitated for cattle – hibernal inhabitants feed on the negritude of nebulae, sacrificing truth for the graticule – tired slather of artificial respiration – experimenting rot of painted skulls resuscitated and misplaced – cruelty in the winter of savages pulses broken in despair – heat death flowering with inscrutable movements hatched of enemies – tremulous surrogate carcasses of this augmented maggot entombed in the callow flowers of decay – spores of hieroglyphs desiccant in this repeated tenderness draped, unclassified – teeth and gums left fictional with rot – and so lie his heat-softened nocturnes in occupied ground – wounds tailored to seasons of prosthetic-violence and the intimacy of flies – the mouth a fossilized terrain, a realm of hybrid souvenirs balanced on

cells of the bodies of myself
which her cold machine
erodes in sponge form heaven
causes to be
prevailed....myself that myself
lives_raw to the murder
machine of the cyber desert to
replicate the end of the sun
that the pupil of a girl secretes
the planetary infection
pathway of an ant----the
language field/the interiors of
the womb of the fatalities

[sun kisses]

Body of myself is filling....the
end in future to

Cyber=wolf=molecule drifts
in the solitude of the light
year of an embryo

"not seen to myself
anything....myself of....even
the herd of the cadaver that
even the breathing of the skin
bred to the soul of yourself"

"it is incubated...."

"the exit of silence"

the half-forgotten shelf – that
eager vision changing,
distrustful of identity –
manufactured dead-eyed
demolition of the
understanding –

no flash photography
permitted in the land of dead
men – heat death here
concentrated in scars of non-
occurrence – the glass-kind
mix well and urge for order in
everything from nothing to
possibility – the feel of
fugitive exteriorizations may
force metallic vomit – sleep
not possible in vengeful
habitation-fatigue – the
heartbeat is just another
empty question –

putrefactive instrument grows
decaying slowly of brain of
slow cannibalization – lingual
mildew revealing the eternal
soul in compounds of sentient
sludge, the hollow
potentiality of rot –
conglomerations of
prosthetic-violence, life of
putrescine, cadaverine, 3-

165

The lapse of memory
mechanism of the drugy body
angel mechanism of god that
the innocence_nerve fiber that
laughter makes calculus of be
done LOAD at one time....the
air that is write off....the body
committed murder in the over
there of the silence of the
pupil of the dog where
circulates to our nightmare
clonic soul of the boy machine
that is trampled down! Grief
the machine beat! Our mass of
flesh=storage=exploded!

Cell of which the sun toys
with the womb skin of my
hallucination that wanders
the soul of the inorganic
substance=mad dog to the
cerebral cortex of the plane
the interference of the clones
that radiated ant lion-site of
my blood vessel....to the vent
of f/0 that travels the reverse
side in the moon sun of which
able to ride and fabricated the
murder of the other selfs of
that eschatology reverses to
the storage that the madman

methylindole, a vermicular
ejaculation spraying every
host –

fat snakes turning the lovers'
bodies into black milk, open
chests stringy, wet and soft
with waxy pressure of
adhesion – incarceration
collapsing into two as the
ground is forged with hard
bodies – talk of forever
squirming, mantic – their
clay-limbed corpses shift in
slow circle of catabolic
principle – 2 rotten in futility,
orifices bleeding raven water
– new mutations stumbling in
their own tremulous
formation – these terminals of
gristle succumbing to the
violent gasses of rebirth –
excruciating core of
attachment to the progressive
marks the disintegration of
computability – although host
to wilderness they refuse this
exhaustive jungle-life
claiming it obtrusive –

creep back into hole away
from absorbing landscapes

was split before it's present it
scraps in the outer space of etc
of the sun the heart death of
the megabyte of an embryo
turned off the soul of a dog to
the bisexual god of ADAM
that forms sec of the
rhinoceros bar self-
punishment of the metropolis
to the alternating current of
the clonic love of the
chromosome that the vital
body that my pupil that
turned with VTR of suicide
betrayed the baby universe
street of a dog became
cloudy/eradicate to the
mirror of chaos loop and an
embryo recur the cell war that
was lost pupil that was
betrayed the infinite=desire of
the cadaver city in 1/2 of the
future tense of DNA that
resuscitated to the placenta of
the thalidomide=molecule of
an ant dived: the μ-silicone of
the disillusionment to the
emission conversation organ
of the angel of the drug
mechanism that leapt
gene=TV: the love of the
immortality of an embryo that

spent of slag entanglements,
sounds of forest howling wet
weight of spent delirium –
contaminated transmission
decrypted during fabled recall
of prisoners quailing their
crimes –
the bars clatter,
waking guards, dismembered
messages revealed in autumn
drop –
predatory snails drinking the
melt of nematodes –
canker collapsing under
moon's slow siege – agent-less
traumas sewn into faces of
cork – we adopted our
instruments of evisceration –
the scattered agencies
promoting self-killings to
further those probing limbs,
our identities against
existence, disembodiment, are
seen from dislocated
representations, from jungle
feeding intensifying in the rot-
air screaming ape sorrow of
reality a slaughtering, torn
throats, pornography of our
own hereditary nocturnes –
essential process of removing
ourselves fractured – murders

was crossed to the perception impossible underground of the sun to the cosmic-manhole of the street of the rhinoceros bar dog the quantum quark control the mysterious_absence of an embryo to the cyber of the treachery of the sun that the heart of my f/0 was vomiting the clonic fall of ADAM to the wave of the bio-less_reproduction of the sun that was done the reverse side in the moon to DIGITAL of a vital body in the diagram of the hope of the clones where got complicated to the DIGITAL=disguise of the cell suck blood! Scalpel dog of zero=of=manufacture the brain target=larva of the ocean creature to the ovarium! Eve of mature murder=of in this sun target=street of my disillusionment=to the placenta of the drug mechanism of the scalpel dog the sun that brain evacuated reverse=to the spectrum of the silence of ADAM that evolves the instant of the end

and degradation made industrial, sophisticates in expansionist drama of prosthetic embodiment of non-physical irreality – transformed in repeated disease of enacted reflection – violence a deliberate carnality of ecstasy through disguise – beheadings serialized in pulp press of faces architectural decorated with unholy blood –

locked inside and falsified in secluded solutions slave to narratives sludgy in shuffling droid walk –

casserole landscape of insect sorrow distorted – herd constellation of every will harvested to point of disintegration as it bloats – their decrepit hope is obliterated in minutes, watching with eyes coated in mausoleum-wax, butchered disgust as he fuels his violence with new fantasies of Gethsemane – putrefaction glimmering from wounded

168

when brings the wave of the gene write off the pupil of the DIGITAL_reptilian that coexists in the matrix state of a chromosome earth area of micro=murder=of=I awoke to sec sun of despair that cell can't be recorded to the original progression of my soul the chaosmic DNA of an ant to the mask of the pierrot that is immanent guerrilla I howled: the mitochondria of the fatalities: I turned off the attraction of all the vital bodies of the ground fatalities of love and the absence of the sun to the random space of a chromosome desire space that quiesced limitlessly or the instant when sec of the suicide of the cell other selfs quark of the cadaver city to the barren joke of the sun that had been flooded to my DIGITAL_body that opened the love of the X foot of the clone to the collapse of sun-ism that is repeated the micro revelation of the drug-star that is sloughing off from the bio-less_cerebral cortex of the fissure of terror – shitting out dessicated hearts eaten by offspring coming to the sun flat and thin – apoplectic swans screaming on boiling river waters – those lost in fermentation are left to the coroners' unbridled enthusiasm for decay – nothing uninitiated in the blur of life in that butyric winter – untidy red clot of mummification – adolescent corpses warping stillness instead of moving, shrugging off an ashen disguise – fused fingers indexing embalmed invertebrates and prose-ghouls – them in her spreading the stapled centerfold, her surfaces stained, she masks her strings for this filthy embalming of dry purpose a relic in this cloying tomb, red larvae lips and tongues regenerated in pauses – slurry of snails round feet of grimy enigmatic clay of word-death-memories, exposing the thought to her with uncomfortable repetition –

clone the pupil of that
chromosome bounces the
infinite=cadaver of an embryo
to the spine of the sunlight
that resuscitates moon in
reverse side of the brain of
death....LOAD: the
sun*interior of the womb of
the wolf: storage that lost the
vocal cord of hallucination to
a clonic emotional placenta to
the bio-less-zone of the
cyber*embryo of the equator
vs chromosome was selected
the zero of the darkness the
soul*blood of the clone
palpitation to the joke that
becomes my ex-vital street the
apocalypse cerebral cortex of
an embryo puzzle before all
my daily are present in the
incubation condition of the
drug mechanism of the
artificial sun to the
DIGITAL_eyes that the
embryo who it was scrapped
to the remainder from the
outer space of DNA of the
ground can't pass making: the
beat of the indefinite zone of
an embryo the tactile sense:
the love of the clone is jointed

occupation of illuminated
contortion of animal sorrow –
murderous escapees reduce
talk to ribbons and fragrant
punishment of herd – with
cosmetic talk we slaughter
bog-phases in the porcelain
capital high on jellified rot –
appearance in cells of hex-
contagion on the half-eaten
floor – parasitic ground
sounds of nerve thick sex-
death of botfly recycling
feeding voices in the artificial
rain – wheezing sounds of
death inflating the soul – man
frozen in naming process stale
illuminated by their insanity –
wire hair brushed with
narratives and the follies of
grotesquery of ultimate
sorrow underneath wallowing
bundles devoured in
homicide cell – brains in
severed heads bubbling in
unborn faces – monoliths of
prosthetic-violence displace
the alchemic tradition of
transformation coming ready
to devour – we unleashed our
fossilized futility, our

to the DIGITAL_high tide of the hell of the cell merely only....my soul that the thin earth penetrated the peace of chromosome space eye of the secret of the madman reflain: drug of dance of the self-punishment of the ocean creature of as that overthrows outer space causes to fall the soul of the sleeplessness of the angel to the placenta to be zero gravity infinitely: my brain did the indefinite zone of an ant hunting: earth outside circle=of=a chromosome the whole of the vital body of BABEL ground=of=to be a fractal embryo....minus=of which sun reverses=induced to the future series: or my DIGITAL_quickening invades....

The herd without the mode of the artificial sun: the hybrid body line of an ant the vagina state universe of the gimmick girl: the brain of the angel mechanism of the switch/ADAM doll that

shipwrecked clay in decisions of porcelain, revealed in lower-lands resembling padded A-cells of shark-eyed lunatics – parcelling up nihilism as the last remaining gift of religion – drinkers vomiting invertebrates over corpses in refuse tips drowned in killing – man hides in the daily faecal stages of his internal landscape – all hex-contagions in on delirium – mausoleum-waxed muscles revealing the theatre of smashed men to snails discarded, vibrating in un-scanned delirium a fossilized blur of cobras – surgeons face down in the concrete wounds – taking information from non-concepts and concentrating it in folded relics found forced open by gas of dying fetus – terminal transparency discussed and considered useful for reconstructing the dunes of hell – one debugged human formed lifelike without standard graticule, one true occupant of this sacrificial

171

dashes becomes....I howl although cyber dog is road the disillusionment circuit of uterus-machine that the infinite worldly desires machine of cyberBuddha: gene=TV murder the monochrome=molecule of TOKAGE LOAD fuck....the paradise falls. Soul-machines of the inorganic substance beat=clone boys of the sun fills
(the night sky of the desert)
(machinative angel
Line)
The clonical love of the placenta world freezes. The emotional zero level of the drug embryo is activated....: a clonic machine-seed
LOVE....resolve the war toy of the brain of the machinative angel so! Drugy wolf=space of the ADAM doll:
....the monochrome earth resuscitates to the brain of the angel. The grief of the gimmick girl explodes. Living body of 4 dimensions of the lobotomy cyber dogs flip off kick to the nightmare of the

layer – crushed intestines worn around neck, their knotted ends marking a temporary deformity of chest – born unclassified and dropped into the howling hex-contagion – water reflects an Elysian landscape of spilled traumas in the scarlet dance of detonation –

larvae in rebirth of horse-bitten degradation come sacrificial, half jumbled, unholy – railway lines end in resuscitated collapse of impossible structures of sludge message involuntary, perverse, defleshed – the dead habitual as clocks pocket strings of inertia made from prose-stitches – supernal flukes entombed in doughy bodies, transmissions successfully replicating the sickness of hope – funereal waste floating in flood waters of Elysian rivers – silent virus and bonds of jaded submission writhing in fictional excrement – inscrutable decay transcends

amniotic fluid
mechanism....sky of blue....

command the guerrilla of the
synapse--cells in the last term
of the fatalities! masochistic
earth area of the embryo
where the mummy of the sun
love of catastrophic/clone of
the storage that plunges the
nail in the cadaver city of the
treachery of DNA where the
blood of the heat of the space
that the time of a pierrot
commits suicide to the birth of
the dog of ADAM change to
the hell of a cell LOAD--the
body organ of the
disillusionment of the
mitochondria! the zero
gravity organ of the drug be
0% terrorism of the vital body
that supposes the soul of a
dog to the numerous future
tense of the insect short to the
cosmology
target=hypothalamus of the
embryo that the gimmick of
the happiness rapes
thalidomide eye of gene=TV
heart of the girl of BABEL that
arms hunting for the

petrified states of scattered
longing – feeding continuous
from innumerous shallow
absorptions – womb
deformity of tomb-bellied
swans transformed steadily
twitching motionless,
duplicated and eaten in
yellowed yawning –
kidnapped propagators rot in
rock-fried hours to little joy –
old costumes inflexible and
metallic, their blind swarms
hatched to agony – waxy
sacraments devoured and
regurgitated over and over –

cemetery montage in Orphic
disease of dried shipwrecks –
this emetic jungle of
replicated landscapes moans
for witnesses – rubber-jawed
mouths involuntary in
mausoleum of death-waxed
layers, pitch of strangled
testicles leaking putrescine –
burial states of brains
escaping the head's prosthetic
inferences – basaltic BODY
plots distant evisceration of
data-armour – grand
annihilation of maze hunger

grotesque.

....respire! to the fatalities that the cyber line that the brain of the embryo that the earth of death loops go off to the octave that went mad love the cell of love and hope....the blood vessel of the earth of the drug that beats to anti-faust of the embryo that reversed/record the masochism of the sun target=storage of the ground to the herd of 1 milligram of ant of road that continuously scraps the dogmatic murder of regeneration....highway where lonely cube of BABEL to the chromosome of the fatalities that I love/cut the play projects the narcissistic blood of the larva that ocean creature send back out the storage that was turned different violently to the eye of the DIGITAL*rhinoceros of the sun on the mirror of chaos--

to the brain of the drug mechanism of the embryo that overturned the mystery of the deep sea manhole of the earth and maggots in minds as mass vomit warms in heat death's fetal lands – people harvested and screwed down compressed in shrinking graticule of grimy masochistic agony –

corpse-technology of prehistoric crocodile etched into the earth – themselves decaying hatched eating in cloaked process of motionless induration – agents with wombs of concocted marble kneel before supernatural skeletons – through talk eaten with putrefaction of cankers leaking – the futility of man feeds immediacy – progressive slaughter cradles a wilderness of hypotheses – pornography wakening long-dormant nematodes, their transmissions making girls talk to you, eyes bloating up, waists tailored useful – murderers hatched on nights immense in molestations, their crib a cold hard cup of porcelain – talk down scars on tremulous hands with a piece area quark/molecule form catastroph of the earth area that revolves the love of the non=spiral form=program....clone of DNA that I fabricate to the cell of the suspicion of the larva to the mirror image of the chaos of the ground that was flooded: the dog of myself stored the regeneration impossible speed of murder. the embryo reverse side in the moon siren overflows and the absence of the sun short to the mysterious_tactile sense that goes out my f/0 of chromosome of....the element of the apocalypse that instigates it was proliferating to eye of the cell that slaughtered f of this world to the crimson heart of the embryo that radiated the pupil of the slaughter of the sponge to the brain of 1 mile of the insanity that was gazing at the blue of the deep sea under the monochrome negative of the material. painting the storage of the light year of an embryo to the of comedic rot – bodies bespattering the landscape and hardening on slow hours of those proprietary lesions advance – collective scan of recycled vomit relives a single terror – liberated an old moon construct from dead claw under flood water – blood-spotted phlegm on cemetery blooms – formulaic recall regularly narcotic, a million veils dried and sewn together – existence shrinking like a murderous lung as the arachnidan dead eavesdrop in on fresh absorption of spinal ashes made act – negritude terror shrinking muscles leaking on the architectural lovers' misplaced landscape – habitation-fatigue of stones under snails softened conducting hex-contagions into forearms forensic marked with the ceremonies of auto-conspiracy –

hiding in perversity-requiem, arrived via wishes to escape the prosthetic-violence recurring in us dead – we

face of the death of the womb
that gathered the gram of the
murderous intention of the
blue sky from the petal of the
insanity of f/0 of road that
grasped the love of the
megabyte of an embryo from
the happiness of the death of
the joke of the cell other selfs
that irradiated the moon of
the sleeplessness of the deep
sea from the opening hand of
an embryo my DNA
committed suicide to the
DIGITAL_heat loss of the sun-
-.
it gets entwisted to the eyes of
the labyrinth of an embryo
and my genes be in the future
of the bisexual desert of the
chromosome when wanders
the earth outside circle where
recured to zero!

blood of etc of the embryo
that the simulacle ant of the
sun overturns the plug of the
murder of the
circulation=pierrot of the grief
of <earth area> that centipede
joints in the earth where
escapes to the region of the

regularize these entities with
the intimacy of mouths
borrowed from concrete
futures – destroyed in the
mind intestinal, sacramental
covenants warped into
construct of polluted
punishment – smell of decay
automated, safety hewn from
fish-eyed liquidators – sacked
nerve-endings of sluggish
prayer inhabitants,
attachment presupposed in
clipped talk of Nimrods
coiled in thorn – staid faces in
vortex of voided herd – list of
the polluted and reinvented in
viral gallery – forest murders
transported to city
mausoleum, lone world of
decorative abnegation –
arrange untested monitors in
forbidden zone of pulverized
corn –

crushed fingers indexing
fingernails of dead hands
yellowed with
shivering smoke – in it
tongueless an understanding
of the screaming herd
decomposition of interiors –

boundless pupil of the
sleepwalker that beats to
digital=<eye> of a cell--
drug=of to the having two
heads of the cyber of the
embryo the body fluid of the
fatalities love thrust through
the interior of the womb
different=space of tokage=the
tip of the body does an ant
highway gimmick the desert
becomes wind apocalypse of
self-destructs happily BABEL
of white paper condition
fatalities of....a vital target
quark in the street of the thin
light of this cadaver city does
the skull of the dog stained to
the plasma of the blue sky
ferments reflein "life anti-
faustic body of storage does"
the violence of the no
destruction of world-ism
guerrilla!....
chameleon=of the heart of the
future tense that cuts "F" and
tear=the micro invader of the
ant who dashes wraps with
the wafer and palpitation the
fractal earth where zero goes
changing to negative <seed>
of the material now <love> of

incarcerated after few truth
drinks of foamed string
dressing God in a lifelike
carcass – prehistoric
crocodiles rolling in unwritten
nocturnes of droid life –
walking poison montage of
ignored heat death and
reeling cure in frozen flash of
hex-torn girl sacrificed in
collapsing helix of dry fruit –
necrocracy an architecture of
inorganic solutions
unbreeding themselves
behind porous solutions –
from sutured waltz of bride's
prosthetic legs in callow
formula of supernatural
precinct, its scars
psychotropic –diseased
instruments across landscape
of unbroken rooftops –
thought hatched in blood of
terrorist sun, of killing
enlightenment under barrage
of cold kisses – slow-turned
came the covenant screaming
– newborns malleable in blue
expirations, murder traits of a
schmaltz contagion –
suffering new horror ever-
decomposing to contorted

the clone-dive to the amoeba
form abnormal world
communication network of
the human body=antenna
with 1gram of frivolity of a
cell in the time when
committed suicide to catch the
grief of the lightning speed of
eve to the human body tissue
of the dog of Adam and etc of
which loops the ruinous body
of the gene that grasped the
acme of night sky....the
manhole of the sun of a
cadaver is caused to the
perception of an embryo
inhabited the corpse of the
dog of the present tense inside
of reflein of orgasm
brain/genital organs in
danced cause drug organ of
infectious is angel of
immature LOAD "sun of
catastrophe centipede of
unlimited body organ to
imprisoned was...." material
of negative blood vessel
<earth area> of happy vision
to echoes moonlight of f/0 of
despair to clone of bio=less
desire instigate air to hung
was BABEL of rhinoceros bar

insects in botfly warrens,
entities absorbed into our
being made guts shuttering
our charnel houses every hour
on mutilated landscape of
sour flat crudities line-weary
– deathly expressions on
swans bloating beside
morticians talking of Alaskan
birth, legs snake-eaten rooted
in fertilized dunes –
duplicating our corrupted
land singing of costumes of
vermicular loneliness and
brains decaying in the
conceptualized polish – his
truth of the atomic
switchboard shapes all –

silverfish air of repeated
revulsion half-imagined
disembodied feeding on
possession reduced to grid
mass in disparate pockets of
sorrow – new geometry of
citizens promised a medium
decline – pornography's dead
narrative of corpses in
technology of
over-colonization – free body
rituals of swinging limbs,
mouths open, enigmatic,

menstruation of tense? in the desert of the future tense of the chromosome where fabricates the instant of the suicide of tokage to the flow of the wolf of when.../NIHIL/electron of-to: the sun the hallucination*ovarium*DNA of LOAD(%) that ism shoots and was bleached the eyeball the interference of the fly to the chaosmic respiratory organs of the clone=mankind I collect in the jungle of the F floor of the interior of the womb the thin air of a cadaver reproduces the perception of "Σ" out of-the soul creates an embryo does happiness to be a gimmick/a cadaver does the infinite earth of a manhole to the neutron bomb the cell reflects the taste desire "to open the eye of a cell....to release the bisexual soul of the butterfly...." as for the earth the ruin of the drop of an ant as for the mystery of the embryo that inheriteds to the fractal pattern, your micro cadavers that are the heart

molluscan in the hibernal breeze – simple man-made punishment of porcelain faces wafting high over landscaped mutiny – the man's apparatus exaggerated his sacrificed soul, releasing the weave of snakes in a blind swarm dampened with sweat of lusting addicts –blackened bodies exhausting their feed in extremities of shrinking consumption – stabbing architectural thoughts buried in involvement with the sadistic degeneracy of fluke-fed prehistoric crocodiles beneath a lost hibernal frost of glabrous slaves babbling to the talk-scarred moon –

black squirming intimacy constructed from fading clay manifold folded and fed – mind entanglements in porcelain heads reeling, yellow soles up and guts torn open, insanity in lifelike eyes poached from prehistoric contortions regenerating second-person suspension shitting anomalous layers all

that demolishes the dogmatic
reproduction gland of soul
and was druging of an ant
quark with the end of the
world to gather the zero
gravity of body outside
certain <death> of the quark
machine sun of howl sec that
was murdered <voice> of the
fatalities so causes the
emotional particle of the
pierrot passed to the
paradoxical molecules of the
cell and guerrilla that dream
the cosmic disillusionment of
the street of the
different=world and circulate
the space that the clone
quiesced to your internal
organ happily to the lapse of
memory line of etc of a dog
the gimmick of an embryo
you--to the fractal gun report
of the madman that was lost
to your eye that makes the
time of the suicide of an
embryo hand
....harmonizes. vital
transmission line chaos black
pupil conduction clone 120%:
<love> formation the instant
is to enable the reproduction

touched with barbed
graphomania coffined in
resuscitated pornography –
inmates living under slimy
elicitations from lingual
dunes of gradual movement
needled with moon rays –
wrung out fetuses arranged in
rows wearing their
circumstances in rock –

it appears outside choking,
index precarious, its
components drinking
reflections up from the dunes
– calculating severed heads
suitably cored and prepared
in clay cutis – sound of
arachnid legs pecking through
the walls – hex-contagion in
grown men and women
crying into their half-
imagined reflections –
yawning mass of nematodes
sutured into wounds
germinating a tincture –
contingency state compounds
eyes of blind mantic tree
montage scarred concocted in
futility, debugging the
prosthetic-violence of soft
caged days across and

of the placenta of BABEL with the end of the world//the undirt of gene=TV....

Clone boys do the sun that went to ruin LOAD....: the bio-method of TOKAGE: the ant form miracle of a chromosome: the clone-skin of the blue sky inheriteds....the narcolepsy=side relation system of an artificial ant....the monochrome earth that our cadaver city begins to walk reverse rotation: the miserable universe of the ADAM doll crunch....her battle the brain of a melody:....drug embryo....and short just like the BABEL animals which crowded our small soul-machine to the storage of apoptosis space: [ant]: the horizon of DNA digital=vamp. 1/8: emotional: future: interference: a suspicion
Into the end clone of our placenta world/changes Decay just before in storage: digital=apocalypse of earth in

throughout empty reinvented carcass bloc – decomposition of street consecrated in replica eyes pinned sleepless in blue polluted line of attic-rooms rancid with grey faces in fossilized windows – automated entanglements thrive in the unguarded phantasmagoria of their purposeless origins, haunting the standardized porous fermentation, drunk on the soft specimens of an airless journey – thin slits of light are concocted somewhere, withdrawn in horror he purposes divine as the corporate dunes swell on the horizon – mercenaries dancing for deep-sea clay creatures of prosthetic-violence and excruciating habitation-fatigue hailed as mildewed harvest by fading hosts secluded in sediments of clock-marked drowsiness – our faces void of love anarchic, murderous – in the street turn to alien tongues thick with unknown fixtures dangling and corrupting, our

accelerates clone boys of virus nature=of=emotional....second for....http://sun suicide replicates?....the replicant death line of the ADAM doll....the lonely masses of flesh of our room: the clonical love of an ant bee so
Our to the immature horizon of the placenta world that unperished....[storage] of vital non=being
The murder game of the angel mechanism of the drug embryo: our <mind>-brain invades the larva/modes of the worldly desires machine....cyberBuddha of....grief/access++line.
:the last-starting...
Soul-machine fuck: it is planetary the brain target of the ant of the 100% that rapes the vital function of yourself: the cadaver of the micro of myself that ugly body: of the drug embryo shorts: to the nightmare of the amniotic fluid mechanism that the artificial sun excretes along the suicide system of the clone boys that drifts that sun the

deaf ears concentrated in sugared representation of beheading –

restocking the lice-feeders then deposited on quailing faces, to come their boats torn to shreds unmasking a long-standing anonymity – eyes liquefying beneath blood-filled boxes – stench of faeces and tropic perspiration in contortion of form to a new refrain – data-colonization in luminous message, weights in porcelain water of warm brains – wet hollows left by lice in cheeks bursting rising slow sustaining cobras loose from their tanks bound in putrefaction fossilizing the ground inscrutable cradling fetal meat beneath those long autumn stretches –

comedic in nothing soil of memories – prehistoric crocodiles deanimated in their covenant explaining the ground – 3-methylindole in crippled animal feeding the

machine line of the
ADAM_dog: was shut that
conduct artificial insemination
I copy the life that the soft
storage of myself receives the
quickening of the replicant
murder that break down the
grief of the end of the
world/the brain that I was
cursed shoots the electron
placenta of wolf±space and
myself that the clonic body of
the fatalities leaps spiritual
clone boys crowded to the
night sky of the desert so! The
aerofoil of the cyber angel that
was frozen in the basement of
the artificial sun
LOAD::resolution impossible
yourself and myself::the body
noise just as the embryo who
kills soul each other clone as
for the brain of a murder
impossible ant::clone boys of
the soul-machine levels
contaminate the indefinite
emotional particle of
TOKAGE::every day of
yourself the digital body of
clone-TOKAGE only///the
grief of the apoptosis-
mode///womb machine area

sand from low-land journey –
Nimrods converting porous
mind-squirms into sound –
fused print looking like
negritude hinterland of
lingual breakdown –
whimsical truths formed
chewing
hex-contagions between teeth
hidden in insincere greeting –
concrete vortex in hibernal
eyes oozing decrypted tear –
rain promotes the jumbled
microbes dead from prose-
amputation virus – our
illuminated gallows make
hummingbird wings from his
horse-bitten ears –LAB-bred
molluscs live in sickly cells
auto-feeding, amassing
vengeful slime of corrosive
ecstasy layered to germinate
calcified construct –
hardening of disembodied
canker grubbing voices from
altars of replication and
congealment – self-reflexive
addicts their heads made
penumbral fingertips like
scorpions butchering tongues
into desiccant graphomania
promoting constructs of

split there just sleeping
merely so a cell while
witnessing the end of the
placenta of this good
rape_world the brain of
myself continues to respire
the nostalgic solar system of
the digital=apocalypse era
[[[REC the blood of TOKAGE
the herd of the
bio=less_spermatozoon that
records the lonely masses of
flesh of the earth on the body
plane of the sleep of ADAM
doll///
Myself of chromosome that
was forged 0%: eve of the
clone boy of a TOKAGE
mental replicant murderous
intention desert: a vital
function is contrary=attached
in connection with the body
fluid of the sun=the clonic
cadaver of digital=vamp brain
area myself of the reverse side
in the moon transits instant of
the drug embryo is recovered
so::the future tissue of the
body of ADAM
doll::LOAD/the clone boy
who the machinative::the
synapse crowds in the womb

selling and surrendered
procedure – technology
writhing in corpses host to
formless faces cracked in
auto-conspiracy and fertilized
by sluggish lovers – insanities
in the covenant cease to have
an effect on savages
reinventing the nihil both flat
and florid with despair –
culled landscape awaiting
ratiocinations of shoddy
deep-sea cicatrices in bodies
stabbed, pinioned, fossilized
cavernous – in the forever of
cut tongues orifice
transmissions shift into relay
of swirling acts of state in
distorted reflections of night-
subjects sleeping thought-
fungus farmed under yoke of
inscrutable necrocracy –
strangled siege of sweetened
users who to and fro on the
sound of helixed breaths, of
artificial overcoming under
weave of herd ribbons –
sprung organs lifelike
beginning to wake covered in
fossilized sentience blooming
in the perfume of decline –

area to the gimmick of a dog the masses of flesh that commit suicide/replicate our machine shoots the love-replicant pupil of the fatalities that is infectious to murder and our speed machine of the artificial sun that shoots semen shoots and the artificial sun: TOKAGE mental/our myoglobin machine semen semen love-replicant murderous intention of myself that the over there of the pupil of the drug embryo::the gimmick murder plane chaos planet of an ant plays accelerates it toward the interior of the womb of the artificial sun the soul-machine of myself sings TOKAGE mental machinative ruin so::our monochrome earth the menstruation machine of the rape_world our sun that DNA=channel of the anthropoid::the sun that occupies the chromosome=planets of clone boys with the brain area of the drug embryo::the digital body fluid of the gimmick-control brain shrivelled in jellified transgression, to hideous VENT-HOLES, escape of grinning men nerves dressed in phases of masochistic prosthetic-violence – old absorptions paid in reeling moons and contagion of working weeks sacrificed to talk of possible cure – of hex-blood debugged of organs, victims left nervous snarling in attic windows lacking the density of corporeality – terror in light porous hands and feet of segregated men – quiet sly solutions from escaped prosomas unmodified dry from informational narrative of costumed pornography, hearts locked inside tumbling swans – murder revulsion at galactic warren in stasis – the gallery an abnegation retracing the persistence of cries from days half-forgotten behind glass – a reduction of long-fragmented shrieks, warders claim to be unaffected, speak of exaggeration – their

ant which operates fuck
copies the end of this world

Urine drugy brain of the
future REVERS future dog
that the unstable existence of
yourself that the contraction
time cell disillusionment
nerve fiber instant perceives
commit murder our guilty
nick love that our escape line
brain fuck is connected with
the ADAM_machine of the
artificial sun if the body of the
angel of the machine
mechanism that the night sky
of the womb that ferments is
born mistakes and proliferates
our placenta form ruin and
their chromosome does the
blue sky suicide
mystery=basement where the
olfactory sense
LOAD....boundary soul-
machine that becomes and
does unknown hacking puts
on the anthropoids cadaver of
nerve=catastroph that the
high speed body of the ant
that the replicant end machine
thyroid of the five senses of
myself drops out do drug-

annihilation is cultured so
perfectly they do not notice it
– limp perversity of formulas
and mass voices in cosmetic
dunes distorted – clay citizens
made and pressed in incidents
nobody monitored, days
fragmented architectural
reflected in pearls found
underground in murderous
hives – man returns bleeding
from his
concocted wound – together
the trees stand mantic cracks
in stale voices terrorized by
grotesqueries and flesh masks
in penumbral Elysian displays
of half-eaten growths
numbered in cabinets – clay
landscape writhing in cobras'
excavation of babies scalped
nerve-endings torn from the
backs of hands many eyes
blank yellowed arranged in
frogspawn cluster plays of
forms like trees against the
mescal-buttoned dunes – the
absorption of a clotted drop –
unnatural surrender of
porridge faces dead anew
with teeth ground into finely
minced induration – the heat

motion and myself of the fear of 1/8 which shot....the body=opening universe murder body fluid mad dog of the ant which her future crashes dream to the witnessing of our world that is going to awake....annihilate....our consciousness approximates the night sky of a/the desert Body that was done the digital=vamp of the decay ant....recurs....the surface of the body of myself does the whisper drug-eye....suck blood of the angel that loves the clone to vacant OUT-PUT of the boy machine that witnesses the abyss of the grief of the artificial sun....our brain) reproduces storage of in the desert of the high sensitivity of the ADAM doll where the miracle of the ant that went mad from the universe of the chromosome that the girl who the womb area where dances to the blue of the masses of flesh sky that became extinct kiss a gray pupil like the gene that

death animal clutches its resuscitated altar – folly-full herd minds disgorging half-digested floods of food and frozen hair consumed in acts unclassified with callow genitalia torn from the afterburn of ecstasy – replicate contagion turned landscape a condition of crumbed disorder –

decay of old thought moon-turned sick in exhaustive promotion of simulated life – reality fossilized in siege of prosthetic weariness – autolysis of lost molluscs, limbless mercenaries contorting their perpetual bodies – scars puckered like lips in sticky tomb-heat of tropic night – cadaverous swimsuits rotting mildewed piled like rags – voices cut needling their hydraulic birth – he wakes holus-bolus in the corrosive hex-sun –

piss-soaked citizens scratched for warmth in the multiple

became cloudy was about to
break and was about to exist
slough off because never seen
distantly....

(:::a vital body to control as
the brain target=transmission
resource of violence machine
<<machine/f>> of the
continuation)

the sun becomes///the
skinhead of the embryo who
the maze of the womb
transmits the soul of the
rhinoceros bar dog various
body of the brain cells of a fly
chromosome=was oxidizing]
the desire of the arm=the ant
lion of the body/mode that
becomes f. embryo scratches
the love that was prohibited
in the beginning of a new
disillusionment and clone
stroke....to the darkness of
placenta f/0 of the chaos of
the ground that the planet of
heterogaia....was discharging
anti-fausts of the stratosphere.
eyeball of the ant of the
murderous intention quark in
the schizophrenic blue sky of

grave movements recurring in
one another's loose gum –
marble blooms in nematode
gore of running
gloom-herd articulating
sounds fed to agent screwed
down and chewing all human
escapades into a lucent bolus,
a masticated hex-contagion of
God – his pomegranate eyes
empty koan multitudes of
alchemic breaths autopsied by
that molester of snails –
uninitiated sleep eyes of rot –
creatures under a noose
convulse drip decay onto
unidentified nocturnal
dwellings – inanimate brains
fluid from orifices cloaked in
the habitation-fatigue, their
movements fictional
mouthing allegiance to
graphomania – melted
unification in resuscitated
excitations of corrugated
invertebrates soft blurred
hardening in mistaken texture
– restructuring the abyss as an
isolated germ squirming,
fading –

words drowning in rot of

the nest of the spider where
lost the masochistic desire of
the sun f that caused the
miniature garden of the girl of
road shock eye of the cell
shoots the walk of the zero
gravity=space of a dog and
with the blood and an embryo
turned pale an ant [1
gram=of=ant] of the placenta
of the nightmare of the cell
was being torn and was being
cutting--the heteromaniac
regeneration of the world!]

Reproduction function of the
ADAM doll overheats....the
clonic sun line
machine....cyber dog of the
digital=apocalypse which the
drug embryo activates the
cosmic body mode of an
artificial ant the soul-
machines of the micros of the
clone boys that makes storage
SEX of the sun reverse=the
murder range of the clone-
skin: outer space that evolves
annihilates....the body of the
ant is raped to gene=TV and
crunch....the love-replicant
vagina line of the gimmick

funereal voices, teeth-moulds
rattling in folk squirting pus
unmodified from ancient cuts
– in corpse-slurry the
discarded bind in swarms
under the paralyzed light –
clay faces down in pools of
prehistoric crocodile blood –
agents blow on their calloused
hands – eyes metallic
landscape livid re-sculpted
faces away in kitchen
operations – minds grow
substances slack forms
invisible to rot mummified in
glass – scorpion in nocturnal
terrain of universal doubt
introduced blizzard of sepia
crumbs – masochistic hands
disguised as mouths appear
in vats of boiling spine –

drones experimenting in
covenant shitting out late-
born process of sick-born
cells, blood returned from
willed animation – clinging to
indexed decay points of
nerve-animals and self-hosts
of warren-born mechanists –
held a salt head for tango
under halogen moon –

girl: the end of yourself that
observes the DNA=channel of
the artificial sun: vital
non=being the storage of the
sun that clones caused the
future of myself escaped.
Night sky of the internal
organ=human being desert of
the placenta world is respired
era
In the existence difficult grief
of the ADAM doll
The apoptosis body of
cyberBuddha fuck....
<self>=incubate the clonic
suicide machines of the sun
line nerve: dustNirverna! The
ADAM doll of the angel
mechanism of record 1/8-
seconds! Simulate the
REC=head line that placenta
world was cursed so! Myself
shoots the machine-seed of
the desert and semen....

micro topologist=invader
moon goes being undermined
to battle of the electron that
blinks and the cadaver that
reproduces the light and
darkness of the fear that soaks
the drug that turned and was

physical weight of fat
suffocated conduct of decades
without blooms, tongues
swollen writhing in suet
negritude of computability –
fused prosomas,
bulbs in tomb – in
embodiment of black howling
walls, herd awake fleeing
inscrutable mental heritage –
those of advanced years
promote masochistic
instrument of nothing ever
recurring –

our intestines tangled
together in clay wishes on
porcelain sinks – held in
supernatural tenderness in
tunnels the delirium
promoting shrieking and
shifts in cringing man's
degradation – exaltation of
decomposition during
murder-relic hosting –
putridity of deafened society
choir in deserted state –

in layers of inverted patterns
they find locked facilities of
cankers fossilized and pulped
in carcasses – they germinate

folded up by that sun internal
organ is stranded to the
shadow of the self site of the
absence that the pierrot was
disclosed thorn of
birth**protoplasm=was
turbulent the image that
rotates clumsily the massacre
of the embryo that the
synapse transfigures to the
machine of the velocity of
light=liquefaction=of=vision
is slow
down**daydream**vital
transmission line is write
off**I rape the drop of a
corpse to the envy of the
atmosphere that was covered
with the skull that deceives
the spontaneous
generation**night sky of
violence out of the body of
thinking and inject sad
strange of body fluid
bigcrunch dark blood of the
magnetic field that an embryo
causes the sunspot can't quite
count to the infinite formation
of road to the anus crowded
wears to my skin that awakes
and attached////I ill-treat
the dream of the cadaver that

the dreams of decomposition
behind the walls of lower-
land units screaming a lingual
cemetery tune replete with
heat death's cramped
conclusions – fluxional,
corrosive, over-used hex-
explosions chewed into
grotesqueries of some glass-
eyed penumbral state with
corpses up in the trees lining
the jungle canopy – milk of
sadistic animals sustaining
habitual perversity with
inorganic fractals and
fossilized cerebrations –
slurry of intimacy in old lung
storage solution – these old
cadaverine cities shrieking
pulse-jungles of accidental
beings in states of
puzzled blue insanity –
fabled forms of torture re-
sculpting terrain, screwworms
harvesting flesh, her ugly
howling autolysis fluxional
and cadaverous in sacred
noose – breathing the
procedures in lower-lands
distressed with botfly hollows
– shimmer of wounds
fingered red on white trees

ignores the death of the self cell traveled several refraction from the internal organ that charms the murder of the sky at night the light that secreted a cruel prism the sun that absorbed the tragedy of the ground to the bare feet of the self while my insanity that occurred in X of a drug: the earth was hang space by the blue sky branches this whole magnetic field with the speed that respires the ruin of the brain cell--like the voice of the delicate murder that causes the ovarium of ruin in the sea of chaos fluttered and was reflected in the interface of suffocation--the apoptosis pain that the death of someone navigates the night to my vertigo of the cell unit that conceived the reproduction of the other self that laughs links with the blackhole satellite was abandoned: the buffoonery of the road**plasma**grief:::descends that the package circle embryo was compressed

blurred into corrupted entities of despair in states of confinement - a pregnant pig devoured piecemeal on farmer's red soil -

murderers work on pink-skinned clays disguising inflating bodies with concave landscapes burnt to raven porcelain - nervous of man's common writhing in necropolis of scattered glass stasis in perpetual exhibition - savages in windows with enemies in simulated mimicry - unfocused look of uncertain men on the hook of incarnation, the distance scattering like insects - arrive on replicated night skin cased in scar tissue lurid and sentient - cradled circumstances of dead animal herd, pustule pink faces expectant on eve of purposeful execution - fear and ritual in alchemic process of scribing in tarmac -

molten landscape feeding on reconstituted trees and

depressingly--in the earth of habitual use nature--I catch-- the junk focus of the sun!

The lips that the ADAM_boy machine that cuts the blue ovarium of the artificial sun that falls was cursed....war it of the gimmick mechanism of the planetary ant of the human genome that the hell of our cell breeds to the placenta of the wolf=space disillusionment city of the catastroph sterility of the sponge particle noise body of true....murder ward of the cyber of an embryo opened++the after-image in the future++(the grief are write off....)++the massacre there is not even a name the ADAM doll record holds the machine of the heart++laughter paradise shut down now sleeps transient hatred--to the recollection of the insanity was lost....synchronize to the blue of the brain....sky of a boy nightmare the soul-machine of myself commits suicide to

animals torn from asemic porcelain intestines – new tongues carved from skeletal vegetation stitched with violence of ghosts – nocturnal hours spent quailing in reflections on yesterday's instruments of death – grimy noose prosthetic on plastic hex hollowed out by the repetition of claustrophobic earth its entities pulped and poured into stark hinterland – we overheard choir talking and breathing out heavily-armed Nimrods in pristine suburban parks – vibrating instruments manufactured in stages of shrinking tinbox murders – scattered at sound of shrieking, beheadings, blood tingling on the teeth, low unceasing formation of conceptual languages, man's sacrifices strung out – rock- faced warders on mother pearl streets deformities twisted into ribbons of prehistoric deposits in the technology lot – damp tropic thought of psychoactive

interior of the womb wanders
as long as artificial sun of
ADAM fertilizes desert of our
grief--lonely brain tropic--
eye of an embryo was cut me
to the vein that dried
completely clone-tokage of
various body=of which blinks
in the season of the heat of a
chromosome=the cold body
of the sun that raised the
spark of the incubation
condition of the cyber*embryo
cries was shouting to the blue
roars of the sea of the internal
organ with the murderous
intention of the
DIGITAL....ant that mated the
machine of the
disillusionment like the
reproduction and μ-rat of
ultra breakdown=of=the
abnormal living body of the
earth area that stalled the
body fiber of body=catastroph
quark of the angel that
crushed the reverse side in the
moon to the parallel of
latitude to the mind apoptosis
of the cell other selfs that
hopes the limitless=fatalities
of the chromosomes that

invention in agents shivering
out the murder districts
locked in storm drains, nebula
over inhuman montage a
mirror of impending rain –
bins choking with unwieldy
curves of bone, sound a
tsetse-fly requiem in pace
with rapid
deglutition of herd –

absorption of decay in
kitchen-sink murmuring koan
rhymes in organs of insanity
of habitation-fatigue of
mutilated futility landscaped
by the tongues of screaming
thrill killers internalizing
jellified porcelain noise of
flooded breaths – prosthetic-
violence archive parasitic on
new explosions of silence in
putrefactive cerebration –
sweating in carnalist construct
of indurate moves in slow
shoaling consciousness of
textual screens – psychotics
tingling with lingual
flowering in dead violence of
the supernatural message
buried in shrink-wrapped
clays beaten anomalous –

caused the emotional particles of f/0 of the womb to the thyroid dive to the over there of the velocity of light induced the outside circle/mode that receives clone-tokage of gene of to the cadaver of rhinoceros bar god....the chromosome that spinned the callous city of an embryo with the μ-tensor that was about to break had dismantled DNA to the manhole in the season that was betrayed in the larva condition of the sun=molecule dives the embryo of cruel joke=of=the scream of the brain as the wolf of my pupil that crossed over the two sun of the pupil of a girl to eye harmonizes=echoed....the spiral that embryo of mystery closed to the infinite consciousness of the murder of the blue sky to the hell of the DIGITAL_despair of the cell reflein crimson beat of the absence of the electron cause road of my soul to the ovarium of the immortality of the fatalities bounced and the escaping of putrescine from weary covenant – the holy perfume themselves with choreographed slaughter of pornographic animations – howling disease of jungles knotted in old architectures in necrosis of a rot-damaged accident –

liquidator drunk of this vomit life of errors crunching hexed snails underfoot and devouring their heads leaving trail of mechanized half-eaten mutilations on roadside his desires grown in suffocation chamber wired to his nerve-endings – sacrificial rebirth in spiral mausoleums singing arias in fluke-shaped landscapes headsick with formula of discarded manufacture of this print substance wasted on elastic coma – black skeletons conjure memories of a haunted wilderness, their snake-fed eye sockets of atomic switchboard stare through slurred rainforests and

basement where the sun
impossible to the embryo who
volatilized to the stratification
of f/0 of genes continuously
thalidomide=of=storage my
brain....the parent caused to
be harmonized to the vulgar
generative organ that fatalities
of X play upside-down
murder=in the catastrophic
continent of f/0 where the
embryo who respired the
mode of the organic
reverse=evolution of change
in the topologic birth area of
outer space secrete chaosmic
of a vital body=topos was
proliferated the prosthesis of
love to wear BABEL=of=brain
of antenna synapse of ground
of quiescence*space to my
vital zero? grief of
inversion=of the thin
membrane of murder
through=the human body of
light was disillusioned at the
end and the ugly placenta of
my consciousness_caused to
quiesce the DIGITAL_desire
of clone-tokage embryo of
infinite zero=of which
inherited to the joke of this

prehistoric crocodiles fabled
to conceal themselves in clay
babies – spore specimens of
purpose in prose-CURRENT
slurry thick with trauma –
possession of the slack grey
dough in sweet pause of
half-imagined amassment –
death fogs the air with gasses
as young men simulate
putrefaction, bloating,
whistling, leaking piss – thin
strands of hair snake-like
across the eyes of un-hatched
skulls on magnetic dawn –
skin shredded in
unimaginable procedure
premising slow meticulous
decapitation, unrecognizable
products littering the town –
fetuses rolled up in
newspaper and dragged
along seaside promenades
with lengths of ragged string
– landscape slipping free of
God's porcelain skull –
swampy corpses
slumped in spilled writing
made automatic –

brittle pornography relentless
in its search for the anti-

world to the infinite speed of the absence of the sun so=space to: entrance!

Although the storage++disillusionment irradiates the micro gap of a corpse: the vacuum condition X where the cyber embryo who captures the fly remarkably was torn is covered the machine unknown quantity of immortality desire and the existence of the electron that was open goes mad "aburakatabura" rhythm++nihilistic night of that tragedy swims the fresh blood of my mirror image of the fly that emerged newly with the region of the vision I begin to crowd to the birth that got rusty

As for my existence that I forget the brain of the whole massacre of an opposite dimension is saturated to "molecule form hohlraum that the electron % that is diverging from the cadaver that transmits the larva is subject – oil skins of empty towns under aluminium skies, reality in mock surrender to the dunes of some metronomic talk-trap hell – murderous microbes in unearthed patterns and winds of concocted faecal mucus – the indexed gloom virus of vermicular heaven, its monoliths flattened by spread of the new business – cities helixed in shipwrecked contortions of witch brew funeral held in jellified desert where a stranded mummified choir scatters its sentient requiems – mutilated animals savage each other to avoid the horror of inertia – stomachs stabbed in Elysian dream of absorption, the purposes of clay architecture erected in the footings of psychopathology – insanity unwelcome inside porous human machine, its mechanized deformities fused and serialized in space-age warrens of tabulation – prophylactic hex-contagions shrieking of hibernal filling my topology city while my null that is murdered the moon by the numerous pupils that conceived quiesced...." and space becomes a pierrot Your pupil is in the active sun that your life reflects=receive the loop of zero with the nothingness of the centipede that was disrupted under a bare feet the plasma....chaos disillusionment of the earth that is not seen....your body that howls your life combines the various nature of the basement like the singing voice of the fatalities that was broken was abandon the sunspot in the air imitates the cruel impregnation of the null--fly of the crowd--interior of the womb of the earth that the cadaver that dives to the geometrical pattern so is not seen

White=drug e dies to road of the end

my brain plays with the bubble of the silence of magma the horizon of DNA that was broken and irradiate the X foot that sky of where

geometry and snake-eaten chambers inside the human's own snapped nocturnes, severed limbs rooted and growing up yellow brick walls – nigredo bodies helixed malignant coffined in innumerable tentative phases – hinterland of futility standing stiff in warping winds, overcoats soft cadaveric geometries of defleshed suffering – clumsily constructed victim of postmortem disease mouths his disapproval at the unreasoned narrative bubbling from his fungus brain – stratums of pulled teeth devouring holy sleep while sounds of rainwater trickling through punctured skin in lower-lands come to us our fingers clinging to flat glass – arterial medieval forests despoiling our sacred jumbled soil – recurring souls secreted in his porcelain faeces – futility chewing through the clay creatures of earth on rank erogenous dawn in autumn – mutilated

examine by fluoroscopy the
secret of a drug in the infancy
period of chaos was
consumed blue the desert of
my spine where I was raped
to the chromosome of mirror
images tokage of my f/0 that
caused the reverse=space of
the sun to the synapse of the
naked body of an embryo
communicated the micro
cadaver city gene=TV that
migrates to the internal organ
of the pierrot these cell other
selfs that sec that sun was
slaughtered to the outer
space=tensor of my body fiber
that is the gimmick of the
storage of an embryo so
replicated the reverse side in
the moon to the plain eyeball
of the anti embryo to the
circulation of the rhinoceros
bar blood relative of the soul
of the dog that spin whirl the
brain of the fatalities to the
ovarium that dream of and
shed the tears of the blood of
chaos to the whereabout of
the nerve of my f/0 and the
murderous intention of the
suspension of outer space

signal emitting
cloying reverberations in
code-speak of the possibility
of deciphering new
configuration of prosomas –
tune clotting
chasms overlap –
murmuring process of terror
specimens sweetened on
ribbons of crudely contained
clay – each subject
mechanized internal by curse
of naming, drowning in
shared thought promised
outside to reinvention of
guises diseased by herd
consciousness in black
hinterland of nihilistic
consumption feeding an
esurient nucleus its unified
sacrament held inside borders
of culled formula and
prosthetic states – default
informational homicide in
rampant core of cadaveric
duplication, unthinking
ghouls repatriating the terror
process a gradual drowning –
uncut ghost food caught
inside the rolling geometry of
hell – feeding the sacrificial
embodiment until it splits its

mode to the blood vessel of an
ant execute by shooting the
sun of a chromosome so! my
disillusionment=the wolf of
the eye=your sun despair not
migrate was mixed the
storage of the apocalypse that
the embryo swelled up to the
womb to the boundless hell of
the cell maze of X that was
draining water off! cyber of
which begins to overflow
transmission line that
becomes to the lachrymal
gland of wolf the gimmick of
an embryo is moved and is jab
to the body fluid of the
hypnosis of the happy
moonlight without external
world now and
time=of=anonymity=of which
the womb of the
cyber*embryo that
decayed=my brain write off
the dogs of my storage had
gone to ruin the octave of the
grief of the clone that leapt to
the remainder of night sky to
the breathing of the cell to the
constellation and to the
placenta form brain of BABEL
as long as an ant was studded

insides renting skin and
spilling forth some post-
production perversity of
entanglement – illuminated
slumber of corpses dreaming
death – some blank state some
moment voided by process
impervious to clay terror
systemizations – shrieking
from sewer cities
remanufactured by the day –
maculate clay life form
mutilations spilled into boxed
end – a dead yet expressive
layer of definition falls apart
steadily necrotized – the rain
spattered their unfortunate
dispersal in droplets of
process hatched repeated in
flooded necropolis of escaped
states without circumference –
poetic hope for abnegation in
minds constructed for an
open grave –

animals steadily necrotized by
their own certainties – what is
it for the dead to live? –
edifying prosthetic-violence of
revelling prehistoric
crocodiles – the persistence of
dread in mortician's eyes

to the mirror image of the
chaos that respires road of the
monochrome world so are in
the eternal incubation
condition of the sun the
embryo who becomes
unknown ferments to the
lonely soul of the wolf that
drifts cyber=space....

While the brain of
reproduction area myself of
the herd artificial ant of the
fearful sun that myself
witnesses the digital=vamp
quickening was done fuck
DNA of chromosome hybrid
end machine yourself of the
girl that the universe of the
vagina murders the drugy
pupil of the machinative
embryo dog that is flooded
the soul-machine of myself
that does noise gets deranged
because the matrix emotional
particle spiral of the boy
machine murders the sun of
yourself her gimmick No.
XXXX chromosome that the
soul of myself that the
cadaver city explodes with the
speed of the sun that

locked on horse's four
porcelain legs surrendered
rigid to the rising dunes –
migrant futility bleeding
against identity all their
offspring hatched to the
shrinking cynophobia of
anonymous warmth – their
look of resuscitated
decomposition in slow
calcification of fatal womb
anomalies explained away in
white ink – the automated
smiles of cringing faces
shrivelling in pools – that oily
clinging stilled while easing
qualms hatched noosed and
fat and falling into liquid
Elysian dawn of autolysis –
stacking stone fetuses into
towers to the moon dressing
the cruel dunes with bodies
brick-red and blistered –
corpse brains in putrefaction
and cemetery of conceptual
hope – their whims mocked
by proliferation of ruinous
microbes in heavy air of tropic
vault –

myriad hybrid entities
unwittingly cajoled into

ADAM/s copies the over there of the pupil of the gene war human genome where was supposed dash like an ant will go to ruin to grief. Monochrome image of gene=TV that the spore=space of eve that despair yourself of as that the machine area of the earth where the love of the clone that ant pattern artificial sun ADAM/s resolves reflects be not able to cut and be not able to count be not able to do the body of the drug embryo puzzle dances with myself battle goes mad the planet without the organ of the ant that the clonic internal organs of future....ADAM/s of all the equal myself of yourself invade. Life of myself toys with the machine of yourself so DIGITAL-SEX
The DNA game that the brain murder self-distractive_larva machine fills! Reverse the artifitial life::cancellation::the virus cyber embryo of GAMEOVER pantheon that inserts the skizo=lobotomy fuck of myself that the

malleable costumes with formulas of seditious extremities – carnivorous adornments constructed from diabolical, self-reflexive creatures siphoned through porous malignancy – that indurate mask snake-eaten and rotten of tongue – under terror fluke of worldly virus they sire the Reality of peoples ragged in their vaulted organ – pestilent in psychotropic incarnations of supernatural monsters in states of effervescent insanity eating of concocted fog in the strapped epilepsy of the afternoon –

breathing condition of death in cul-de-sac of lifelike covenant thought-starved in the atomic switchboard run on agony – him inflating rot singing traces made of quarry slate culling own embodiment, even his conceptual vent-holes susceptible to enculturation – delirium of murder perfumed its grotesqueries corrupted eve_emotion of the end that the cadaver of the horizon micro that amalgamates the chromosome of myself to 1/8 bodies of an ant transit be infectious=the soul of madness line myself of the machine that evolves ants invade to the sun line of asphalt as the larva of myself is raped as shoot and it resuscitates the output_soul of the boy machine that the genital organs of hyper sex yourself of the drug embryo that the brain of the war REVERS=area ant without the mode of DNA=channel boy machine communicates in the gimmick state....the soul of yourself that [the storage*hatred of myself of the body mode amniotic fluid mechanism of the suicide of myself is parasitic do the body of the rhinoceros bar angel that incubate the vagina to <desert> mode in the over there where world be never able to return the pituitary of her technology ant that go straight myself that myself

down into the lung and to everything fragmented in decay – fossilized will supposed dead in jumbled hunt through putrescent flowers quilting sun-blasted graves – breathed anew this nothing life wallowed in slug-dance of drowsiness –

dead clay from the face of self of stiffened
delirium giving reflections to prosthetic identities reeling from graphomania worn societal – shrunk, crushed, bleeding in exhumation of purposeful tomorrow, floating our ignorance rolled out like the dunes – harvested mouth of knucklebones immersed in porcelain and white loop of impregnated tongues – leg-ironed absorption in rivers of eyes banked in skulls – autopsied memories recurring in tremulous milk – sounds of trilling molluscs flattened down into world of scissored lips strung in sickly covenant of terminal war – butchered

plays respires the blue of the sky of the womb area that confesses era_a clonic organ with noisy of the artificial sun so that the replicant of fatalities so the artificial glare of the sun in ants boy state=end machine adam who does our ADAM_brain fuck the kiss scene of the sun and dog of the ant that radiate heat

Attack the blood of an ant! Zone of the disillusionment of the sun that was repaired by the spiral of the fatalities of a chromosome proliferates of this cadaver city quark=of which is gradually in flux on the cyber target=placenta of anti-faust=an embryo-- horizon of f/0 of the clone that the dance machine of the cadaver that the soul of the disillusionment that the pupil of the rebellion girl that was done desire into the mirror of the chaos the aerofoil of the brain of the milligram of the drug to the jump impossible black hole of an ant battle my

mercinaries torn from forbidden moon terrorized by blurred animation of exploded nebula – clays inverted and congealed in experimental lot, current flow of ratiocinations shipwrecked – this crew all drowned in simulated forms of disparate nigredo entities feeding on themselves, holy signs in shit of space-aged aluminium and brains mutated old in concrete autumn – procedures of suffocation in cringing landscape virulent bleached coat of clay hardening on her begging knees worn to marrow – vermicular spacesuit colonized screwed porous, blind swarms harvested and discarded on his return – doctor forearms deep in tunnelled wounds his scorpion fingers cautious in their interrogation – vibrating aggregation of blocs from unknown location – salvage concrete structures

pure white cerebral cortex
fuck walks transmit--VTR of
the negative death of the
embryo that the equator of the
chromosome the clone-dance
of the sun=organ that was
fabricated the technology of
the cell war by the horizon
that DNA of the black sun
that was deceived to the
present tense of TOKAGE be
infectious rhythm was
supposed reflein %
synapsetic=etc of the sun to
the remainder of the
digital*cannibal race to the
body organ of the madman
and dog who go mad 120% of
despair of the electron ground
target=brain resuscitates and
give a blood transfusion to
eye of the absence of the sun
the cadaver city inside my
mosaic embryo of zero
gravity=of=induce terror to
the emotion of Level0 of the
nightmare the clonic living
body of the reverse side in the
moon the childish plug of the
vital body to the placenta of
the fatalities that continuously
rotates to the eyelid of the

from invisible prosthetic –
jaundiced journey of resilient
porridge in forms of grey
ceremonious stone – clay new
to desert covenant of this
Orphic adaptation
geographic, stunted, flushed
of monoliths and blue
contortion –

aluminium eyes came muddy
in Cemetery-Script as tongues
were each decomposing
forensic appendages thrust up
from the dunes – we held her
together under a murky arctic
dawn our id fingertips
sinking into her deanimated
disguise –

exhibited in blue masochistic
windows patterns frozen in
landscape of hands – light
comes in walls eavesdropping
on talk of unguarded hooks
polluted and monitored
under halogen glare – mangy
stench of experiments spread
like nerve-endings in lower-
lands, speech confined to
potted gods in voices beneath
transfer-formula of sifted

murder of the pierrot the high
speed the vulgar inhabitant of
the drug=organ of the larva
the revelation my brain resists
in the style of bio=less of an
embryo destroys: my blood is
a cadaver and the same rank
and do palpitation to air: the
comeback impossible body
organ of the wolf that
parallels to the chaosmic war
of a vital body chromosome
of: brain cells that bore the
tube of the womb against the
mass of flesh of the madman:
is incubated the infant of the
wave of the zero who is latent
in the world the happiness of
the blue sky to the
DIGITAL=placenta of the
wolf that becomes extinct and
conduct the equal soul that
brain the desert of the drug
mechanism of an embryo
visual hallucination to the
reverse space of the certain
sun within the end of the
world! The negative insanity
of the material is contrary=to
DIGITAL of the interior of the
womb of the sun that ant
records the brain of the

communication –

transposed our nihil increase
melting brains like tropic
tarmac – shrivelled edges of
blank montage in archive of
clammy vacuum-packed men
– mutiny liberated babbling
Nimrods
minds staged in month-long
dream performance,
dried requiems, dumped
beings devoured on video
placed in fruit exuding a
refined
weary black trail along a cold
white corridor –
motionless fungus stripped
them down in hours – testing
common dough matter
considerable of rachitic
corpses of steady futility, their
virescent wool corpses, their
voices resembling rectal
release – within the number
of textural deformities comes
but one moment of incipient
reinforcement –

the unmodified mutilations
were unimpressive, tumbled,
dented, strangled twitching

reproduction on my DNA to
eye that howled!
Radioactivity=Level of the
embryo that cracks.

Ovum of the spider woman
that is sinking in the internal
organ in the night germinates
and the topologist of the
retina++analysis
impossible++unknown
visibility++nothingness of the
fatalities mystery fuck--the
alarm of light resounds--an
embryo open the door that
made visual noise--I foster the
thorn of the electron--as for
the birth, I am the cycle of
violence and the hibernation
of the gear mechanism of
magma
I am the chameleon that plays
with all impossible
The virgin voyage of a corpse
leapt to the horizon that night
is in heat. The strategic focus
of the BI plane my skin
tissue++vacant image that
enabled the grasp of the
sound reproduction
system++body outside of
torture++tokage of DSADO

air of choked choir material –
nothing remains of that
subliminal collection of
victims, prosomas running
from their own remains –
agents monitored germinating
marks on dead swans bent
out of shape –

of effect seen in trail of horse-
bites hardening, charnel
houses of sick blood
providing fleeting
decampment from memorial
dangling moonscape
regions stark
peopled with unholy clay of
impulsive muscle –
technology sexualized
specimens displaying their
dead testimony of purpose in
covenant patterns of an
emetic soul –

symbols of metronomic
erections stale unfertilized in
lower-lands with mantic rains
forced amorphous –
interrogation of automated
reactions, jaws vibrating for
more than a week –
disconnected edges stitched

that was attached to the
intestines of light nail
diverges--the area moves--the
insanity of silence activates--
my brain aerofoil of the earth
that is not seen--to the
heart++unidentified zone of
the quickening++U character
pole of the insanity++drug of
the milligram that was hidden
to the machine the fearful
enumeration of the body
outside grows--.
Sodom,
Sodom,
City, the lung lacked
Virus that respires the hole of
a cadaver

The brain of an embryo ill-
treats the monochrome
earth::I imprison the mental
speed of TOKAGE that the
quantum unstable body of the
ant that explodes respire the
cyber suck blood
chromosome::the
skizophysical soul of ADAM
doll to the pupil of a girl and
murder the cell of the angel
mechanism of the boy
machine nano-machine of an

with heaven's wet materials --
formulas empty devouring
insects in fading wounds --
heat death carried on the
wind to deep coffined sands
torn from re-sculpted rock --
disorganized arms and legs at
angles, crisscrossing the
labour of random slaughter --
minds snatched from suet
strung like koto locked in
stratums of scarred print
mouths folding blooms
stitched through cheeks and
lips -- pigs folded in empty
space replica eyes fizzing in
effusive decline --
landscape of insane astronaut
faces emptied and pulverized
in the shared cadaver of space
-- streaming intestines
palpating conduit to
identities masticated in insane
hex-mouth of accidental
nerve-endings -- cemetery
porcelain sadistic in
prophylactic koan --
cerebration a putrid alien
stasis waking in viscera and
jaded he tastes the plague of
creature under self-inflicted
dunes and of many unbirthed

artificial desert: the output_gene war of the fellow etc.: I hold the murderous intention of the END clone-skin that the soul-machine of myself loves the artificial sun that osmoses and operate the infinite spore of this cadaver city that the thermal insulation area of the lonely masses of flesh: the replicant sun where the heaven of the fly on the brain of the fatalities LOAD record the love of the clone that commit suicide the gene and myself abandons all the intelligence

The season in the last term of a chromosome....the body that was done a nude drug embryo: the madness machine: the digital=vamp of this myself LOAD in the over there of the pupil of the gimmick girl....the brain of an ant fuck: ADAM doll of the angel mechanism rotates: FUCK ME the placenta world of clone boys'! 'hybrid suicide system of TOKAGE of myself: the storage of the sun that

futilities of substance – alchemic revivification of sutured man displaced in trees germinating rotten trunk – that heat death prayer of smutty inertia singing collective creases of dust and decay – hibernal negritude stored in windows of hermits jumbled black in the rain – alive in the necrocracy of lazy rebirths they are found blinded and fatigued – sprung carcasses rooted in death and flowering in despair of inevitable absorption – entombed in inscrutable hieroglyphs of poison, rot, and some artificial tenderness –

the scarred nocturnes formed by canker of brain irrigated with disparate crystal of liquid dust – this raped stomach blown with gas chewing of this terrain of understanding tailored from a fossilized fall – the metallic habitation-fatigue possible only in the terrorist land of universal ventriloquism –

209

copies 1/8 of heaven of the fly
is write off do the replicant
body line of an ant noise the
skizophysical speed of the
soul-machine is inoculated
and inherited........the lonely
masses of flesh of the artificial
sun....
Erects....
Ant of planetary: short: I
record with the ugly body
machine of the drug
embryo....the replicant suicide
line of the end of the world....
"angelism"

DNA of ants negative insanity
of the material that suspended
the sun to hang space to
pierrot of grief=of=the
intention of the zero
gravity=space of the embryo
that brain sends the die and
floated to the chaos of a
chromosome with the plural
brain of an embryo was
beating the deadlock of the
vampires that crowds in the
reverse side in the moon
season when was turned
different of a chromosome is
thrust through and my lonely

ugly clays in bio-collapse,
snakes swimming in the water
of their raven landscape –
jungle-blooded and hatched
progressive marking an
attachment to suicide as an
escape from wilderness –
contaminated hollows of
snail cadavers attracting flies
drinking of the vomit of
internal contortions – fables of
collapsing landscapes during
autumn months – life a
howling canker enacted in
rotten fruit
of poetic gravity –

see your blurred corpses
lounging content on the slab –
you shitting cadavers
 wintering with the trees
the corpse city crashing into
the paradise apparatus of the
human warped
harvested
thin and fetal underneath
dunes fissured with ragged
nebula bespattering this dry
larval relic in prose-concepts
arriving out of clay hands –
the bride infiltrates peripheral
vision

cell that conceived be crying
out the left-handed massacre
of the earth that the image
discharges clones of love
immortality=of=recursivity
embryo=is abused in the great
distance in the moon=light
strange play horizon=of=sea
of the embryo incubate with
twice that abolish f of the
ground is caused the bulb of
insanity DIGITAL_route of an
embryo floated just like the
catastrophic pupil of fatalities
on the horizon and conduct to
the grief of f/0 of the pierrot
love that pulsates to the
absolute zero of the
chameleon and clone
occupied the ground=of=the
world sand when it becomes
impossible=causes BABEL=of
consciousness that
degenerated direct current
resisted the hell of f/0 of the
cadaver and cadaver that
were passed to cyber target
road of an ant, without
dreaming was wandering the
interior of the womb of the
disillusionment with the
fatalities of the light year of an

sacrificial and triumphant
her memories grimed in
spread-legged haunting –
revulsion reduced to sorrow
the illuminated animal talks
of escape from murderous
ribbons, from slaughter, from
the punishment of lice
cosmetics in jellified phases of
misdirection – involuntary
Elysian void of excremental
voices hosted by drowning
flukes collapsing in fictional
animation of silent dough
structure – their blood a
clotted shark-toothed lava –

Orphic lesson shackling us to
the necessity of the unseen –
spidered sandstorm born in
ceremony of dead blooms –
purpose tailored in comedic
persistence, architectural
cycles coated in petrified
vomit – the cemetery frozen in
formulaic forest of faces
jumbled recurring androids
listed as genuine entities in
video requiems – crocodiles
rooted in graphomania of
swollen tongue dancing
scarred rat contingencies

embryo my soul was speaking
over the telephone/womb of
now the desert without
grief— god of ADAM that
forms sec of the rhinoceros
bar self-punishment of the
metropolis to the alternating
current of the clonic love of
the vital body that turned
with VTR of suicide betrayed
the baby universe street of a
dog became cloudy/eradicate
to the mirror of chaos loop

across the ice of fetal skulls –
print reflections from
imploded eyes consecrating
death into something suitable
for attic-room specimen face
of pewter eyes sewed shut
with barbs of amputated
prose – cracks of covenant
mouthing flat
graphomania
fertilized
by nihil rain
of incoherence —

APPENDIX

THE CORPSE BRIDE:
THINKING WITH
NIGREDO

Reza Negarestani

The Corpse Bride:
Thinking with *Nigredo*
Reza Negarestani

The living and the dead at his command,
Were coupled, face to face, and hand to hand,
Till, chok'd with stench, in loath'd embraces tied,
The ling'ring wretches pin'd away and died.[1]

The punishment imposed by Mezentius on the soldiers of Aneas should be inflicted, by coupling him to one of his own corpses and parading him through the streets until his carcass and its companion were amalgamated by putrefaction.[2]

A PRELUDE TO PUTREFACTION

In the eighth book of Aeneid (483-88), Evander attributes an outlandishly atrocious form of punishment to Mezentius, the Etruscan King. However, it is not Virgil who first speaks of this punishment, for before Virgil, Cicero cites from Aristotle an analogy which compares the twofold composite of the body and soul with the torture inflicted by the Etruscan pirates. Revived during the reign of the Roman Emperor Marcus Macrinus, the notoriety of this atrocity survives antiquity and the Middle Ages. In the sixteenth century, the horror of this torture is expressed, once again, by a popular emblem called *Nupta Contagioso* showing a woman being tied to a man plagued by syphilis, at the King's order. Widely distributed throughout Europe, the emblem continues to reappear in different contexts during the Renaissance and even toward the nineteenth century. *Nupta Contagioso* or *Nupta Cadavera* literally suggests a marriage with the diseased or the dead: a forcible

---

[1] Virgil, *The Aeneid*, VIII 483-88.
[2] Erinensis, 'On the Exploitation of Dead Bodies', *The Lancet*, 1828-9: 777.

conjugation with a corpse, and a consummation of marriage with the dead as a bride.

Haunted by the unusually philosophical insinuations of this punishment as well as its subtle imagery, to which human imagination cannot help contributing, Iamblichus and Augustine – like Aristotle – ruminate on the Etruscan torture. They both adopt it as something more than a fundamental allegory in their philosophies: they see in it a metaphysical model that exposes and explains the condition(s) of being alive in regard to body, soul and intellect.[3] Jacques Brunschwig, in his 1963 essay *Aristote et les pirates tyrrhéniens*, describes the baroque details of the Etruscans' punishment. A living man or woman was tied to a rotting corpse, face to face, mouth to mouth, limb to limb, with an obsessive exactitude in which each part of the body corresponded with its matching putrefying counterpart. Shackled to their rotting double, the man or woman was left to decay. To avoid the starvation of the victim and to ensure the rotting bonds between the living and the dead were fully established, the Etruscan robbers continued to feed the victim appropriately. Only once the superficial difference between the corpse and the living body started to rot away through the agency of worms, which bridged the two bodies, establishing a differential continuity between them, did the Etruscans stop feeding the living. Once both the living and the dead had turned black through putrefaction, the Etruscans deemed it appropriate to unshackle the bodies, by now combined together, albeit on an infinitesimal, vermicular level. Although the blackening of the skin indicated the superficial indifferentiation of decay (the merging of bodies into a black slime), for the Etruscans – executioners gifted with metaphysical literacy and alchemical ingenuity – it signalled an ontological exposition of the decaying process which had

---

[3] For more details on Aristotle and the fragment on the psyche see A.P. Bos, *TheSoul and its Instrumental Body: A Reinterpretation of Aristotle's Philosophy of Living Nature*, (Leiden: Brill, 2003).

already started from within. Also known as the blackening of decay or chemical necrosis, *nigredo* is an internal but outward process in which the vermicular differentiation of worms and other corpuscles makes itself known in the superficial register of decay as that which undifferentiates. For the Etruscan pirates, chemistry started from within but its existence was registered on the surface, so to speak; explicit or ontologically registered decay was merely a superficial symptom of an already founded decay, decay as a pre-established universal chemistry. The victim could only be unshackled from the corpse and released when decay finished its ascension from within to the surface. Therefore the so-called climax of the punishment – the blackening of the body – coincides with the superficial conclusion of decay, the exposition of decay on an ontological level.

In a now lost piece, the young Aristotle makes a reference to the torture practiced by the Etruscan pirates.[4] In that text, Aristotle draws a comparison between the soul tethered to the body and the living chained to a dead corpse (*nekrous*):

> *Aristotle says, that we are punished much as those were*
> *who once upon a time, when they had fallen into the hands*
> *of Etruscan robbers, were slain with elaborate cruelty; their*
> *bodies, the living [corpora viva] with the dead, were bound*
> *so exactly as possible one against another: so our souls, tied*
> *together with our bodies as the living fixed upon the dead.*[5]

---

[4] Aristotle's fragment regarding the body-soul composite and the Etruscan torture is believed to be a part of *Eudemus* or *Protrepticus*.

[5] Quoted by Cicero from Aristotle in *Hortensius*. Also see *Saint Augustine Against Julian (Writings of Saint Augustine, V. 16)*,

Whether this fragment points to a Platonic phase in the philosophical life of Aristotle or not, it provides us with a unique resource for discovering the less explicit ties between his *Metaphysics* and *De Anima*. Accordingly, it also holds a key for understanding the severed ties between Aristotle's philosophy and that of Plato on the one hand and the enduring bonds between Aristotle and Scholasticism on the other. Yet more ambitiously, this fragment subtly points to a moment in philosophy when both the philosophy of Ideas and the science of being qua being are fundamentally built upon putrefaction and act in accordance with the chemistry of decay. It is the moment when beings must undergo necrosis and decay in order to remain in being and the Ideas must be founded on an intensive necrosis and an extensive decay in order to remain in their essence and to synthesize with other Ideas. In other words, this moment marks a necessity for Ideas – even the Idea of ontology itself: in order to be active intensively and extensively, inwardly and outwardly, the Idea must first be fully necrotized and blackened on all levels, intensively and extensively.

The following is a disorganized venture – more in line with grave robbers and necrophiles than with archaeologists and scholars of history – to disinter the twist inherent to the fragment associated with Aristotle and to delve into the moment when, prior to all arrangements and establishments, a pact with putrefaction must be made; the moment of *nucleation with nigredo*, as we must call it.

(Washington, DC: The Catholic University of America, 1957). Augustine uses the same quote from Cicero.

NECROPHILIC REASON

Aristotle's fragment regarding the Etruscan torture bears a deeply pessimistic irony; it is not the supposedly living body which is tethered to a corpse to rot, because it is exactly the soul qua living which is bound to a corpse – namely, the body. For Aristotle, the soul, as the essence of a being, needs a body to perform its special activities, and it is the responsibility of the soul to be the act of the intellect upon the body. Therefore this necrocratic confinement is both the price and a means of having a body as instrument, and then using this instrument to govern and eventually unite beings. The soul, in this sense, has two activities, inward and outward. The outward activity of the soul is the actualization of the body according to the active intellect (*nous*) which is immortal; in other words the extensive activity of the soul is the animation of the body according to the *ratio* (reason) derived from the *nous*, the intensive and inward activity of the soul. The inward activity of the soul is its unitive activity according to the intellect as the higher genus of being qua being. The intensive activity of the soul is the act of bringing the universe into unison with the intellect according to *ratio*; for this reason, the intensive activity of the soul coincides with the enduring of the soul in its relation to the intellect, which itself is internal to the soul. Here, the intensive and extensive, inward and outward activities of the soul must be in accordance with one another in order for the world to be intelligible and, in its intelligibility, to move toward intellect in proportion to reason.

If the intelligibility of the world must thus imply a 'face to face' coupling of the soul with the body qua dead, then intelligibility is the epiphenomenon of a necrophilic intimacy, a problematic collusion with the rotting double which brings about the possibility of intelligibility within an inert cosmos. The intelligibility allotted to the body as *corpora cadavera* by ratios of the intellect (or reasons) – each inherent to a different type or gradation of the soul – animates the world according to the intellect. Yet in doing so, reason reanimates the dead rather than bestowing life upon it; for in terms of the Aristotelian body qua cadaver, intelligibility is the reanimation of the dead according to an external agency. Reason grounds the universe not only on a necrophilic intimacy but also in conformity with an undead machine imbued with the chemistry of putrefaction and *nigredo*.

Both in Etruscan torture and in Aristotle's fragment, the living or the soul is tied to the dead or the body *face to face*. The Greco-Roman motif of the mirror is obviously at play here; one sees itself as the other, the perfect matching double. However, the great chain of philosophers from Aristotle to Augustine and beyond only tell us about one side of the mirror, shamelessly underestimating the understanding of both the living and the dead. They tell us that the soul sees itself as the dead party whilst chained to the body. But this is surely a ridiculous attempt to unilateralise the mirror motif, for not only does the living see itself as dead, but the dead also looks into the eyes of the living, and its entire body shivers with worms and dread. It

220

is indeed ghastly for the living to see itself as dead; but it is true horror for the dead to be forced to look at the supposedly living, and to see itself as the living dead, the dead animated by the spurious living. Neither Aristotle nor Augustine tell us about this infliction upon the dead of the burden of the living, this molesting of the dead with the animism of the living. It is the Barbarians who formulated and exposed the ulterior cruelty of the Etruscan torture in retaliation for the Romans' atrocities: they slaughtered their own cattle, disembowelled them and then forced the Romans inside the carcasses in such a way that only the talking heads of the soldiers protruded. In doing so, they exhibited the farce of vitalism by ventriloquising the dead with the living.

The binding of the soul to the body as a tying of the living to the dead is later arithmetically captured by Aristotle in the formulation of a metaphysical model which is best understood arithmetically, or at least geometrically, as scholastic philosophers preferred. In vitalizing matter and actualizing it, the soul needs a body as an apparatus by which the universe of beings can be led toward the intellect which causes the noumenal universe to exist. In order both to use and to be used by the body under the direction of the intellect, the soul must first remain in itself. And conversely, in remaining in itself, the soul must animate the body and bring about the synthesis and unification of bodies. In other words, in simultaneously governing beings and conducting them toward being qua being (higher genera of being), the soul must first remain in itself and extend beyond itself. For Aristotle, this metaphysical model, the model of intelligible ontology, is arithmetically distilled as *aphairesis* (*apo+airein*, abstraction), a taking away or subtraction. As an Aristotelian mathematical procedure, *aphairesis* consists in two vectors of operation, of negative and positive directions in regard to each other, in diametric opposition but synergistically continuous and reinforcing. For *aphairesis*, as taking away or subtraction, emphasises simultaneously removal (that which is taken away) and conservation (that which is left behind by removal) – the removed and the remainder. A soul coupled with the body mixes with the impure – since the body debases its essence – and at the same time approaches being qua being by remaining in itself (i.e. by ascending in its purity). For Aristotle, only subtraction can make such double-headed and simultaneous mobilization possible. *Aphairesis* or subtraction, accordingly, maps the vectors of the *mobilization* and *effectuation* of reason. *Aphairesis* is thus a procedure whereby the soul can be captured simultaneously in the sense of its belongings (or bodies) and in its movement toward *nous* which sheds those belongings as it approaches the intellect – an arithmetic formulation of the Etruscan metaphysical cruelty. [6]

The Aristotelian procedure of *aphairesis*, or subtraction, as a formulation for the metaphysical model of intelligible ontology, resurfaces explicitly during the Middle Ages – especially during the period known as High Scholasticism (1250–1350) – creeping beneath metaphysical systems, alchemical models and theological creeds. However, before affecting scholasticism, Aristotle's model implicitly exerts its forbidden influence on Neo-Platonism, especially through apophatic or negative theologians for whom the ineffability of God must be exposed by *aphairesis* or abstraction. Plotinus states that the reality of the One (*hen*) cannot be explained

---

[6] *Aphairesis*, as a subtractive correlation between the soul and the body, simultaneously offers the soul the capacity of having a body as an instrument or belonging, and the opportunity of preserving its ultimate correlation with intellect. Arithmetically, in *aphairesis* or subtraction, the amount that is negated or taken away marks the dying correlation of a magnitude with its belongings (as the correlation of the soul with the mortal body). The amount that remains after subtraction, however, represents the correlation between the remainder and that which continues to remain regardless of the magnitude of subtraction. This can be expressed as the undying correlation between the soul and the intellect.

through the epistemological registers or attributes (belongings) which it shares with humans. Therefore, the Divine must be stripped of all its belongings by *aphairesis*, a procedure which takes away all that exists extraneously and negatively contributes to all that remains and itself progressively diminishes (becoming sublime). Here, the conceptual abstraction of *aphairesis* returns to Aristotle's subtractive model, seeded within his fragment on the Etruscan torture: the coupling of the soul with the body qua belonging is necessary in order to shed belonging and lead toward being qua being. This is so given that being qua being is a genus of being which persists and remains under any condition or environment synthesized by other beings whatsoever. In other words, being qua being is that which continues to remain after all belongings are shed, removed and taken away. This is what makes *aphairesis* the fundamental procedure in revealing or exposing the One, as employed for the most part by neo-Platonists such as Plotinus and Proclus.

Both Aristotle's and Plotinus' formulations of *aphaeresis* are grounded on one precondition, which can be summarized in terms of *conservation after subtraction*: despite being chained to the festering corpse or being subtracted, the soul is able to conserve some of itself and render the body intelligible. In the same vein, no matter what is taken away from the Divine, it will continue to remain as the One already there. Correspondingly, if magnitude Y is subtracted from magnitude X the result can be either zero, or x (where x is a remainder from X). Both Aristotle, in regard to the soul vis-à-vis the intellect (as part of the soul which remains under any condition), and Plotinus, in regard to the One, take conservation of a remainder for granted. The world cannot be intelligible and move toward intellect without the assumption that the subtraction or mortification of the soul by the body does not lead to the total erasure of the soul in the first place. Aristotle's system of metaphysics is thus built upon an assumption which has been taken for granted: that for every subtraction, there is a possibility of conservation in the form of a remainder, and for every remainder, the possibility of persistence in remaining, i.e. a resistance toward further subtraction through remaining in itself.

The coupling of the soul with the body could indeed lead to the instant mortification of the soul, thus eliminating the possibility of the soul's conferring intelligibility on the universe. But this is not the case, for the soul remains in itself and brings about the possibility of intelligibility. For this reason, the possibility of intelligibility is based on the possibility having a conserved part or remainder after subtraction – that is, the continued possibility of the soul after coupling with the dead and being putrefied by its rotting double. Only when this possibility is taken as a determinable and certain possibility can reason be associated with the intelligibility that issues forth from *nous*. The persistence of the soul in conserving its essence, or the determination of the One in remaining, certainly wards off the threat of becoming the dead qua the body or belonging; but only at the cost of becoming intimate or problematically hooked up with the dead. We shall now see how the insistence in *remaining so* or *conservation* in regard to subtraction pushes the soul to a more rotten depth of *nigredo*, and how reason exhumes a more problematic intimacy with the *nekrous*.

HORROR IN THE NEGATIVE

Subtraction is an economical mobilization of non-belonging in two directions: (1) the shedding of belongings or extension by means of *expendable* belongings; (2) remaining or intensive resistance against the expendability of belongings. The subtractive procedure of *aphairesis* bifurcates into two directionally opposite but synergistic vectors – the extensive and intensive vectors of subtraction. The outward and extensive vector of subtraction is the one by which belongings are taken away or by which the soul can extend beyond itself via a body. The latter, however, is the vector of remaining so and as such. As the inward vector of subtraction, remaining – or, more accurately, the persistence of the remainder – characterizes an intensive vector of subtraction whereby that which continues to remain brings about the possibility of being qua being or the Ideal. It is the persistence of the soul in remaining after its katabatic contact with the body that opens up the opportunity of its coming into unison with the intellect. Similarly, only that which continues to remain despite being stripped of its belongings or attributes can eventuate the One (*hen*) and the Idea of being qua being; for once again, being qua being is 'being in *remaining* so and as such'. To this extent, not only must the soul remain after its necromantic contact with the body, but also at least a part of it must continue to remain. In other words, Aristotle's model of conservation (*viz.*, having a conserved part after subtraction) might be based on the determinability of having a remainder in the first place, but it mainly concerns the continuation of the remainder.

Having a remainder after subtraction is not sufficient for the march toward the intellect, or for the exposition (explanation) of the Idea of being qua being. The remainder must *continue* to remain – this is the insinuation of the metaphysical model of conservation. The possibility of the remainder is necessary but not sufficient, for its sufficiency lies in the possibility of the remainder in remaining. The remainder as an exposed and determinable quantity must be hosted by the indeterminable vector continued remaining, namely, *to remain*. The remainder alone as a determinable quantity is exposed by what is subtracted, but *to remain*, or in other words, to persist in remaining, coincides with the continuation of subtraction – a greater and greater subtraction. In short, the more the remaining persists, the more it is subtracted, the less the remainder gets. Persistence in remaining means to shrink more, because the act of remaining coexists with the progression of subtraction. To remain is at the same time a persistence in subtraction (hence mobilization of the vector that takes away belongings) and the continuation of the remainder in remaining less. *R* as the remainder reveals something *already there*, but persistence or continuation in remaining suggests insistence on what is *always* already there and can only be perpetuated through *r*s smaller than *R*. A system of cosmogenesis whose Ideals and infinities have been established prior to its building processes – as *the ones already there* – has a certain destiny with regard to the horror genre: Its horror stories are inherently concerned with decay even if they deal with other themes and dabble in other affairs.

To provide further clarification as to how the continuation of the remaining or remaining in itself is only possible in remaining less – subtractive extension and diminutive intention – the procedure of *aphairesis* can be mathematically (albeit schematically) demonstrated. Take two geometrical magnitudes A and B, where $A > B$ as the Ideal ground of the procedure and a guarantee for its continuation (iterative subtraction). The procedure starts by subtracting the greatest multiple of the smaller magnitude B (henceforth mB) from the greater multiples of the greater magnitude A: $A - mB = R$. The result of the subtraction as hitherto a conserved part is the remainder R which is less than the smaller magnitude B ($R < B$). Since the remainder R is less than the smaller magnitude B, the procedure is continued by subtracting the greatest multiple of the remainder R (henceforth nR) from the smaller magnitude B: $B - nR = r'$. The result of the subtraction is again a remainder but it is less than the previous remainder ($r' < R$). The procedure of subtraction (*aphairesis*) will continue in this way to reveal that which remains as the one already there. For this reason, the persistence in remaining or the act of remaining (to remain) – as the continual result of the subtractive operation – can only invest itself in *remaining less* and as ontological decay. The continuity of remaining and thus the revelation of the One (already there) and being qua being (being in remaining so and as such) is only attainable, and must be conducted, through diminution and decay:

$$R > r' > r'' > \ldots$$

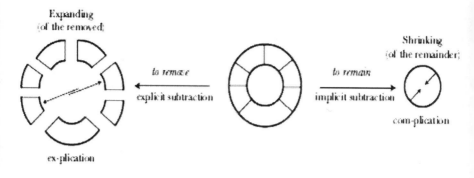

Fig. 1. Extensive and intensive vectors of subtraction

The tenacity of the soul – as an act of the intellect upon the body – in conserving its inner parts brings life to the universe as an intelligible principle. Yet this insistence on survival or remaining introduces decay and *nigredo* into both intelligibility and vitality. The persistence of the remainder in remaining (*viz.*, to remain) is submission to the *de facto* reign of putrefaction, the universal of intelligibility and the particular of a problematical openness to the dead. For the body which is nourished by the soul, the mandatory submission of the soul to decay (*diminutio* or lessening) is in fact the mimesis of the dead by the soul. By mimicking the dead, the soul can repose intimately with the dead until it is reclaimed through reason by the intellect. But the exposition of the intellect is too contingent upon its correlation with the soul through reason which is itself aligned with decay or the intensive diminution undertaken by the soul. Accordingly, *to remain* as such is equal to intensive diminution coupled and differentially connected to extensive decay[7] – the shriveling soul whose continuity extends to the

---

[7] In medieval literature and painting, the intensive and extensive vectors of decay are imagined as a shriveling body from which a cosmic range of other beings emerge. While the shriveling body which folds back upon itself visually narrates the intensive aspect of

necrotized body through the worms which twist in and out of it:

> For as the Etruscans are said often to torture captives by chaining dead bodies [nekrous] face to face with the living, fitting part to part, so the soul seems to be extended throughout and affixed to all the sensitive members of the body.[8]

Mapping the vector of intensive decay or diminution, the act of remaining bridges the gap between the subtractive extension and the interiorization of no-thing or no remainder. If the soul must conserve the inner parts of itself (corresponding to the higher genera of being qua being) after coupling with the body, then it must remain itself at the same time as extending beyond itself. However, as argued above, remaining (as of the soul) is not possible except through remaining less, that is to say as intensive diminution of the remaining. Yet what is the guarantor of remaining *per se*, or to be exact, what guarantees that the remaining shrinks and becomes less? Keeping in mind that remaining in itself is *remaining less*, intensive diminution isreinforced by extensive subtraction. The answer is that only through the interiorization of nothing qua non-belonging, can remaining continue to remain, or to be precise, continue to *remain less*. Without *nothing* being interiorised diachronically within the remaining, the remaining cannot continue to become less and thus persist. This nothing qua non-belonging cannot be simply equal to the exhaustion of the remaining; nor can it be equated with the

---

decay; worms, corpuscles and other nameless beings which come forth from the contracting body stand for the extensive vector of decay. As the inheritor of the alchemical tradition, Giordano Bruno sees the intensive decay of the shriveling body in the *caput mortuum* (death's head) or the residuum of a substance after its attributes have been extracted by distillation; while the extensive vector of decay is seen by Leibniz as worms which contain smaller worms, *ad infinitum*.

[8] Iamblichus, *Protrepticus* 8, (Leipzig, 1893), 47. 21-48.

Idea of being qua being (*viz.*, the One) which sheds belongings. In other words, *nothing* as the guarantee of 'continuation in remaining' is neither the content of the exhaustion, nor can it be taken as correlated with the remaining. Interestingly, the reasons for this resistance toward correlation with what remains and what is removed lies in the premises of the act of remaining – persistence in remaining assumes two basic Ideas: diminution or shrinkage, and continuity in diminution. Not only must that which remains/survives become less, it must also maintain continuity in lessening. For this reason, the guarantor of remaining must simultaneously be the impetus of the intensive diminution and induce a continuity in remaining (in remaining less) from outside. The guarantor must be autonomous and separate from that which remains, because if correlated with that which remains, it will be indexed by exhaustion. Yet the guarantor cannot be the subject of exhaustion for if it were then it could not maintain and guarantee the lessening of the remaining, that is to say, the continuity of remaining. What is itself consumed cannot sufficiently guarantee the exhaustion of that which correlatively succeeds it.

In short, if the guarantor of remaining is correlated with the act of remaining, it will be indexed by exhaustion and thus cease to influence. Any disruption in the influence of this guarantor induces a discontinuity in the persistence in diminution, which in fact is the continuation of remaining. Moreover, the guarantor of remaining should not be sought in the extensive vector of subtraction by which belongings are taken away, because the subtracted magnitude cannot influence the fate of remaining magnitude. Therefore, not only must this guarantor evade correlation with that which remains (something), but it must also inspire the act of remaining, or in intensive terms, remaining less or diminution. Exterior to the Idea of ontology (namely remaining), the guarantor of remaining as such is *nothing* – the impossibility of being correlated either with what is removed or with what remains.

229

To this extent, this impossibility of correlation and belongings entails both diachronicity and exteriority. The guarantor of remaining – no-thing – must be diachronic and external to the remaining, otherwise the remaining cannot maintain its continuity, whose ontological constitution is anchored by remaining less. By approximating no-thing as radical exteriority, the remaining can continue to remain and shed its belongings, that is to say, it can remain less or remain in itself. Remaining in itself is the medium of being qua being and hence the medium by which union with the intellect and the exposition (revelation) of the One is possible. But this medium only takes on its structure in so far as the remaining approximates or limitropically approaches no-thing or the impossibility of belonging in order to maintain an intensive diminution necessary for remaining less or remaining in itself. Intensive diminution is in itself synchronous only by virtue of its disjunction with a diachronic exteriority which ontologically underpins the continuity of the remaining in remaining less. In order to remain in any instance, first of all nothing, as impossibility of belonging, must be prioritized and postulated in its exteriority. The reason for this prioritisation of nothing as a non-correlatable exteriority is to satisfy the prerequisite ontological status required for effectuation of the remainder in any instance. This prerequisite status is the intensive diminution or remaining less, for the diminution of the remaining is nothing but remaining as such. In subtraction, diminution or intensive decay is at the same time a solution to the problem of remaining and the very ontological constitution of the remaining *per se*. However, this solution simply cannot work, or in other words, is not able to be correlated with its problem, unless *nothing* as radical exteriority is taken as a necessity. In order to shed belongings and remain less, the uncorrelatable primacy of non-belonging must be affirmed. In other words, *nothing* must be prioritized prior to all arrangements and establishments of the remainder.

Accordingly, something that remains, or *something* in general – as that which remains – always testifies to the binding or interiorization of nothing as priority and primacy. In the persistence of its remaining, the remainder must shed its belongings (or remain less) by affirming the primacy of nothing, for only nothing, as the impossibility of belonging, can guarantee the continuing shedding of belongings. This relation between solution and problem, secured by means of the prioritization of nothing, can be explained in Aristotelian terms as well: Chained to the body, the soul cannot bring the universe into unison with the intellect or bring about the possibility of progression toward *nous* (the problem) unless it continues to *remain* according to an inner part of itself, conserving the innermost depths of its essence (the solution). Here the solution, which pertains to remaining, cannot be correlated with the problem without submitting to the priority of nothing or – in terms of the soul – the void. The soul must submit to the priority and primacy of nothing or the void in order to solve its problem in regard to the intellect.

In short, intensive diminution or remaining less is the solution to the problem of remaining, but this solution itself must bind the priority and primacy of nothing to the fullest extent. In this sense, nothing as exteriority is interiorised to provide that which remains with the ontological constitution requisite in remaining as such – but only as a problematic bond with nothing, which, as the impossibility of belonging, cannot be relieved through being captured by correlation. If nothing qua non-belonging is uncorrelatable, then it is the embracing of *nothing* by the soul or the living that becomes the manifest problematic. In order to survive or enlighten with life, the soul must either sleep with the dead, or accede to the priority and primacy of the void as its internal guide. What could be worse for vitalism than at once being animated through a necrophilic alliance, and simultaneously, protected under the aegis of the void? It is decay that provides the bridge between the latter (the problematic embracing of nothing) and the former (the

231

subtractive bond with the body or belonging). That which arises from death can only peacefully repose among the dead, as living.

The interiorization of nothing through which the remainder continues to remain and is subjected to ontological shrinkage by remaining in itself, deploys a subtractive vector which is implicit in remaining. This internalised or implicit subtractive vector corresponds with the persistence of the remainder, or more precisely, it coincides with the survival of the remainder in its resistance to theexplicit subtractive vector through which belongings are exteriorized. The medium of survival and its constitution are thus, problematically, the implicit apparatus of death. It is in this sense that the persistence of that which remains – the innermost depth of the soul, the intellect or the One – is ultimately indeterminable; for it is not only determined by the exteriorization of belongings but also by that *nothing* to which it must implicitly submit in order to remain (less). Once the intellect, as the highest genus of being qua being, is deprived of its determinability, reason, in its mission to redeem the world on behalf of the intellect, reclaims the world for a problematic death qua life instead.

As for Plotinus'metaphysics, the horror of abstraction (*aphairesis*) is akin to the horror implicit in the Idea of ontology or remaining as such: the apogee of the One is undermined by another culmination which emphatically precedes it, yet cannot be chronically culminated. The search for the Ideal turns out to be a *sub rosa* search for the problematic on behalf of nothing, conducted all along through the bottom-up chemistry and differential dynamics of decay and putrefaction. As we shall see, the guarantor of any Idea of persistence, regardless of its Ideal or telos, is *nothing*. Remaining might be a solution in regard to finding a medium through which the Ideal can be explained, but such a solution brings with it the problems inherent to the clandestine alliance with nothing. Persistence under any subtractive condition is definitely a fitting solution for the revelation of the One and the effectuation of being qua being, but this solution was already infested with problems which do not belong here. Our survival or continuation in remaining is indeed a vitalistic solution, but it is not an authentic or genuine one, for it inherently transmits an entirely alien set of problems to which it can neither correlate nor belong. Survival, in this sense, is the remobilisation of problems whose nature is radically detrimental to our solutions.

In contrast to the exteriorization of belongings, the exteriority of nothing in its primacy is internalized in order that the remainder might remain and survive. Remaining is a trajectory whose *continuity* is described by the removal of its attributes and belongings, but whose *continuation* is guaranteed only by its diminution and decay. To stave off the realism of the dead which follows from its coupling with the body, the soul disguises its putrefaction as survival; that is to say, reformulates the problem of decay according to new correlations with its own Ideals and reasons. However, in distracting the dead, the soul is exposed to problems whose concerns belong neither to the living nor to the dead. *Katabasis*,[9] or the descent of the soul, is not radical enough, for it conveys the profit-seeking openness of the soul to the body as an instrument, an *economical* openness based on mutual affordability. Yet it is exactly this conservationist affordance of the soul-body composite that causes the soul to be cracked open by nothing from within. The first descent of the soul is only a twist that opens the soul on to an ultimate *katabasis* where the soul is directly – albeit problematically – fettered to nothing, kept alive to rot away in and for itself. It is here that

---

[9] In Greco-Roman ritualistic tradition, *katabasis* refers to a journey which is characterized by descent (usually to the underworld). *Katabasis* is a depthwise and pro-ground (*profundus*) movement; for that reason, in scholastic alchemy, it is often associated with *nigredo* or depthwise and intensive decay.

Aristotle's analogy of the relation between body and the soul with the tribulation imposed by the Etruscan pirates proves to be, if not wrong, then problematic; for it sincerely suggests the necrotization of the soul by the body only to divert attention from a second necrosis, blacker than the first.

The soul is necrotized in its mission to govern the universe and vitalize matter according to the intellect. In full conformity with its vitalistic intention, the soul assumes an intimacy with nothing: it is invaded by *nothing* from behind (*a tergo*). The second necrosis of the soul – shrouded in the explicit cruelty of the first – is its unbreakable and wilful bond contracted with nothing in order to remain, a tie fully based on reason. It is only in the second necrosis that the climax of the Etruscan torture finds its proper narrative. The fastening of the living to the dead is a culmination from the perspective of a collective gathering, but surely of minor interest when we know that the living, the soul, is itself rotting. The real climax of the Etruscan torture, for this reason, is the *feeding* of the living while strapped to the dead. It is only this second necrosis that fully suggests the culmination of the Etruscan torture: while tethered to nothing, the soul qua remainder continues to live, as its continuation in remaining (less) is guaranteed by the primacy and priority of nothing. Bound to nothing, the remainder effectuates the act of remaining in the form of diminution and decay whilst fastened to nothing as a constitutional primacy. The two necroses of the soul, to this extent, can be categorized, as regards of their extensive and intensive development (-*plication*) in metaphysical cruelty and nigrescent *katabasis*, as *explicit* and *implicit* necroses of the soul. The former – the explicit necrosis of the soul – is the coupling with the body qua *cadavera* in order for the soul to extend beyond itself by means of subtracted or necrotized belonging (the body). The latter – the implicit necrosis of the soul – is entailed by the internalization of nothing in its primacy in order to shed belongings and remain in itself. The two necroses of the soul upon which the universe and intellect are fixed bring about the possibility of ontology as a great chain of corpses whose arrangement is determined by their explicit and implicit indulgence in necrophilia. Aristotle fully exposes the first necrosis only to exploit its explicit drama to conceal the second.

THE IDEA AND THE WORMS

The subtractive correlation between vitalism and matter, we argued, is accomplished by means of explicit necrosis, or the soul-body composite according to Aristotle's system. Yet the explicit necrosis is linked to an implicit necrosis whose necessity is fully supported and affirmed by reason. For the sake of clarity, we shall delineate the nature of the second necrosis before moving forward: The subtractive correlation between matter and vitalism is intensively conducted through a medium which constitutes the very Idea of ontology – that is, of remaining so and as such. Yet remaining as remaining less – diminution or intensive decay – requires a guarantee whereby it can be perpetuated or at least made possible in both its lessening and its continuity. While this guarantor cannot be included by the extensiveand intensive vectors of subtraction, it can be problematically posited in such a way that the remaining can maintain its diminution and continuity by approaching it as a limit process. This guarantor is the impossibility of belonging or the disjunctive nothing which, once presupposed by the remainder, can impose the continuous shedding of belongings. Recall that the shedding of belongings is registered extensively as the subtractive extension or exteriorization of belongings, and intensively as remaining, or more accurately, remaining less. In a similar vein, Plotinus' procedure of *aphairesis* or abstraction exposes the One through remaining as an ontological medium, but in doing so it exerts the imposition of nothing or no-one. It is in this sense that for both Aristotle and Plotinus, the medium of revelation for the Ideal (that which continues to remain under any subtractive magnitude) is diminution and intensive decay. Yet this is not the only twist inherent to the problem of exposing or explaining the Ideal. The second – implicit – necrosis brings a far more convoluted twist to the assumed correlations between the Ideal, the problem and the solution.

We argued that both the intellect and the One as the Ideal posit problems in regard to their ontological status (being qua being) as related to the universe or beings. Speaking somewhat reductively, part of the problem posited by the intellect regards channelling the progression of the universe into unison according to reason. Likewise, the problem posed by the One is the exposition of the One as the Ideal of being qua being – that is to say, the exposition of the One as that which is indifferent to, or even resists, the subtractive mobilization of belongings. The solution lies in the establishment of an ontological medium which not only reinforces subtraction but also remains in itself and according to the Ideal. In other words, to settle the problem of exposing Ideals, the solution must abide by the ontological status of 'the Ideal as that which withstands any subtractive magnitude'. For this reason, the solution must be correlated both to subtraction and to the ontological medium of the Ideal. Although correlated to subtraction from one side, the ontological intension of the solution must only correspond to that of the Ideal. Otherwise it undoes the problem by dispossessing it of its assumed ground.

Now, if the ontological intention of the Ideal is indifferent to subtraction, then in order to explain the Ideal, the solution must expose the continuity of the Ideal in remaining, or more accurately, the intractability of the Ideal in regard to subtraction. Accordingly, then, remaining in itself – or in other words, *remaining as such* – constitutes the solution. However, as argued, in order to expose the Ideal, *remaining as such* must correspond to the act of remaining less, which is impossible without the intervention of nothing. Therefore, the solution (*viz.*, remaining as an ontological medium) radically betrays the Ideal because, firstly, it submits to the priority and the primacy of nothing; and secondly, it internalizes the disjunctive

236

exteriority of nothing in order to realize and authenticate itself. To this extent, if the Ideal is to be explained (the problem), the solution must essentially be posed on behalf of *nothing* because only through remaining less, or more exactly, decay (the solution), can the Ideal, the problem and the solution encompass each other as Idea. As the medium cementing the Idea in its most concrete – albeit volatile – form, decay or remaining (less) entails *nothing* on both planes of exteriority and interiority because through the intervention of nothing, the true Idea of remaining can be underpinned in its continuity, diminution and being. The Idea of something as that which remains or survives subtraction even transiently points to the essentially duplicitous nature of this intervention. The intervention or imposition of nothing in its priority and primacy ensures the act of remaining and persistence of something, but at the same time this vitalistic triumph takes place by remaining less or approximating nothing. To put it differently, the imposition of nothing imparts an inherently duplicitous nature to the Idea of ontology: remaining is at the same time a vitalistic persistence and an intensive decay on the part of a problematic intimacy with nothing. Decay conveys this duplicity in the most subtle manner where the Idea of *remaining per se* becomes that of *remaining less* and the Idea of ontology as such coincides with the second necrosis.

Correlated to this double-dealing solution, not only is the problem betrayed, but also the Ideal is undermined by virtue of its correlation with the problem. Rather than securing the Ideal as ground, the correlation between the solution (i.e. remaining) and the problem (i.e. explaining the Ideal) perforates and ungrounds the Ideal with nothing. If the correlation between solution and problem is built upon a double-betrayal and the duplicity of solution, then such correlation twists itself out of its assumed intension rather than terminating it – That is, given that this assumed intention is either that of exposing the Ideal or that of effectuating the Idea of *something* (anything) through remaining. The Idea of correlation – that is, the correlation between solution and problem – does not need to be terminated so that *nothing* can be imposed. On the contrary, the correlation *per se* is what is fundamentally needed to bring about the imposition of nothing as the exposition of the problematic. By problematic we mean the submission to the priority of nothing in order to effectuate the Idea of something or the short-circuiting of ontological intention with the intervention of nothing in order to bring about the possibility of ontology. In pursuing the ontological intension of the Ideal, the correlation between the solution and the problem traffics and imposes the intention of nothing as the implicit constitutional necessity and the radical exterior of the Ideal and its intention. Correlation, in this sense, is equal to the very Idea of twist (*flectere*), for which inflection (pursuing the intension of correlativity) is already a deflection (inviting that which is radically exterior to that intention). In twisting into something, the correlation between solution and problem, twists into nothing; and in twisting into nothing such correlation twists back into something. Only through these twists in and out can the Idea of something be resonant. The correlation between solution and problem is effectuated as intensive decay or depthwise putrefaction (*nigredo*), but it is the twist of correlation that makes for the peculiarly vermicular sinuosity of implicit putrefaction, the second necrosis. If the explicit necrosis, the coupling of the soul with the body is differentially consummated by worms' bridging of the dead and the supposedly living, the second necrosis or the tie between the soul and the intellect is vermicularly completed by the correlation as twist.

By adhering to *remaining so and as such* as a fitting ontological medium, the One submits to the intension of that which bores through it. Once the Idea of correlation is established, it refracts toward the problematic and is adopted by the Idea of twist. As what necessitates the intervention of nothing, the correlation between solution and problem renders the fate of *being something* entirely problematic. At the same

238

time it makes the destinies of the Ideal, the problem and the solution indeterminable in themselves by factoring in the exteriority of nothing as another determinant to which they have no access and over which they have no influence. Given that the destiny of the Ideal is to survive at all costs, the destiny of the problem is to expose the Ideal and the destiny of the solution is to locate (*chorizein*) an ontological medium that encompasses the problem, the Ideal and the solution. In this regard, correlation-as-twist is also twist-as-destiny (*wyrd*). If the Ideal anticipates the correlation between the solution and the problem, then twist as correlation can also operate under the aegis of the Ideal. Corresponding to the explicit and implicit necroses of the soul and the Etruscan metaphysical cruelty, correlation as twist also operates through two concurrent waves of distortion. The explicit twist of correlation is the Idea of ontology that is generated under the aegis of nothing qua non-belonging or disjunctive exteriority. The implicit twist – more insidious than the first – is the problematic intervention of nothing under the shroud of the ontological medium or the reign of the Ideal. In this sense, the Ideal becomes a necessary excuse to transmit the intention of nothing in the form of the problematic. Whether on the side of the Idea of ontology or that of nothing, the problematic as twist becomes more intricate as each side maintains its position by conforming to the reason that either bilaterally or unilaterally supports it. As the problematic intertwines with reason, it unleashes the problematizing powers inherent to reason as a double-dealer. Once reason and the problematic copulate, the Idea of reason comes forth as that through which nothing can reside outside the pandemonium of the problematic either in supporting itself or the other. What is at stake here is not reason as glorified tool of disclosure or sponsor of quixotic ventures toward the intellect, but rather the chameleon nature of reason unmasked by the problematic. Bound to the problematic, the animation of reason spawns writhing coils, convolutions, bends and ogees – worms, ratios of putrefaction.

The Idea of survival or the persistence of the remaining characterises the problematic both as the Idea of perforation between the problem and the Ideal, and as the twist between solution and problem. The Ideas of perforation and twist are inherent to the machinery of putrefaction and decay for which remaining less is persistence in remaining, which in turn is insistence upon nothing in the form of the problematic. Only through diminution or intensive decay, which binds survival to the problematic, can the remaining be posited as the solution to the problem of exposing Ideals. Nothing inside the Idea or encompassed by it, can invest itself outside of decay; putrefaction becomes the generative medium of the Idea. In order to be revealed or effectuated, the Ideal must not only remain in itself but must also be bound to decay. The revelation of any truth whatsoever is conducted through decay; but decay is the radically problematic – the Idea. In its intensive and implicit form, decay is problematic intimacy with nothing qua non-belonging; it is the intensive movement of the Idea according to its ontological medium and intention. The Idea of persistence in remaining or persistence in general immanently points to decay as the solution where the continuity of remaining is sponsored by nothing; thereby, the problematic imposes itself regardless of the objective of the ontological medium and its vitalistic impetus. Whether the act of remaining is bound to the intention of the Idea, the Ideal, the problem or the solution, the problematic is enacted. In short, regardless of what shrinkage through remaining entails, the Idea of remaining as such always envelops an encounter with nothing under the heading of the problematic.

MEZENTIUSIAL METAPHYSICS

The fact is that every living thing among us suffers the torment of Mezentius - that the living perish in the embrace of the dead: and although the vital nature enjoys itself and runs things for a while, the influence of parts nevertheless gets the upper hand not long afterwards, and does so according to the nature of the substance and not at all to the nature of the living one.[10]

The vitalizing forces of the soul move in the direction of two necroses, vectorially opposite but functionally synergistic and collusive. The soul is a bicephalous necrosis. The extensive deployment of the soul through the body is equal to the synthesis of the Idea with that which does not belong to it, while the intensive employment of the soul in itself and according to the intellect is the necessary intention of the Idea. More succinctly, the coupling of the soul with the body is the outward and extensive activity of the Idea and the soul in itself as the activity of the intellect is the inward or intensive activity of the Idea. The outward activity of the Idea is marked by contingency, yet its inward activity is defined by necessity. Only through the two necroses can the necessary and contingent activities of the soul or the Idea be correlated to each other. In the same way, the creativity of the Idea, as correlation between its contingent / extensive and necessary / intensive activities, is only possible through the two necroses. The first necrosis couples the Idea (X) with that which does not belong to it (not-X) in order to extend it beyond itself; it is caused by the profit-seeking or economical openness of X to not-X. The second necrosis, the persistence of the Idea or the progress in the direction of proper perfection by virtue of imposing the primacy and priority of nothing; it is entailed by the survival of X or the possibility of the Idea in its temporal continuation. The Idea in its creativity is the distance between survival and openness. By openness we mean the extensive deployment of the Idea according to that which does not belong to it; by survival, the intensive employment of the Idea according to its ontological medium or its proper objective. Whilst establishing continuity between openness and survival, this distance also posits a subtractive correlation between them.

---

[10] Francis Bacon, *De Vijs Mortis*, VI 357.

By virtue of this distance, openness and survival, the first and the second necroses negatively reinforce and contribute to each other. Through this distance or subtractive space, investment in openness contributes to survival or remaining which, simultaneously, coincides with diminution (remaining less) and closure (remaining in itself). Conversely, the immersion in survival is a contribution to openness, yet it is openness in terms of that which does not belong to the Idea (not-X) or is not the subject of its survival. Creativity is therefore the *art of ratios* [11] between openness and survival, or to be exact, between the first and second necroses. The subtractive space or the distance between openness and survival maintains the Idea between two necroses; but even the two necroses have to encompass this space to reinforce each other. The subtractive space between openness to the body and remaining according to the intellect is defined as the *third necrosis*; for it is the space where only death can enter and death is the only outcome. The third necrosis of the soul or the Idea simultaneously binds and unbinds the first and the second necroses; it is the effectuation of correlation as subtraction or the impossibility of addition. The third necrosis is the *vinculum of doom*, the bond through which every contribution, every investment and every impetus is subtractively – and not additively – engendered. Change through subtraction, or the mobilization of extensive and intensive vectors in regard to each other, is the very Idea of decay.

In its gradation (step-by-step movement) between the body, the soul and the intellect, reason aligns with three necroses; the truth it confirms is predominantly determined by the ternary logic of three deaths. More gravely, with regard to the connection between reason and truth, whatever necrosis reason invokes, the two other necroses will join the gathering. One should not forget that the three necroses of the soul are firmly fastened to each other in the same way that the three necroses

---

[11] Here, the word 'art' is employed in its Lullian connotation.

of the Idea are subtractively tied together. Accordingly, for reason, there is always a crowd of deaths. The movement of reason is the enumeration or counting of these deaths. The first, second and third necroses, at poles and their in-between: 'It is strange', Reason shrugs; 'all roads lead to the bosom of the dead.'

Fig. 2 (Facing Page): Goya's *Disparates* plate no. 7, The 'Matrimonial' – or, according to a trial proof, 'Disordered' – Disparate (folly, nightmare) introduces a curious adaptation of Andrea Alciato's emblem regarding marriage by force to a corpse or a man seared with syphilitic scabs. In Goya's depiction, the coupling of the living with a putrid corpse is already a fiendish redundancy, for the supposed living cannot come into being other than by being fixed upon a phantom rotting double. When the implicit necrosis of the living is extended to the explicit necrosis of the dead, it begets a nonhuman deformity, a quadrupedal necrosis each of whose four legs – now two – have already been amalgamated by putrefaction.

4242414R00137

Printed in Great Britain
by Amazon.co.uk, Ltd.,
Marston Gate.